THE
FRIEND

ALSO BY TERESA DRISCOLL

Recipes for Melissa
Last Kiss Goodnight
I Am Watching You

THE
FRIEND

TERESA DRISCOLL

THOMAS & MERCER

Text copyright © 2018 by Teresa Driscoll
All rights reserved.

Published by Thomas & Mercer, Seattle

www.apub.com

Amazon, the Amazon logo, and Thomas & Mercer are trademarks of Amazon.com, Inc., or its affiliates.

ISBN-13: 9781542046664
ISBN-10: 1542046661

Cover design by Tom Sanderson

Printed in the United States of America

For my lovely dad, who is greatly missed

TODAY – 4.00 P.M.

Why a robin? I don't understand . . .

I am in the train toilet – feet wide apart – leaning over the tiny, stainless-steel sink, trying very hard to . . . *just . . . breathe . . . goddammit . . .* and trying also to work out what the hell a robin has to do with any of this.

More than two hundred miles away, my child is in a hospital bed being cared for by strangers. He may or may not have had his spleen removed.

There is appalling confusion which a series of phone calls has done little to resolve, because he is with a friend and astonishingly the medical team cannot tell them apart. Obscene and surreal, this identity thing, but only now does it hit me that in brushstroke terms they are quite similar: brown hair, brown eyes and, thanks to a recent growth spurt in my son's friend, pretty much the same height, too.

A nurse with a soft Irish accent has been trying to coax sense from me through the fog which seems to hang all around my body, making it difficult to think straight. In one phone call she is wondering if my son has any distinguishing marks.

Moles? Freckles? A birthmark?

I have been told already that the boys' clothes were removed by paramedics, but for some reason I find it comforting to run through the list with the nurse anyway: a green T-shirt with a dinosaur logo (a favourite which I ironed specially last night) and black jeans folded up at the hem because they are too long. I keep meaning to stitch them up for him but I am not really that kind of mother and . . .

She interrupts me gently to ask about his hair.

Curly? Straight?

I tell her that he has an unusual crown – a bit like a question mark. I used to trace it with my finger when he was asleep in my arms as a baby.

There is a pause on the line during which I find that I am inadvertently tracing a question mark on the edge of the sink, and then she is saying, sorry, but she's checked the hair and she can't really see what I mean, and I am no longer listening, thinking instead about the day my son decided to cut his own fringe. He was about three – a year ago – and he came into my room with wide, frightened eyes beneath the crooked mess, scissors still in his hand.

And in this horrid, tiny place, I can for a moment see his perfect face staring right back at me through the smudges of the stainless-steel surround. *Can you fix it, Mummy?*

The train is rocking – *ta-tum, ta-tum* – negotiating a corner then picking up speed, so that I have to set my legs even further apart to steady myself. Someone starts to knock gently on the door of the toilet cubicle, asking if I am all right, but it is such a ridiculous question that I am aware of an alien noise emerging from my mouth as I close my eyes to the blur of pictures pushing their way through this fog – the times and places when I should have seen this coming.

Stopped it.

It has taken us just six months to get here and I cannot believe I have allowed it . . .

And then the nurse's voice is back on the line – *ta-tum, ta-tum* – and more animated. One of the boys has something drawn on his arm in felt-tip pen. A doodle which looks like some kind of bird – a robin possibly, as the chest has been coloured in bright red.

And she wants to know if this means anything to me.

A robin redbreast?

CHAPTER 1

BEFORE

We met on a Thursday. Two boys. Two mothers. Much later, and especially on that train, I will torture myself for the curiosity and excitement I felt; the enthusiasm with which I so easily opened my door to it all.

But at the time there was no clue to the future – the consequences. At the time I did not know that someone was going to die, and so I was lost in the humdrum of a day so very ordinary that at the critical point of our meeting I was distracted by the parsnips.

I had been to the farm shop for eggs, taking just my handbag, but the parsnips surprised me – so fat and firm. I bought too many for the free but flimsy paper bag, and so came upon the kerfuffle on the village square with Ben balanced on one hip and parsnips spilling in all directions.

At first I didn't notice the lorry, just the small crowd gathered by the pub, several familiar faces shaking their heads in practised dismay. It was only as I stepped forward, more parsnips escaping the split bag on to the ground – *damn* – that I realised what had happened.

It was not the first time; in our four years in Tedbury Cross, I had seen two identical accidents – lorries misjudging the twist of the hill by the pub and ending up wedged between the wall of the public bar and the side of poor Heather's cottage.

'Poor Heather' was a local artist of the struggling variety with the highest insurance premium in the village. When, just a couple of years earlier, a significant part of her kitchen wall had to be rebuilt, she determined to throw in the towel. But word of the lorry threat had spread. Two buyers pulled out in swift succession, and with homeowners more afraid of 'blight' than nuclear war, the parish council launched a loud but wholly futile campaign for a bypass.

'Oh, no' and 'not again' were the mutterings through the crowd as I tested my stomach muscles, trying to reclaim parsnips without dropping Ben. It was only as I stood back up that I noticed her. My mirror image. This striking newcomer – a woman of similar age in precisely my pose; a small boy balanced on her own hip.

She was dressed head to toe in black, with silver ballet pumps and accessories – a city chic which stood out immediately as she pushed large square sunglasses back from striking blue eyes. I noticed Nathan, a local architect and family friend, staring while sucking in his stomach, and had to bite my lip against a smile.

'Your removal van?' I stepped forward as our boys eyed each other from our hips with a shy curiosity.

'I'm afraid so. Not a very good start, is it?' Her son buried his head in her neck. Ben did exactly the same to me, each boy pretending not to steal glances. Very funny.

From across the square, several voices were by now shouting conflicting directions at the driver of the removal van, temporarily imprisoned in his cab by stone walls on either side.

Left hand down hard . . .

No. No. He needs to straighten first. Edge forward. Then reverse.

'We're supposed to be moving into Priory House.' She pulled a face. 'At least that was the plan. I'm Emma, by the way. Emma Carter.' She began to stretch out her hand but her son wriggled a protest, so she shrugged an apology, looping her hands together to hitch him up to a more comfortable position.

I smiled. 'Look – I'm just opposite. Why don't you come in for a cup of tea? I'm Sophie, and this is Ben.'

'Oh, that's very kind but I couldn't. Really. I need to help sort this mess out.'

'Trust me. This is going to take quite a while. And there are more than enough cooks already. Chances are there will be a TV crew along shortly. I'm afraid it's not the first time this has happened. There's a bit of a campaign going to get something done.' Her face changed and I felt a punch of guilt. 'I'm so sorry. I've alarmed you, Emma. Seriously, you both look as if you could do with a drink. Why not lie low at mine? The boys can play. It's no trouble.'

'But I feel so *responsible*.'

'Nonsense. It's hardly your fault. Come on.' I moved to the left to explain the plan to Nathan, trailing more parsnips in my wake, which made Emma laugh out loud. A few more heads turned, several people stepping forward to rescue the vegetables, so that we were both smiling at the absurdity as I led the way to our cottage.

As I opened the door, it hit me instantly – that strange frisson of excitement in the company of a stranger. I noticed her looking straight down and remembered exactly how I'd felt the first time I saw it. The *floor*. Sometimes after a holiday it could still surprise me. The flagstones. Not the angular precision of the diamond-cut slate in the smart kitchen shops we would visit sometimes in that former life in town, but this softer, paler evidence of a life which has borne witness. *Endured*. The stones all rounded and smooth – the contours worn away by hundreds of feet over hundreds of years so that on our first viewing I wanted to crouch down and stroke it. Desperate to run my fingers over the cool, smooth stone. I was too embarrassed back then – the estate agent grinning from ear to ear while Mark mouthed behind my back that I was not to show so much enthusiasm. *Bad for bartering, Sophie.*

'Lovely place.' Emma put her son down, straightening his clothes before stopping me in my tracks by kneeling to run first the flat of her palm and then her fingers across the floor, tracing the shape of fossils in the corner of one of the larger stones before sitting back on her heels.

'I am so jealous. This is simply gorgeous.' Again she traced her fingers across the same stone, a favourite of mine, and I noticed that her hands did not match the rest of her at all. Short, untidy nails and dry, rough patches of skin. 'Such a shame so many of these floors were dug up. Priory House has carpets, unfortunately. I was hoping there might be something interesting underneath but I've checked. Concrete.'

'Yes, I know.' I was a tad disorientated, a flutter of something I could not yet understand, and so I turned away, leading the boys through to the kitchen to pour them some apple juice before kneeling down to greet Emma's son at eye level.

'So, what's your name, young man?'

'Theo. It's short for The-o-dore.'

'Is it now? Well, that's a very nice name. I've never met a *The-o-dore* be-fore.' I emphasised the rhyme but there was no response, not the smallest of smiles, and so I turned to my own son. 'OK, Ben. How about you show Theo the toys in the playroom and share nicely, yes? And remember, I've put new batteries in the trains.'

And then I stood back up, only to feel it even more strongly. That forgotten but not unpleasant combination of nerves and anticipation. A stranger. A change. A breath of fresh air.

'So you know Priory House, then? Oh, but what am I saying . . . You probably know *all* the houses in your village, Sophie.'

'Sorry, I wouldn't sit there. Cats' hairs. Coffee or tea, by the way?'

'Oh, tea please. Then I can read your leaves as a thank you. Oh, God. Look.' She was kneeling at the window seat. 'Someone else is squeezing into the removal van's cab now, through the window. Do you think that's a good idea?'

'If it's one of the farm hands, it's a very good idea. They can turn trailers on a sixpence. Sorry – didn't quite follow what you were saying. About the tea, I mean?'

Emma turned back from the window. 'My party piece. Reading tea leaves. Picked it up from my gran. I do palms too. You're not anti?' And then, seeing my frown, 'I'm sorry, Sophie. I've embarrassed you.'

'Not at all.' A lie. 'OK. Yes, actually, you have. To be perfectly honest, I think I've only got tea bags.'

She was laughing at me as I began rummaging in a wall cupboard.

'It's OK, really. Don't go to any trouble. Builder's tea is fine – the stronger the better – though I wasn't kidding about the reading thing. We can do that another time.' Next, turning again towards the window, 'Sorry – did you say something about a TV crew turning up?'

'Quite possibly. Bit of a running saga – lorries and that road. Depends how long he's stuck and how busy the newsroom is. Though if they let one of the farm boys take over, it may not come to that.' I gave up the fake rummage, well aware we had no loose tea, and so dropped three tea bags into a blue china pot, leaning out of the way of the steam as I poured from the kettle.

'This is very good of you, by the way. Rescuing me and Theo. Wouldn't happen in Streatham.'

'So you've come from London?'

'Not directly. Via France, actually. I had a few months there with my mother.'

'Oh, right. I see.'

'I doubt it. A bit complicated, actually. There isn't a *Mr* Carter in case you were wondering. Never was. I do hope that won't ruffle feathers? For Theo, I mean, in a little place like this?'

'Don't be silly.' I could feel the flush as I carried the teapot and two of our best mugs to the table. 'So – a few months in France? That sounds lovely.'

And then Emma surprised me again – an unmistakable wince, with those striking eyes flickering as she fiddled with her long, dark hair. An odd and unexpected fracture in the show of confidence.

She was buying time, and I felt sorry for her sudden discomfort as she pointedly looked away towards the playroom where both boys were lying on the floor, fitting lines of trucks behind engines on parallel rail tracks. We both watched. I waited.

'They seem to be getting on well. Theo was nervous about the move – me too, actually,' and then Emma's tone was at last steady again, 'though I rather think I'm going to like it here,' her smile returning, not just to her mouth but to her eyes, which I only now noticed had tiny flecks of different colours in them – green and brown streaked through the blue. A detail so unusual it made me suddenly self-conscious again – aware of this really strange and unexpected mix of feelings. Curiosity, and something rather odd.

Something which, in that moment, I could not quite put my finger on.

TODAY – 4.30 P.M.

So what exactly is a spleen *for*?

I stare out of the train window, struggling through the filing cabinet of my brain for a biology lesson or a snippet from some documentary which might help, but find nothing, remembering instead the woman a few seats away with the annoying child . . . and the iPhone.

It's less than a minute before I am standing in the aisle alongside her. 'I'm sorry to intrude, and I really wouldn't dream of asking if I wasn't absolutely desperate, but I need to look something up and I have this terrible phone today. I'm very happy to pay you?'

'Excuse me?'

'Is there any way I could borrow your phone? Please. Just for a minute. It's my son. He's only four.'

'Your four-year-old has a mobile?' Her tone is all startled disapproval.

'No. No. I'm not explaining this very well. I don't want to ring him; I need to look something up *about* him. He's been hurt and – look, I don't want to embarrass myself here.' I have to pause, the words catching in my throat and my eyes warning her . . . *Not. To. Bloody. Ask. Please.* 'Look. I'm desperate. This is my spare phone and I don't have a data package.' I hold up the clunky, ancient model.

'Right. Oh, I see. Yes. Well.' She glances at her own daughter who is colouring in a picture of a fairy in hideous shades of pink felt tip. 'Of course. Yes. I suppose.' She is tapping away at the phone, setting it up for me . . . and I try hard to conceal my envy that her daughter is sitting there. Sighing. Bored.

Safe.

'I'm really grateful. It won't take long.'

Five minutes later I'm back in my own seat and words swim in front of me.

. . . an integral part of the immune system.

The spleen, as I feared, is important. A fist-shaped organ which sits under the rib cage and above the stomach. I am scrawling notes in the back of my pocket diary. The web page said something about filtering systems. Platelets and red and white blood cells. If you don't have one there is a higher risk of infection for life, which means you may have to take penicillin or other antibiotics every single day . . .

And he's only four.

On the phone it was the ward nurse who let slip about the surgery. Later she backtracked – said she should not have told me until the consultant made a decision and they sort out which boy is which . . .

Suddenly I feel quite sick. The squeamishness over this word – *spleen, spleen* – makes me feel weak and pathetic and not strong enough for my son. I close my eyes and find I am wishing with all my heart that it is his friend's spleen that is sitting in some stainless-steel tray on the side of the operating theatre, which is wicked and cruel and makes me terribly ashamed but it is a thought I cannot help because this is what motherhood is suddenly.

My child. My baby.

And in this moment, on this wretched train, no energy to care about anything else.

CHAPTER 2

BEFORE

The worst irony? I moved us to the country because I thought it would be safer.

My plan, not Mark's. My insistence, actually.

For the first two years of our marriage, we really did love London. The theatres. The restaurants. The bridges. The buzz.

We shared the cliché of a bay-windowed North London flat with black marble worktops, squashy white sofas and regular muggings outside the local kebab shop.

Ours was the metropolitan dream, loved at first and then loathed in equal measure by a gang of friends who segued, pregnancy by pregnancy, from the easy pleasure of tube stations and exotic foodstuffs on our doorsteps to unforeseen fights over too much crime, too little storage and the state of the local state school.

As baby hormones raged in turn around the group, all our friends surprised themselves and each other by drifting away to entirely different lives – Ryan and Elaine to run a holiday complex in France; Sally and Eden to new teaching posts in New Zealand; Hermione and Ian to the dreaded suburbs; and Simon and Stella to the divorce courts.

And then – our turn. 'London is no place for a family, Mark. It's too dangerous.'

'Rubbish, Sophie. It's a great place for a family – think of the museums.'

'We never go to the museums, Mark. And I'm serious. Have you seen the local school? Knives are practically on the kit list.'

'We'll go private.'

'We don't believe in private.'

'Hypocrisy is permitted post-partum.' He was staring at my bump as I stood there, five months pregnant, in the black-and-white kitchen of our newly inconvenient one-bed.

Mark's plan was very simple. We would move to a bigger garden flat with laser-beamed security.

It took me just a few weeks to convince him otherwise – a shameless campaign involving a caveman's quota of rare fillet steak and a lifetime's quota of oral sex.

'I'll feel safer in the country, Mark. A different person. More cooking. Less stressing. It's what the baby needs. What we all need.'

And so while Mark continued to argue for the suburbs, I worked on our complete reinvention. If I was going to take the agreed career break for the sake of family life, I would do it with bells on. I had fallen in love with Devon as a child and optimistically imagined Mark could relocate his business to Exeter over time. At worst, Bristol.

'You're insane, Sophie. Devon? Do you have any idea how long it will take me to commute from Devon? We'll be weekending forever.'

And then the brochures began to arrive – tumbling through our London letterbox – with thatches and barns and *fields of dreams* for hammocks and llamas. Also golf. So that, as the bump grew, so Mark's resistance finally shrank until Tedbury was suddenly in both our sights.

A 'village of the year' with a thirteenth-century church, and a pub, shop and primary school, Tedbury offered the rare bonus of a traditional square with six magnolia trees which for a brief spell each spring rained pink confetti on the residents as they walked their dogs early in the morning and parked their cars late at night.

I'll be happy in the country. I know it, Mark.

How the phrase came to haunt me, tossing and turning in bed after meeting Emma.

All the boredom and all the frustration? One hundred per cent my fault.

I left London dreaming of this very life, and yet the moment I quit my job as a senior copywriter for a corporate advertiser . . . you guessed it, I missed it. And the very moment I had the longed-for child bawling in my arms with colic, I was the one thinking *what have I done?* Pining for the buzz of the city. The 'Mind the Gap'. All of which made me feel this terrible and crippling guilt watching Mark slog up and down the motorway.

He tried to share the blame. Mark genuinely planned to move the business, then later got cold feet. But I'm the one who miscalculated the most.

I'm the one who did not bank on the fox eating my chickens, on the damp wood which would not burn, on the rain clouds which seemed to cling to the moors like cotton wool to a Christmas tree. And on the fact that baby number two was point-blank refusing to happen, stretching my career break into this lonely and never-ending limbo.

Every few months I had the same thought: *Go back to work, Sophie . . . The second baby isn't coming,* only to have the idea dashed by my period running late. One tantalising week. Two. Dreaming. Hoping. And then always the same debilitating disappointment . . .

'So – what's she like, then?'

I opened one eye to find Mark perched on the bed.

'What's who like?' I was momentarily confused; had not heard my husband come in last night.

'Have you not been listening, Sophie?'

And now – more guilt, wondering what had happened to Mark's chin. Didn't he have a nice chin once? Where had it gone?

Did other wives do this? Look at their husband after each spell apart and think, *Goodness. Have you always looked like this?*

'Sorry. Sorry. Not quite awake. Who do you mean?'

'The mystery woman everyone's talking about in the pub.'

'Pub?'

'You were already in bed asleep when I got in.'

'So you had a quick one.'

'Three.' He kissed me on the forehead, exhaling a dragon's breath of stale beer by way of confirmation. 'But I secured a new contract this week to keep you in this charmed life. So it was a celebration. Anyway – Nathan was in. And all he could talk about was a furniture van crunching into Heather's yesterday and some mystery woman he clearly now has the hots for. Reckons she's some jazz singer. He says you rescued her, so I am under strict instructions to get the full story before golf.'

'Oh, you're not playing golf with Nathan *again*?'

'So – what's the deal? Is she famous, then?'

I could feel the frown as I sifted through our conversation. I'd had a very pleasant hour with Emma, but no, not a word about music. In fact, no talk about work at all, which suited me just fine.

'I didn't recognise her. And she didn't say anything.'

'Oh – you're hopeless. I'll make coffee.'

'She's quite unusual, actually. Glamorous but with definite Totnes tendencies. She wanted to do some kind of *reading* for me, which was odd. Romany grandmother or something. But I liked her. In fact she could be just what this place needs. Though much too nice for Nathan. I'll have to warn her off.'

Mark was now, in deference to Totnes, making mock-hippy peace signs – the nearby town a strange portal to an even stranger past.

'Is he sure she's a singer?'

'Big on the jazz scene, apparently. Been on *Jools Holland*. But then, you don't follow music.'

'I do so.'

'No, you don't. And I wouldn't go meddling regarding Nathan.' I raised my eyebrows; Mark raised his hands. 'Right. *Coffee*.'

He disappeared on to the landing, closing the door as I shut my eyes again and heard Ben's footsteps. Next the sound of Mark whizzing our son into the air, followed by aeroplane noises and giggles. Ah yes. I smiled, remembering why I married him. *Daddy can make breakfast. Daddy can play aeroplanes. Daddy can . . .*

And then suddenly Mark was waking me a second time – whether ten minutes later or an hour, I hadn't the foggiest – standing next to the bed with a tray and an expression of puzzlement. As well as proper frothy coffee, which confirmed a reluctant battle with the espresso machine, there was the newspaper plus a small bunch of flowers, and more mysteriously a packet of Darjeeling tea. A dark green, Tardis-like box with gold writing. Nice quality. Proper leaves.

'Flowers?'

'And before you say *you shouldn't have*, I didn't. They were on the doorstep with the tea. So what's all that about, then?'

'Our new singer.'

'*Tea?*' He pulled a face, staring at the gift, but I decided to tease – shrugging bewilderment and readjusting the pillows.

An hour later, showered and dressed, I appeared downstairs to a familiar clattering from the under-stairs cupboard – Mark apparently searching for his golf equipment. This was both surprising and entirely fruitless, as the bag was in the garage. I'd watched him transfer it the previous weekend with a running commentary about how much more convenient it would be *to just pop it in the car boot.*

I said nothing as a series of crashes was followed by swearing. I put the flowers in water and mouthed quietly to Ben to *fetch your shoes, darling.*

'Sorry? What was that? I can't find my golf equipment.' Mark's voice from the depths of the cupboard was followed by a single, extremely large crash, the sound of breaking glass and an ominous silence.

I put Ben's coat on very quickly and ushered him to the door.

'Try the garage, honey. We'll see you later.'

The stroll to Priory House was precisely as I feared – both entirely familiar and entirely strange. The crunch of the gravel, the smell of the wild flowers just in blossom along the route, the moo from a cow by the hedge irritated at the intrusion on her breakfast – and yet along with these familiar sights and sounds, an awareness deep in the pit of my stomach that it was not Caroline who would open the large stable door, not Caroline's kitchen table we would sit at, with its familiar smears and stains. The table at which, just a few months earlier, we sat waiting for a blue line on the test stick; the blue line which never, ever came . . .

Emma's arrival meant I would have to deal with Priory House in its new clothes rather sooner than expected. And so I tried to picture how it might feel. Same space. Different sofas . . .

'Are we going to see Caroline, Mummy? Has she come back?'

'No, Caroline has moved – remember? We're going to see the new lady and her son, Theo . . . You know – you met him yesterday. They're going to live at Caroline's.'

On the doorstep I had to take Ben's hand to stop him pushing his way in. Caroline never locked the door.

'Why are we ringing the bell, Mummy? And where will Caroline live when she comes back?'

'She's not coming back. Remember? I told you.'

'Is it because you called her a cockroach?'

'That's enough, Ben.'

Then a puzzle – Heather opening the door.

'Oh heck. Sophie. You'd better come in. Sorry. Emma's got her hands full.' She smiled at Ben and led the way through the dining room to the kitchen, in the middle of which Emma was pulling china and bowls from one of several large packing boxes.

I was surprised at the camaraderie, given the new dent in Heather's wall. 'No pistols at dawn, then? No mud wrestling? I feared you two might be talking through solicitors . . .'

'Heavens, no. Emma's been marvellous. We've done all the paper-work with the removal firm already. *Fully insured*, thank God. There's nothing much broken so far here, and it doesn't look as if there's any structural damage at mine. Just some pointing to be done . . . *Plus*' – and here Heather turned to our host, eyes wide – 'Emma reads fortunes.'

'So I hear.'

'She's done my tea leaves and my palm. *A-ma-zing*. As good as that bloke on the Barbican. Come on, Sophie. You must have yours done immediately.'

I widened my own eyes as a warning. 'Well, actually, we're not stop-ping. I just came to say thank you for the flowers, Emma, and to offer a favour. I wondered if Theo would like to come and play sometime?' Then, lowering my voice, 'In fact, if he's not too shy, he'd be welcome now. Give you some space to crack on with the unpacking. Don't worry, though, if it's too soon. Just a thought.'

'I'm not shy, but I don't want to play trains again.'

'No. No. That's fine, Theo.' I winked at Emma, remembering the dispute over the bridge collapse. 'Well, there are lots of other toys at our house, Theo. But it's up to you. If you'd rather help Mummy unpack?'

The two boys now eyed each other in their own tacit conspiracy.

'I've got dinosaurs,' Ben offered, hopefully.

'Any man-eaters?'

Ben nodded.

'OK. If there are T-Rexes, I'll go.'

'Great – we can play *Jurassic Park*.'

'You haven't seen *Jurassic Park*, Ben.'

'I have.'

'We've been over this, Ben. No, he hasn't,' I reassured Emma and Heather, winking again. 'Sore subject.'

Emma ruffled Theo's hair, laughing as he pulled away, and then reached across to flick the switch on the kettle, insisting we stop for a drink first – ushering the boys into the garden for football.

'Don't worry – no tea. No *reading*. I'll make a pot of coffee, Sophie. Then you won't feel on the spot. Librans *so hate* that.' Emma was grinning while I glared at Heather.

'Don't look at me like that. I didn't say a thing. I don't even know when your birthday is, Sophie, I'm not on Facebook. See, I told you she was good.'

Emma, meanwhile, wiped her hands and sat at the table waiting for the kettle. Also, evidently, for my reaction. 'I'm sorry, Sophie. I shouldn't tease but I'd put money on it. Libran? Yes?'

It was true. October 20th. Though, for a reason I could not entirely understand, there was no way I was about to confirm this.

'Actually, I have a question for you, Emma. Just to make sure I haven't missed something. Do you sing?'

'*Sing?*'

'Yes. As in, for a living . . .'

CHAPTER 3

BEFORE

Four days later and Emma stared down at Tedbury below her, suddenly working something out.

Yesterday she'd bought postcards from the local shop: a romantic and improbable version of the village, the image all soft focus with a strange mist. Photoshop, she assumed.

She bought a batch, telling the postmaster she would use them as change-of-address cards, then binned the lot the minute she got home; no intention of telling anyone where she was.

And now? From this vantage point, Emma could see that the postcard was no photographer's trick after all. Far below her, the early-morning mist pooled in the valley exactly as depicted in the image, while on this higher ground the cows chomped obliviously at their breakfast, bathed as she was in contrasting sunlight.

OK. So a trick not of photography but of topography. Emma smiled, aware this mist would not last long and thinking of the grandmother she had to thank for the treat of being introduced to it; the woman, tall and lean, whom she had come to know as Granny Apple and who taught her to rise early for mushroom-gathering. *It is the curse of a house, Emma,* she'd explained as they foraged barefoot through the dew all those years ago. *Houses breed the delusion of more comfort indoors than out. And yet – see. Just look how wrong they are. How much they miss.*

Ah yes, Emma thought. *How much we miss.*

'Is it smoke, Mummy?'

In France, she had walked with Theo in a little rucksack on her back, but he was beyond that now – a small, yawning voice alongside her. Talking. Moaning. Always talking.

'No, Theo. It's mist.'

'Does it hurt?'

He had moaned especially about coming out this early, but she remembered another of her grandmother's tricks now.

'Pancakes when we get back. Our reward.'

'With maple syrup, Mummy?'

Emma ignored the question, picturing for a moment not the frying pan on the stove outside her grandmother's dilapidated caravan but the pancakes in France – the skill with which the women at the market rolled them out so thinly on the large, hot grill plates, Theo stretching up on tiptoes to watch. The smell of caramelised sugar and warm chocolate wafting through the air, just like this mist; and then, with the thought of France, the tightening in Emma's stomach which accompanied any thought involving both her mother and her grandmother – the women who could not sit comfortably together. Not in the same room. Not in the same sentence. Not even in the same daydream.

'Can I have maple syrup, Mummy?'

Emma pretended not to hear. Eventually, she had learned, he would give up asking questions.

Instead she was picturing broken glass and crockery all over the floor of her mother's kitchen in France and, with the memory, an echo in her head of her own voice, angry and uncontrolled.

Who did this, Theo? Did you do this again? You must own up to Mummy and Granny right this minute if you did this.

'Come on then, Theo.' Emma tilted her chin up. She would need to be more careful around her son in Tedbury. 'Pancakes with maple syrup.'

Much more careful.

Aware now that the lane could probably be seen for miles, she lifted the flat of her hand for a high five, intending to offer a piggyback home. Yes. The kind of thing Sophie might do. She was pleased with herself for thinking of this, but Theo did not respond, instead wrenching away his hand. Something, she realised, had caught his eye in the hedgerow a few feet away. Crouching down with one knee on the ground, he very gently parted the long grass at the foot of the hedge, his eyes wide with concentration as he reached forward with uncharacteristic control and care. His face was just softening in anticipation when there was a riot of barking from further along the lane, and both their heads turned at once as a large dog appeared – bounding to join them and diving head first into the very same section of the hedge.

'Theo!' Emma lunged forward. The dog was a golden retriever, but for all the breed's gentle reputation its highly animated state was alarming. With Theo wailing in horror, the animal reversed, low to the ground, wiggling its bottom and with something very clearly in its mouth.

'He's eaten it. Oh, Mummy, he's *eaten it*.' Theo's distress was still incomprehensible, Emma having no idea what had caught his eye. As she tried to calm him sufficiently to explain himself through the sobbing, there was a loud and at first disembodied voice calling, 'Bella! Bella! Here girl,' from further up the lane.

Emma turned to see Nathan, the guy from the village square that first day, swinging wellington-clad legs over a stile. The dog responded immediately – first a turn of the head and then complete obedience, bounding through the mud to her master, tail wagging and leaving Theo still wailing.

Emma, crouching low to put both arms around her son, watched as the dog offered up something which Nathan was very carefully examining, pulling a face of concentration and then surprise before rummaging in his pocket. 'It's all right. Stay, Bella, *stay.*' Leaving the dog by the stile he strode towards them, wrapping his find very carefully in a handkerchief.

'I'm sorry about that. But she's all bark. Look, it's still alive,' and then, crouching down to Theo, Nathan gently opened the white handkerchief to reveal, to Emma's astonishment, a small, quivering bird.

'I'm surprised it hasn't died of shock from the barking, to be honest. But she's trained to retrieve very gently. See. She didn't break the skin.'

He peeled the handkerchief back just a little further to reveal the bird opening and closing its beak silently as if trying to chirrup. There was dark blood on its left wing which Nathan quickly covered as Theo winced.

'That wasn't Bella, I promise you. It's dried blood, not fresh. The bird must have been in a fight. Sorry – I don't remember your name, little chap?'

'Theo. It's short for Theodore.'

'Right, well, I'm Nathan. It's short for Nathaniel.'

There was no response – not the tiniest smile – and so Emma, eyebrows arched, mouthed an explanation over her son's head – *he's very fond of birds* – as she struggled to wipe away the evidence of his misery with a tissue.

'Sorry about the kerfuffle, but it's nice to meet you properly, Emma.' Nathan stretched out his hand to shake hers, holding it firmly along with eye contact. 'I was on the square when you arrived.'

'Yes, I know. Sophie has been telling me all about you.'

'Has she now?' A pause, still holding her gaze, unblinking, before grinning and turning back to Theo.

'Well, Theo. Looks like you've saved yourself a robin.'

'A robin? But I thought they were for Christmas.'

24

'No, not just Christmas. They're around all year. And very territorial. Fights are quite common, actually.'

Emma stood up. 'So you're a bit of a twitcher, then?'

'Oh, no, no.' Nathan began brushing down his trousers. 'Not me. Drinking companion in the pub – Tom. Not much he doesn't know about birds.' And then, brightening suddenly, 'I tell you what, young man. Why don't we get this bird back to my place – I'm just up the road – then we can give Tom a bell and see what he thinks.'

Theo checked for his mother's reaction. 'We were going home for pancakes.'

'Well, as it happens, I do a very good pancake myself.'

'Do you now?' Emma returned Nathan's stare and then glanced at her watch. 'Oh, go on, then. Why not?'

The barn, about a third of a mile along the lane, was one of those rare conversions which did not sit directly opposite a farmhouse, enjoying its own two acres and with them an unexpected degree of privacy. It was an upside-down affair, steep steps to an entrance of magnificent double-width oak doors leading into an open-plan sitting room and kitchen-cum-diner.

'Wow.' Theo was eyeing the long and open stretches of polished wood floor. 'Can I take off my shoes?'

'No, Theo.' Emma was clocking the expensive-looking ceramics on low tables. Direct hits for skidding in socks.

'Oh, please.'

'I said no.' She spoke with practised determination, mother and son surveying the room together while Nathan held the bird high enough to deter Bella's enthusiastic sniffing, eventually handing the bundle to Emma – *would you mind?* – and leading the dog down the stairs, apparently to the back garden.

A couple of minutes later, Nathan reappeared with a shoebox in which he coaxed Emma to place the robin. 'We'll give Tom a call.' Nathan quickly washed his hands then picked up a phone and walked across the kitchen area to open cupboard doors as he dialled. 'In the meantime, pancakes . . . You two make yourselves at home, please. If you can forgive Bella, Theo, she's in the garden. Plays a good game of catch. There are several balls on the lawn. It's just down the stairs and through the big doors. She's very friendly, honestly.' He turned to Emma, suddenly frowning and then blushing. 'Though if it makes your mother nervous . . . ? The dog is perfectly safe, I promise you. I know that some parents—'

'It's fine. So long as I can watch from the window?'

Theo seemed to be checking his mother's face closely, and when she nodded encouragement, he shrugged and headed down the stairs. Nathan then tucked the phone under his chin, chatting away to Tom while simultaneously gathering ingredients for the pancakes – to Emma's surprise needing no prompting from a recipe as he confidently measured out the flour and began cracking eggs, all the while explaining their find to Tom. 'Yes. Bella gave the poor thing quite a fright. I know they don't often make it but a little lad found it and he's a bit upset . . . Sorry? . . . Yes – half an hour is fine.' He glanced at a large clock on the wall. 'I've popped it in a shoebox for now . . . OK. See you then. My shout at lunchtime. Bye.'

By the time he turned, Emma was watching him keenly. Both the house and the man had surprised her. The room was understated – not the dark wood and leather she would have predicted, but light and airy with large cream sofas and a series of very distinctive naive paintings hung around the whitewashed stone walls.

'Lovely place.'

'Thank you. Though I wouldn't do open plan again. Seemed a good idea at the time but you get tired of living with the smell of the last meal.' He was smiling, beating the batter with one hand while replacing the phone with the other, all the while staring at her, not at all self-conscious.

'So you like to cook, then?'

And now Nathan peered down at his paunch, pulling an expression of feigned surprise which made Emma laugh out loud.

'While I hear *you* are something of a crystal-ball gazer.' His tone was teasing as he reached for a small frying pan hanging from a utensil rack above the range cooker.

'And how did you come to hear about that, then?'

'Oh, this is Tedbury, Emma. You can't fart in Tedbury without a paragraph in the parish magazine.'

Emma had now wandered over to the window to watch Theo playing with the dog on the lawn. 'Of course, the singing keeps me very busy.'

'Touché – though I would argue that particular misunderstanding was not my fault.'

The error, he explained, had been traced – according to Heather – to a local estate agent who seemed to believe he could talk up local house prices affected by the lorry 'blight' by spreading rumours of 'stars' moving in.

'Last year it was the lead singer of a boy band. This year a jazz singer . . . which everyone, of course, presumed was you.' Nathan stopped whisking his batter as he turned to follow Emma's gaze to the garden. 'It's OK. There's nothing down there to harm him. Just the chainsaw,' he added, grinning as she checked his face. 'So, if Sophie has been talking about me, I expect you've heard all about my wicked past, then? She's a nice girl, actually. We're on the fair committee together. I like her. Just a shame she doesn't approve of me – her husband's a very fine golfer.'

'I should warn you she's been sweet to me, Nathan. Very welcoming, so you're not to be rude.'

He began pouring the first batch of batter into the pan, swirling it around. 'Funny how the first pancake is always rubbish. Why is that?' The batter hissed as he watched it closely.

'We lived in France for a while. Visiting my mother. That's where Theo got into pancakes.'

He did not reply, concentrating on the job in hand and rejecting the first pancake into a bowl – Emma watching intently as he went on quickly and expertly to cook several of perfect colour, which he placed on to a warming dish. 'Right. We're in business.'

'Actually, Sophie did warn me about you. She said you'd been married twice quite disastrously and had something of a *reputation*.'

'Oh dear.' He was smiling again. 'Well, the lovely Sophie is probably quite right. If I had met a version of Sophie some years back then I would probably have been all right myself, truth be told. But then she is the kind of woman who sees everything in black and white, wouldn't you say?'

'Now, I warned you not to be unkind.'

'Oh, I'm not. I like her too. Honestly. Very bright and very funny. Takes the piss mercilessly out of the fair committee, which gets my vote. I just said that she had very little experience of the *grey* in life.' And now his face was much more serious. 'While I have always . . .' A pause then, frowning. 'Well, let's just say I have always found the grey bits of life the most interesting.'

He seemed to be checking her face for a response, but this time Emma pointedly turned back to the window and so Nathan twisted on one foot back to his stove. 'Which is why I had to learn to cook. Having made such a lousy husband. Now, do please pick some music if you like. Over by the fireplace. And we'd best call the young chap in for his breakfast.'

Emma had by now walked right up to the glass to see Theo revelling in the control he had managed to exercise over the dog – making her sit and fetch in turn, pointing his finger at her in an exaggerated gesture of chastisement. And then, as she watched him repeat the sequence, there was a familiar feeling of impatience deep inside her.

She could see it written on her face, reflected in the glass, and so deliberately relaxed her features, softening her mouth. In truth, she was itching to get on with things in Tedbury, but after all that had happened in Manchester and in France, she knew she needed to take more care.

To slow down.

'I'm very glad I bumped into you this morning, Nathan.' Emma turned suddenly, deliberately widening her eyes. 'Yes. Very glad indeed.'

CHAPTER 4

BEFORE

LIBRA
Today you must leave it alone. Walk away from it. Be
strong, be sensible and above all else, be less bothered.
Practise the art of 'not caring'. There's your solution.

'Are you sure you don't want me to come with you today? I can hold
off on the meeting?' Mark's voice was pulling me back into the room.

'Sorry?'

'The appointment? You want me to come?'

'No, no, Mark. There's no need. It's fine.' I snapped the newspaper closed and felt the flush of embarrassment. I never read my
horoscope . . .

'You're not just saying that?'

'I'm not just saying that. Honestly.' At least, I never *used to* read
my horoscope.

I pushed the paper away and poured us both more coffee.

'But what about Ben – won't it be awkward? With little ears?'

'It's OK. Emma's offered to have him.' I felt the smile inside. 'He
and Theo are getting on so well. It's a real shame Theo's that little bit

younger and they won't start school together. Actually, I was thinking of having Emma to dinner soon. You'll like her. And I'd like to introduce her to a few more people. Help her settle in properly. You know what people here can be like.'

'Of course. Whatever you think. Maybe we could invite Nathan – he's taken quite a shine to her. And you'll ring me after the appointment?' Clicking his briefcase closed, he was slurping his coffee and trying not to let me see him check the time on the clock opposite. Our Monday routine. Him pretending he doesn't need to hurry; me pretending I don't mind.

'I'm fine. You go or you'll hit the traffic. I'm fine – really.' Not fine at all . . .

Be less bothered.

I found a smile as he kissed the top of my head, and then sat very still as he left the kitchen, aware of the pulse in my neck as I listened for the familiar sequence of sounds. The slam of the boot, the start of the engine, the tyres on gravel then a pause as he checked the lane before pulling out. And then silence.

Sometimes I could sit for a long time consumed by the quiet after he left. Just me and the house – Ben playing in his room upstairs. I remembered those awful days even further back, when I would sit, not just immobile but as if anaesthetised, watching Ben, a baby in his all-in-one padded blue-and-yellow suit, strapped into the car seat on the floor. Waiting.

There was a bunch of plastic keys attached by Velcro to the bar of the seat – also a multicoloured spider made of towelling. Each pair of legs a different shade. Blue. Red. Yellow. Green. Ben would play with these toys while he waited, more patiently than I deserved. *Waiting for what*, I would think, staring at him back then.

What are you waiting for?

Today I put my hands together, as if praying, tapping my lips. 'Come on, Ben. Get your rucksack. We're going to Theo's.'

Technically, I thought, sitting in the waiting room staring at the amateur art for sale on the walls, *we attend the wrong doctors*. Tedbury, on the road between Modbury and Aveton Gifford, is supposed to fall under the Modbury practice, but I did not realise this when we first moved in and registered at a different clinic a few miles away. No one challenged me and I was grateful for the mistake now, not keen for everyone in the village to know our business. All these appointments.

There were a dozen or so pictures around the walls today, some of them surprisingly good. A watercolour of a boat – quite striking. Sixty pounds but the frame was dreadful. I was wondering if it would be worth reframing, mentally walking around the house, imagining which wall it might suit, when a beep confirmed a new message on the flashing neon sign. My name in red lights. *Dr Elder. Room Four.*

'So . . .'

I sat down and began tracing a line on my trousers where the brown cord was completely flattened over the knee. A picture of Emma in her black-and-silver outfit popped into my head, and I glanced down at my worn flip-flops and unpainted toenails.

Dr Elder is nice. I like her. One of just two female doctors at the practice. Sometimes I have to wait more than a week to see her, but there is no way I can face any of the men. Not over this. Dr Elder is in her forties, with four children beaming from a leather burgundy frame on her desk: two girls with strawberry blonde hair, and younger twin boys with freckles marching across their noses and the top of their cheeks.

I wondered how the hell she managed the job. Nanny? Au pair? Wondered if I should have done the same – gone back to work rather than expecting baby number two to turn up to order.

Dr Elder was frowning as she glanced between a paper file on her desk and the screen. I felt my pulse in my ear. And then at last, 'Well, the good news is everything's fine.' A beam finally as she turned towards me. 'The blood test confirms you're ovulating perfectly normally. And I see we spoke last time about your husband's result. Also fine.'

I felt my shoulders change shape and nodded. In truth, I would like to have delivered the relief Dr Elder clearly hoped for, but this did not come. Fact was, I knew already I was ovulating 'normally', having spent the price of a small car on tests from the chemist.

'So why's nothing happening?'

And now the doctor tightened her lips. 'Well, it's as we discussed last time. Sometimes there's no obvious explanation.' She was glancing at the photograph on her desk. 'Sometimes they just make us wait.' I checked the photograph again myself. Neat steps in the head heights. No sign of waiting in Dr Elder's world.

'But I fell pregnant with Ben so quickly.'

'And it's been?' The doctor was once more checking the notes.

'Two years, four months.' I immediately regretted speaking up so quickly, tears pricking the backs of my eyes.

'And have you spoken to your husband about the options we discussed last time?'

'Yes.' This was a lie. 'He still thinks we should just wait.' I did not say why.

'Well, I can see this is very difficult for you, Sophie. But in the vast majority of cases, your husband is absolutely right. You're young still. And I know it's easy for me to say, but the best thing I can advise is for you to try to relax. Take a holiday. Distract yourself. Try not to focus so much on this' – looking again at the screen – 'so, remind me, are you working?'

'Not at the moment.' And now a hot ache in the back of my throat. Also the stinging once more behind my eyes. 'I was planning to go back after the second child.'

'You know there is nothing at all to suggest that history will repeat itself, Sophie. We will be watching . . .'

'I'm not afraid.'

The kind smile again. 'Look. Why don't you give it a bit longer. A couple more months, say? Then if there's still no good news, I'd like to see you with your husband. We can discuss all the options so that you both understand exactly what treatment would involve.'

'Yes. That sounds fine.'

'So, is there anything else I can help you with today?'

Only later, on automatic pilot in the car, halfway home with no memory of the first part of the journey, did I realise that I did not say goodbye to Dr Elder. Or thank you. It reminded me of church as a child, when I would sometimes find myself at the end of a prayer with no recollection of chanting the beginning. Did I say it? Or was I remembering last Sunday? Or the one before that?

On the doorstep of Priory House, the hot ache in my throat was still there, so it was no surprise – though no less embarrassing for that – when in the kitchen the dam burst at Emma's innocent inquiry, 'Are you all right, Sophie?'

There was no sound, just a stream of silent, angry tears which I fought to stem by screwing up my face very tightly – body turned towards the window on to the garden. Mortified.

And then, before Emma could respond, the humiliation was complicated by Ben suddenly appearing in the doorway. 'Mummy, oh Mummy – what's the matter? What's happened?'

I was frozen, Ben's eyes widening until Emma lunged at me, grasping my left hand. 'Mummy's got a splinter, Ben. From the front gate. I'm going to have to get it out for her. Have you ever had a splinter?'

'Yes. From the climbing frame in the park.'

'So you know that it hurts, then. And that Mummy's going to have to be very brave.'

'Are you going to use a hot needle?'

'I'm afraid so.'

And then, pulling a face of disgust, arms rigid at his sides with tight, white fists, he was gone.

Fumbling in vain for a tissue in my pockets, I eventually accepted one from a box held out by Emma.

'God. I'm so sorry about this.'

'Don't be silly.' Emma walked me by the shoulders to a chair at the table. 'Right. Sit. Strong coffee.'

I blew my nose loudly. 'Thank you. And that was very clever of you – with Ben, I mean.'

And then, as Emma began to busy herself over the drinks, I began to formulate a cover story. But even as the first idea took shape, Emma sat across the table with such an extraordinary and expectant look in her eyes – the little streaks of green and brown seeming especially vivid – that the truth instead spilled from my mouth as if my lips were just too tired to hold it in any more.

The waiting. The false starts. The day I sat right here in this kitchen with Caroline – my period two weeks overdue. So sure that time. Allowing myself to get excited. But no. Always, in the end, the bloody test said *no*. And then the worry that it was somehow bound up with that awful time after Ben was born. The depression. *Post . . . natal . . . depression.* The long, dark time before it was properly diagnosed, when I stumbled from day to day like a zombie. Not dressing. Not washing. Mark having no idea what to do. Ben sitting in his little car seat. Puzzled. *Waiting . . .*

'I'm so sorry, Emma. I don't normally do this. Spontaneous combustion. Look – I should go.' I stood.

'You are going nowhere. Now sit back down and breathe slowly. I mean it. In and out, really slowly, until you calm down.'

And so, yes. In. Out. I did as I was told. In . . . Out . . . And before I knew it, the whole story was spewing from me. How I lied to the doctor. That Mark was point-blank refusing to consider fertility treatment – afraid we might have twins and that if the postnatal depression returned, twins would be too much, for me and for him. While I – an only child – was positively desperate for a brother or sister for Ben.

'I mean, I know Ben should be enough, Emma. Look at you and Theo. You're completely fabulous together. And some people don't get any children at all' – talking faster and faster now – 'and a part of me feels guilty getting so obsessed with this, but is it really so wrong of me to want another baby? Is that really so very terrible of me?'

Emma said nothing.

'I even read my bloody horoscope this morning. Can you believe it? How sad is that?'

'Look – the readings thing, Sophie. Calling birth signs. I should never have said anything. I mean – it's just a bit of fun. Not something I would ever do seriously, not over something important . . .'

'No. No. I didn't mean it like that.' I hung my head forward, cradled it in my palms. 'Oh God, Emma. I did, actually . . .'

And now we both laughed and Emma passed the box of tissues again.

'Listen to me. I promise you, Emma, I didn't use to be this bonkers.' I blew my nose hard again. 'It's village life. I'm going slowly mad.'

'So you haven't worked since Ben? Not at all?'

I shook my head. 'I was in advertising. Not an industry that understands *part-time*. I had this idea I would have two kids close together and go back full-time later. The plan was to relocate Mark's company once the family was complete.'

'And you would never consider a nanny?'

I winced again, picturing my eight-year-old self holding the au pair's hand as my mother searched for the car keys. A pile of luggage in the hallway. The usual quick kiss goodbye, the scent of perfume which lingered in the hall with the promise of postcards. All those postcards . . .

Why did it have to be so hard for the mothers? Work? Don't work? *Black. White.*

'No. Didn't fancy the nanny route. So anyway: my choice – my fault. The move here. The career break. All of it. And I actually don't regret that – for Ben's sake, I mean. I love him to bits. Of course I do – it's just I never envisaged it would be this *hard*.'

I was searching Emma's face for a response but there was nothing.

'I'm sorry. I've embarrassed us both' – standing up again – 'the doctor's right. I've become completely obsessed with getting pregnant. She's doing the whole "take a holiday" routine. Reckons I need to *distract* myself.'

And that's when Emma's expression began to change. For a moment she looked away to the window, and then back at me with a flicker of a smile as if something had just occurred to her. Next she was darting over to a drawer in the dresser where she began rummaging furiously.

'Look – you are to say if this is a terrible idea.' She was trying a second drawer now, raking through the papers, until suddenly, 'Ah, here they are,' returning to the table with a bundle of cuttings which she spread in front of me. There were various features and articles cut from newspapers and Sunday supplements. 'Like I say, you mustn't be polite. Absolutely no pressure, but I was planning to make the most of the summer before Theo starts preschool. There's *tons* I want to see with him. Look' – she turned a feature on the Burgh Island Hotel towards me – 'I just have to see this place. Art deco. And Castle Drogo. Also Agatha Christie's house – the National Trust have got it now. And well – you mustn't feel you have to say yes.' It was her turn to speak faster and faster. 'Not everyone's into buildings. And Theo and I are used to our own company. To be honest, I worry about him, too. Not enough friends. Like you say, an only. But if you'd consider joining us . . . Tagging along with Ben. I mean if it would help you as well, as a *distraction*, to keep your mind off things, keep you busy over the summer, well – we'd just completely love it.'

I looked down at all the cuttings strewn across the table and then back at Emma, her eyes wide and hopeful, just as Ben reappeared in the doorway, his little fists still clenched white at his sides.

'Are you all right, Mummy? Is the splinter gone?'

'Yes, darling. Come here. I'm fine now. Emma has *saved* me.' I reached out to take Ben's hand, pulling him into my side and mouthing a thank you at Emma, surprised at how much better I felt already. Relief tinged with that slightly out-of-body numbness which follows any proper bout of crying, remembering just in time to clench my 'injured' hand as Ben's shoulders visibly relaxed.

As did my own.

TODAY – 5.15 P.M.

What the hell?

The train is at first slowing. Brakes screeching.

I glance around the carriage as we finally shudder to a halt.

Passengers are leaning this way and that to peer from different angles through windows.

'Why have we stopped?' I realise the question is ridiculous but do not especially care. We are right between stations – the last just ten minutes back. This makes no sense . . .

There are embarrassed shrugs. The passengers with window seats continue to strain their necks but no one can see ahead of the train.

'We can't just stop. We seriously can't stop here . . .' I am clenching my hands so tightly that the nails bite into the flesh of my palms. Several passengers are now glancing at each other, their expressions suggesting they are every bit as alarmed by me as by this unexpected stop.

I don't care; rage and turmoil bubbling in my stomach. All the news from the hospital remains so confused. Still the staff do not know which boy is which. During the last phone call I suddenly had this idea I could send a photograph, borrow that woman's phone again. But it is too late; both boys are now in surgery. Which means we have no idea which boy may be losing his spleen, which one is in gravest danger . . .

Finally there is a crackling over the intercom. A weak male voice next. Driver? Guard? Who knows . . .

'I'm very sorry, ladies and gentlemen, for this unscheduled delay. We apparently have some signalling problems ahead. We are just waiting for an update and I will let you know as soon as I have more information.'

I look at my watch. Nearly two hours still to go.

I look out of the windows again. Left then right, trying to work out where the hell we are.

In the middle of nowhere, that's where. A cow turns from a field to catch my eye as if to rub this in.

Surrey? Somerset? God knows . . .

I take out my ridiculous phone and walk through to the little connecting corridor between the carriages.

I dial the number the police sergeant gave me earlier. Infuriatingly, the automatic doors keep triggering and I have to move to stop them. At last the phone is answered but it is a different officer. *Jeez.* I waste precious time trying to explain everything. Who I am.

Eventually this new guy is understanding me. He says there will be more information when I get to the hospital. They can perhaps send a car to the railway station if that will help? When I arrive. Though there are usually plenty of taxis . . .

'No, no. That's the problem. That's why I'm ringing. My train's stopped. Stuck in the middle of nowhere. I don't know why . . .'

'I'm sorry.' There is a pause. 'Goodness. How frustrating. Very stressful for you . . .'

'But can't you do something?'

Another pause. 'I'm not following. What would you like us to do? How do you think we can help you?'

'Well. I don't know.' I move and the stupid automatic doors are triggered again. For some reason the word *helicopter* comes into my head.

'A helicopter. Can't you get a helicopter? To meet the train. To get me to the hospital. The police have helicopters, don't they?' I am looking out at the field next to the train. The cows. I can picture myself charging the cows to make a space for the landing . . .

'A helicopter?' The tone with which he says this makes me want to cry again. I do know I sound ridiculous but I don't care . . . I'm beyond caring what anyone thinks. 'I'm sorry but that's not a resource we could use in this circumstance. But if the train is delayed, we could perhaps send a patrol car to meet it. So where are you?'

'I don't know. They're not saying what's happening.'

He tells me to ring back and update him as soon as I know more, so that they can make a decision.

Again I ask him what they know about the accident. What exactly happened to my Ben? To both boys?

There is a much longer pause and I have had enough. In desperation I ask to speak to Detective Inspector Melanie Sanders. I tell him she will want to know about this.

For Christ's sake. Does he not realise what happened in Tedbury before? Back in the summer . . . My part in it? I look down at my hands and fight the panic as I remember the scene. The blood. The knife . . .

My tone is near hysterical but again I am fobbed off. He says the priority today was getting the boys to the hospital. The treatment. They are trying to piece together what happened but DI Sanders is busy. I will be told more when I get to the hospital myself.

'But I'm stuck on this bloody train. I need to know *now* . . .'

More platitudes.

'Listen to me. You have to keep her away from the boys.'

'I'm sorry?'

I lower my voice. 'Emma Carter. She's involved in the accident. I think she's having surgery too. I don't know. Patient confidentiality. They won't tell me. But you have to keep her away from the boys. Both boys. My son, especially. I insist that you keep her away from my son Ben. Do you understand? I want you to write this down.'

There is a complete change now in his tone. A series of questions that I can't answer. I can tell that he thinks I am hysterical, unhinged even. He is reminding me that Emma Carter's son has been hurt too. They are hoping she will be able to identify which child is which when she is conscious . . .

'No. No. That's the point. You mustn't do that. You mustn't let her near them . . .'

He is saying that he understands how very upset and frustrated I must feel and he will get the investigating officer to ring me back once there is any more news. He is making a note of what I have said. There will be a full update at the hospital.

'So you're not the main investigating officer?'

'No.'

'Then just piss off, why don't you . . . Just piss off.'

I hang up and try the ward again. *Come on. Come on.* It is engaged.

Next I try Heather. Straight to voicemail.

And then I cannot help myself. I open the window, reach out for the door handle. Locked. As I look down at my hand, I can see it all again.

The colour red; the feeling of the blood, thick and warm all over my fingers. That look in her eyes. *The knife . . .*

Next I feel the breeze. The rain. I move my case to the door so I can stand on it. This will be difficult . . .

Oh, good grief. Look at that woman. She's climbing through the window.

I work out that the drop to the bank of grass is not as bad as I feared . . . On the third attempt, I manage it.

I get off the train.

CHAPTER 5

BEFORE

'So – what got into you?' I was staring at my husband in our kitchen, the debris from the dinner party filling every surface.

I normally like this time after entertaining. That feeling of release and relief when you have just waved off the final guest and retire to the kitchen, feeling a little bit drunk but pleased and proud and still smiling at the banter, happy that you made the effort.

'Look – I'm really sorry, Sophie. This bloody cold.'

I looked at him again, narrowing my eyes.

'I apologised to your guests; I honestly did my best.'

'Well, if that's your best, Mark – heaven help us all. And forgive me for thinking they were *our* guests. You know – in *our* home . . .'

The dishwasher was already full so I ran hot water into the sink and started to line up the wine and water glasses, turning away from him.

'Can't we do this in the morning?' He was tipping the contents of a Lemsip sachet into a mug.

'The row or the dishes, Mark? And you can't have another one of those yet. You had one in the middle of dinner.'

'That was hours ago.'

'Mark – is there something going on at work? Something you're not telling me?'

'Why would there be anything going on at work? I've got a cold. End of.'

I glanced at the kitchen clock. Eleven thirty. Hardly a triumph.

I'd invited two couples to meet Emma tonight. Nice people. Gill Hartley, who works for the council, her writer husband Antony and local teachers Brian and Louise Packham. The Hartleys were normally stayers – 2 a.m. not at all unusual – but I was not surprised that even they'd cut the evening short. At one point Mark had disappeared for so long for his Lemsip, I actually feared he had gone to bed.

'It was a good evening. You did an amazing job as always, Sophie. Great food.'

'While my husband was like Houdini.'

'Oh, I wasn't that bad. Come on. Give me a break, I've had a really terrible week. I've probably got the flu the way this is going – I didn't want to stink out the dining room with hot lemon. I drank it in my study. Anyway, you know I struggle to cope with Antony Hartley and his poetry at the best of times.'

'I thought you liked the Hartleys.'

'I do – but I'll eat my own child before he earns a penny farthing from that pissing about. It winds me up.'

Mark stirred his Lemsip and then threw the teaspoon into the washing-up bowl. I felt him move behind me and then his arms were around my waist, while I stood rigid, angry and ridiculous in my bright yellow rubber gloves.

'And you can forget trying to get round me. I don't want your germs.'

'Look – I'm truly sorry, darling. You're right. I'm not myself. It was just bad timing. Dinner party after a bad week. But I didn't want to ask you to cancel. I'll make it up next time.'

'If there is a next time. I rather think everyone will give you a wide berth from here on.'

'Oh, come on. I wasn't that bad.'

'Yes, you were. Jesus, Mark. The idea was to help Emma settle in. Meet some new people – not cross-examine her about her CV. What does it matter what she did or where she worked before she moved here? Why did you have to go on and bloody on . . .'

Mark let go.

'You didn't like her, did you?' I turned to monitor his reaction. He shrugged. His eyes said I was right.

'No – come on. Spit it out, Mark. What's wrong with her?'

'Oh. I don't know. I just thought she was a bit—'

'A bit *what?*'

'Oh, never mind. Just a vibe.'

'Vibe? What does a *vibe* mean?'

'Nothing. Never mind. It's just this cold.'

'It's Tedbury, isn't it? Anything new and interesting in Tedbury and there has to be some *vibe*. Something to carp about. Something to belittle. Something to compare unfavourably with London while I'm at least still trying to make a go of it here.'

'And now you're just being ridiculous.'

'So what then, Mark? Were you just pissed off that I didn't postpone because Nathan couldn't make it – your precious golf buddy? Is that what this is really about? Never mind that Nathan with his track record is the last thing Emma needs . . .'

'And that's your call, is it? Other people's lives? To pick my friends and decide who Nathan is allowed to like?'

I stared at the floor.

'Look. I'm sorry that Nathan isn't your cup of tea but Antony Hartley isn't really mine. To be frank, maybe I'm just fed up with all these creatives wafting about the countryside, waiting for inspiration to paint pots and piss about with poetry while some of us are out there actually grafting for a living. You know – up and down the sodding motorway.'

I winced. The weekending was a nightmare, granted, but it was only ever meant to be temporary. Long ago we had agreed to delay sorting the geography until after the second child. And it was Mark who had changed his mind about moving the company.

'I'm sorry. I shouldn't have said that about the driving. And I didn't mean *you* not working, Sophie. I meant Antony, and now this Emma. Oh, look, can we just drop this – please. I'm feeling completely crap, that's all. Overtired. I'll apologise to your friends again, I promise.'

'You don't sound as if you have a cold.' *Your friends again.* I thought of Gill and Antony in their pink two-up, two-down cottage near the church. Money was always tight with them, yet they had hosted us often and generously ever since we moved to Tedbury. Nice wine. Nice food. Nice people who talked books and art and all the things I loved, who had made a good effort with Emma tonight, Antony deep in conversation with her about Sartre and existentialism, rules and rebels.

And then I pressed pause to study my husband's face which, in fairness, looked unusually hot, perspiration glistening from both his forehead and neck.

I started to feel guilty, realising I should have postponed until Nathan was free. But the truth? I wasn't overly keen to gift Nathan a platform with Emma. Nathan was charming, yes, but had never grown up, learnt to keep it in his pants. Mr Infidelity throughout both his marriages.

'Well, I like her. Emma. She's a breath of fresh air.' I let out a sigh.

'Whatever you say.' He looked unconvinced.

'So how about you just take your germs to bed, Mark?'

'Our room or the spare room?'

'I'll let you choose.'

CHAPTER 6

BEFORE

Libra
Not every hour is equal. Ask an insomniac how long the
night is.

'Your husband doesn't like me, does he?'

It was a couple of weeks after 'dinnergate'; I was watching the waves crash on to the rocks, and tilted my head to follow the foam into the rock pools where the boys liked to fish with their nets for hermit crabs, slipper limpets and, on lucky days, starfish.

I was not sure how to answer Emma's question, thinking instead of this morning's horoscope. My new guilty pleasure. Today's was spot on: hours are not equal at all. Some people you can know for years and yet not at all.

While others?

I blinked finally and turned to Emma, my eyes smarting from the wind.

'Mark just hates the weekending. All the driving. Don't take it personally, Emma. His problem is with Tedbury, not you or the Hartleys or anyone else. He never really wanted to move here. I rather twisted his arm. The plan was to move the business too but that hasn't worked out . . .'

Emma held my gaze, then found a half-smile before turning away.

I thought of the Hartleys. A couple of days after the dinner, Gill had invited me and Emma for coffee. Gill had a week off work and had made a spectacular apple cake which she warmed and served with home-made ice cream and espressos in beautiful little orange cups.

'So, how's Mark's cold?' Gill was being polite but I could tell from the glances she exchanged with Emma that they had talked about it. The disastrous dinner party.

I have always liked Gill and was sorry not to have given her a better night. She worked for the council in Plymouth while Antony studied. It was no secret that she wanted children though Antony apparently didn't; tough for her. Just occasionally I would catch her looking at Ben with real sadness in her eyes.

I glanced at the two boys now myself, working on an enormous sandcastle several feet away, a punch of guilt as Ben suddenly stood rigid while Theo ran with two buckets to the water's edge to top up the moat.

It was my fault – Ben's appalling water phobia. A fall into the pool on our very first villa holiday; I had turned my back for just a moment . . . He was standing on the sand right now with his fists tightly clenched and I could feel his tension, his fear, as he watched Theo wade into the water to his knees. Sometimes Ben even refused a bath. *I don't like it. I don't like the water all around me. Please don't make me . . . I want a shower.*

I closed my eyes to see the picture more vividly: Ben choking and gasping as Mark hauled him from the pool. Barely two. Petrified. His little body shaking head to toe as we wrapped a towel around him . . .

My fault. My greatest shame.

I opened my eyes to watch Theo return from the shoreline to touch Ben's arm for reassurance before handing him one of the buckets of water. He was such a sweet kid, Theo – as good for Ben as Emma was for me.

I turned back to her. Yes – I wished Mark had taken to her so she and Theo could come over at weekends too. Emma had met Mark a few times since the dinner but there had been no improvement, and I sighed, realising that I had to let it go.

My friend. My choice. Not the end of the world.

Emma returned to the task of sorting shells from a small plastic bucket, and I reached up to smooth stray hairs back into my ponytail. Further along the beach a dog was digging for Australia – a nearby toddler in a buggy was wailing as the flying sand landed on his face. His ice cream. His pride. I watched the mother scoop the child up on to her hip as she tried to rescue the cone; the child pink-faced and furious as the owner of the dog appeared, arms outstretched and all apologies.

It had been just a couple of months with Emma like this – sitting, talking or walking, drinking and playing tourist – and my horoscope was right because our relationship had already trumped the level of ease I had reached with almost any other friend. Even Caroline.

I saw Emma most days midweek now, at least for a coffee. She would ring each morning to tease me. *Of course, if you're too busy hoovering to come out and play, Sophie* . . . And, yes, I was disappointed that some of the older clique in the village had not warmed to her. I was especially disappointed that Mark had not taken to her. But they were all stuck in that groove where everyone plays the game of superficial politeness, following the rules of small talk and minding your own – which Emma most definitely did not.

It was probably what I liked about her most: this knack of leaving you nowhere to hide. She had a way of looking at you ever so directly and asking the questions that mattered, peeling back your layers and exposing the core that you normally managed to keep from people.

She also had this incredible energy, Emma, which had been the boot up the backside I needed. She came at you all guns firing but with a quirkiness and energy I found infectious, and somehow rejuvenating. She was the only person I had ever met who could say 'lighten up' with a look in her eyes which confirmed an absolute motivation for enjoyment and not offence. Also – and this was a key factor for me – she was completely missing the gene for embarrassment.

Take our first trip here – to Burgh Island. We both desperately wanted to see the hotel but I thought we would just pick up brochures from reception. I was thinking that maybe we could spoil ourselves and return for lunch, properly scrubbed up, when the boys were in school and playgroup in September.

It's amazing, the hotel. Stunning period interior – a tribute to a thirties heyday when the place was the darling of the beautiful set. All white and whimsical art deco on this transient island setting. When the tide is out far enough you can walk across the beach to the hotel on its hilly outcrop, but at other times there is an extraordinary tractor contraption offering rides through the water – a platform on stilts keeping passengers just dry above the waterline.

I'd visited once before when we first moved here, again to pick up a brochure. I'd hoped to return for dinner with Mark, but somehow, like so many things, we never got around to it.

But on that first visit with Emma? Oh, my word. We let the boys play on the beach first; I was bundled in this huge, ugly old sweatshirt only to find Emma marching up to the hotel, suggesting lunch. Especially crazy as there was a sign specifying *Residents Only*.

We can't do that, Emma – will you, for Christ's sake, come back. It's residents only now . . .

At the desk, Emma was pure charm; the staff delightful but firm. They were sorry but luncheon was not possible. And then Emma was doing this whole fantasy spiel about how she was in PR and marketing, working with a London media firm, looking for hospitality venues.

I was mortified – standing there with the sand-sodden children alongside couples in floaty silk dresses and smart linen suits – but Emma was incredible. In the end, she managed to swing coffee on a terrace while the staff brought her a media pack.

'Don't frown, Sophie. You'll get lines.' Emma did not look up from the plastic bucket as she said this and I was smiling again, thinking how differently I felt, not just about Tedbury, but the whole of Devon since she'd arrived.

'You know, I've lived here four whole years and not really made the most of it.'

'Sorry?' Emma was still transferring shells between buckets, sorting the colours.

'Until you moved here . . . I wasted it.'

'Didn't you get out and about with Caroline?'

'No. Not really. I was just thinking about that. How much time we frittered away. Caroline didn't have children so she didn't really understand about Ben. What he liked. What children need. At the time I told myself it didn't make much difference. But it did, actually.'

Emma was looking at me very directly. This was another thing I liked about her – the proper eye contact. She did this every time we got together to plan the next outing. Wide-eyed and enthusiastic. One month and we'd pretty much worked our way through the cuttings from her drawer already.

A boat trip to Agatha Christie's Greenway on the River Dart. A steam train ride from Totnes to Buckfastleigh. Picnics on Dartmoor, allowing Theo to paddle in the streams with poor Ben watching and waving but too nervous to join him. *I'm fine. I'll stay on the bank.* Damn that villa holiday.

'You know what? I feel so much more like my old self since you arrived, Emma.'

'Well, that's very good to hear, Sophie – especially today because I have something important I want to bounce off you.'

'Bounce away.'

'You know I'm seeing Nathan?'

'Er, knock, knock, Emma. This is Tedbury.'

'So people are gossiping?'

'Posters go up tomorrow.'

Emma laughed. 'Well, sod the talk. I don't care about all that. The important thing is that you don't disapprove too much. I know you warned me off but I promise you – I've completely got his ticket. It's just I find him rather fun and it's *nothing serious*.' She tilted her head. 'But I don't want you to be upset.'

'I'm not upset.'

'Good. Because Nathan was telling me what happened with Caroline. The deli. And it got me thinking.'

I found myself sitting up straighter and felt the frown return. The debacle of the deli was not something I cared to discuss these days.

I really liked that I didn't have to talk work with Emma. It had become my worst nightmare, anyone asking me *so what do you do then?* I was still unsure about pitching for any kind of job while Mark and I were on such different pages over fertility treatment, and Emma seemed happy to be taking time out from work, too.

I had no idea how she could afford to do this, to be frank. She was a tad light on detail about that – also her time in France. I assumed there was family money sloshing around and she was embarrassed about it. Meanwhile she referred to herself jokingly as *the last thing the south-west needs . . . another bloody artist.*

My instinct from the off was that she was being unduly modest. Heather was certainly green after Emma unpacked properly and these extraordinary pieces of her own ceramic work emerged. Emma finally confessed she had taught at art colleges in both London and the North, staging several successful solo exhibitions at key galleries.

Now, looking at her in the wind, her hair blowing back from her face, I wondered where this unexpected conversation was going.

'OK. Go on then, Emma. You said the deli got you thinking?'

'Yes. Well – you know me, brain always whirring. When I heard that it didn't work out for you and Caroline, it stirred up a bit of an idea. Nathan mentioned that you still have all the kitchen kit? Stored in one of the outbuildings?'

I couldn't help myself; I closed my eyes and turned away.

'So you're still too cross to talk about this. You still blame Nathan?'

Deep breath. 'Look – I blamed Nathan because I didn't want to blame Caroline. Or myself, I suppose.'

'But it wasn't really his fault?'

'No. Look, Emma – no offence, but I'm not really sure I want to talk about this. OK?' I fiddled with my ponytail. The truth was that I didn't want Emma to see this side of me. The extent of my naivety exposed, my disappointment raked up. To admit to her that I still *dreamt* about it. Ridiculous. Embarrassing.

'I put way too much into the deli, Emma. Imagined it would solve everything. Get me over the blip after Ben was born. Help us settle into Tedbury properly.'

She waited, trying to read my face.

She looked at me so intently that I almost imagined she might see it too, the image from my dream so vivid. The feel of the thick cotton apron – blue-and-white-striped, new and crisp – against the back of my neck. All my produce laid out in bright, shiny dishes. Three large bowls of signature pâtés: mackerel with a twist, chicken liver and my own game recipe. Warm bread in baskets. Signs trumpeting tinned produce imported from France: rillettes, confit de canard and duck mousse.

In the daylight hours I did not let myself think of this any more. I had shredded all the plans and financial papers. The business plan. The lists of products and suppliers. The growth projection for years two and three, by which time I had hoped we would be able to supply meat and organic vegetables from the local farms. Our own-recipe sausages. Our slogan: *A taste of Tedbury – keep it local.*

'I'm just surprised you never mentioned all this to me, Sophie. What did Mark think?'

'Mark warned me not to mix business and friendship. In the end he bit his lip.'

An understatement. To his credit, he never said *more fool you.* He'd strongly advised against me putting a penny of my own savings on the line – suggesting the protection of a limited company and a nice, tidy bank loan. Everything official from day one. But I threw myself into the deli in the same way I threw myself into the move to Devon. *Look – this is Caroline. We're friends, Mark.*

I took a deep breath and told Emma everything just in case Nathan had put his own spin on things.

Six months I spent putting that deli plan together – most of the initial enthusiasm from Caroline but most of the hard, practical graft from me.

When Caroline owned Priory House, it had a converted single-storey barn at the end of the garden which she let for a modest rent. After several tenants bolted owing rent and bills, she'd fancied an experiment. A 'foodie' project together.

My cooking, I am proud to say, had become a talking point locally. Already a fair cook before we moved here, I filled my boredom with professional courses and often cooked for village fundraisers. Caroline's thinking was we could try a pop-up stall selling my pâtés, my pastries, my pickles – local produce too, from the farms and smaller growers.

And then when the current tenant in Caroline's little barn suddenly left without paying his electricity bill, it was game on for something bigger.

Discreet enquiries confirmed the parish council would be very much on board for a proper village deli. There was just one planning concern – the pedestrian access. Which was where I made my first mistake – funding not just the architect and official papers for a change-of-use application, but some preliminary work to lay a better path around the side of the cottage to create an entirely separate walkway for the little barn. At the time it had seemed only fair, given Caroline would be providing a ready-made building for the joint venture. This faith then extended, once the change of use was agreed, to paying for some of the basic equipment required: the coffee machine, the refrigeration unit, the oven.

We used a firm in Totnes to handle the plans and legal work but Caroline later asked Nathan to run his eye over the conversion before the local builder installed the kit.

And that's when the whole thing turned very sour very quickly. So traumatic were the ensuing exchanges between me and Caroline that I didn't get the full story until she left the village.

Turns out Caroline believed her barn was permanently bound by a neighbour's covenant restricting any extension. But Nathan, on reviewing all the papers, had discovered a loophole. The original covenant was time-limited and had lapsed; there was nothing to stop Caroline pitching to convert the barn into a two-storey home which would produce a much better return than a deli.

Planning consent was duly won and Caroline swiftly secured a sale to a property developer happy to take on both homes as a project. With the handsome proceeds, she bought a villa in Portugal for reinvention as a 'life coach'.

Cockroach, more like became my favourite phrase.

Emma laughed.

'But it was hard, Emma, seriously – watching them convert the barn into a house when it was supposed to be my deli. I was furious.'

'So all this equipment you paid for. You still have it, Sophie?'

'Yes. The Packhams have it stored in their parents' outbuilding. I keep meaning to put it on eBay. Or find an auction.'

'Well, stop right there, because I have had the most marvellous idea. How about we resurrect the plan. You and me? But not just a deli – a bistro-cum-gallery. I was looking at Nathan's place – the way he shows off the art on his whitewashed stone walls – and I was thinking a barn would make the most superb gallery space. And then when I heard about your deli plan, the two things started to sort of gel in my head.'

'Oh, no, no, no, Emma. I'm completely done with all of that. Plus Mark would go mental.'

'I'm not asking Mark.'

'But in case you hadn't noticed, the Priory House barn is occupied by your neighbours. It's a house now.'

'Oh, I don't mean there, silly. I've been talking to Albert about his single-storey place along Hobbs Lane. It's lying empty. Completely idle. Got a loo already installed and patch of land alongside ideal for parking. And it's the perfect size. He says I can have it for a very reasonable rent but I don't want to do a project on my own. It would be no fun.'

All at once I could feel my pulse in my fingertips. Feel the blood shifting in my veins. I didn't know what to say, what to think.

'Look, I know this is a bit sudden. Even a bit cheeky, given it was your idea. But it would just be perfect for us, Sophie. Solve the boredom when the holidays finish. You could cook. I could do pottery demonstrations. We could rent out space for artists to display in – it would draw in the creative crowd during the shoulder seasons and tourists in high season. Be nice for the locals too.'

'But artists don't eat out. They can hardly afford to eat in, according to Heather.'

'Trust me. If we pitched this right, it would be perfect. The whole creative vibe would be our USP. Off-season we could do a budget-busting lunch for artists and locals – soup and a snack. Then a broader menu during the tourist season, complete with the cream tea palaver. It would be a hoot.'

And now my mind was whirring, a storyboard appearing as I closed my eyes again. A logo with coffee cups and easels. Paint brushes and paninis . . .

'No, no. I'm done with all of that. You need to stop, Emma.'

'All fifty-fifty this time. Written agreement. Nathan's drawing up some plans and putting in an application for the parking as we speak. Parish council are on board again.'

'You're kidding me? You're already on to all of this?'

'All you need to do is say yes, Sophie. Otherwise I'll have to find someone else, which would be a complete killer. The Hartleys were saying they were looking for a project, but I'd much rather do this with you.'

And now I felt this even more powerful pang inside, imagining how easy Emma would find it to coax someone else to resurrect this dream. My dream. Emma, with her optimism and flair. Emma, who in contrast to Mark with his bloody cold at that disastrous dinner party had all the other guests eating out of her hands – the Hartleys especially. And though that had been the whole point of the evening – to help Emma make new friends – I found myself remembering my mood when I had that row with Mark. Was I jealous? Was that it? To see Antony and Gill hitting it off with Emma so very quickly? Emma reading their palms, while I felt boring somehow and Mark did his disappearing act.

'Look, I've probably not been entirely fair to Nathan. Over the business with Caroline, I mean. I suppose he was just doing his job.'

Emma smiled. 'So, you'll think about this?'

'I didn't say that.'

'Excellent. I'll bring the paperwork round tonight.'

TODAY – 5.25 P.M.

'Excuse me. Please . . . You need to get back on the train.'

I ignore the remark and stare at my phone. Only one bar now. I scramble a little further up the bank but it makes no difference.

'Hello? Can you hear me, madam?'

I am aware now of a range of different voices from the train behind me. The guard's voice is the loudest – firm but, for now at least, calm. But I don't turn around to face all the others. The mix of voices, passengers mumbling among themselves. The sound of more door windows being opened.

I am looking instead for a road. A path. Anything which will tell me where I am and if there is some other, quicker way back to Ben. But there is nothing. Just grass and banks and cows . . .

And then suddenly the commotion from the train changes gear.

'Right. That's enough. You two . . . back on the train. I mean it. We can't have more people leaving the train . . .'

I turn now to find that two other passengers have climbed off the train on to the bank. A middle-aged man with grey hair. Quite striking. Tall. Kind face. Also a woman alongside him, younger, with her hair in a high ponytail.

'Seriously. I am going to have to call this in. It will delay us all even further.' The guard's voice is now much louder and increasingly alarmed.

'Please, madam. It's not safe. You have to get back on the train . . .'

He is looking directly at me, eyes wide and a mobile phone in his hand.

'We could be delayed for hours. I can't be stuck here. I have to get home.'

'We've been told ten minutes tops now.'

'So why didn't you say that over the intercom? Why did you just leave us all sitting there, not knowing anything?'

'We were waiting for confirmation.'

'Rubbish. What about that train the other week where the passengers were left for hours with no air con, no toilets. No intercom. Nothing. We can't just sit back and let you lock us on a train and treat us like this, you know . . .' I am enjoying the rant; I am enjoying putting all my anger and frustration into this new place.

By now there are scores of faces at the line of windows watching me. The man with the grey hair is watching too, but his face shows less disapproval.

I am aware of my hands beginning to shake and so I clench my fists to stop this. I also feel a tiny bit giddy and so move my feet wider apart to steady myself, not wanting the guard to see.

'We have rules, madam. Protocols. We have only been delayed fifteen minutes so far . . .'

'*Only!*' The disapproval is shouted from someone out of sight – on the train behind the guard. I can't see who but I am grateful for the support.

The guard turns and uses his arms to signal calm before glancing back to the couple on the bank and then me.

'Look. Final warning. I need all three of you to get back on the train. Please. Otherwise I am going to have to escalate this. Call for assistance. The police. An ambulance . . .'

'The police?'

'You are causing a serious incident here, madam. Putting yourself and others in danger. We absolutely can't allow this. Please. This is your final warning. Get back on the train . . .'

Suddenly I feel the panic rising in me. Ambulance? What does he mean – ambulance? It's not an ambulance I need, it's a hire car or a helicopter.

Now the man with the grey hair draws a little closer to me.

'Are you feeling unwell? You look very pale. Unsteady. I'm a doctor. I'm happy to help if I can.'

He glances at the guard. The guard's face changes.

I don't like the way they are looking at me.

'I'm not disturbed.' I lean forward as I say this. 'Is that what you think? That I'm disturbed? Some headcase?'

'No. Of course not . . .'

I wonder for a moment if I *look* disturbed.

Suddenly I see the scene through different eyes and I am starting to panic a little at the guard's reference to an ambulance. Could they cart me off? Would that be allowed?

Further down the train I see so many faces staring at me through the line of windows and then among them, finally – *his* face. It is as if time freezes for a moment, then the window is opening and he is calling my name. I am both shocked and relieved, confused and overwhelmed by this myriad of emotions all in the same moment.

The next thing, Mark is off the train, hurrying along the bank to stand near me.

'This is my wife. Oh my God . . . *Sophie.*' His eyes are locked on mine but I raise my hand to stop him.

'Your *wife?*' The guard is clearly as confused as everyone else. 'You weren't travelling together . . . ?'

'I didn't know she was on the same train . . . She doesn't have her usual phone.'

I am staring as Mark says this, trying very hard not to cry.

'We've been called home for an emergency.' Mark is looking at the guard.

'I have to get back to Ben, Mark.'

'I know. I know that, love . . .'

Mark turns again to the guard. 'Our child has been in an accident back in Devon. He's having an operation. We've only just been phoned by the police and we don't know exactly what's happened.'

'Oh goodness. I am so, so sorry.'

The doctor's face changes also as he locks eyes with me. 'You must feel very shocked. Very frustrated . . .'

I am really fighting tears now. For some reason I don't want this kindness because it makes things feel worse.

'We need to get back to Devon. My wife has had a very bad time lately. A lot of shocks actually, even *before* this . . .'

Mark is using a very gentle tone, like the doctor, and I am willing him to stop now. Maybe he is trying to prevent them calling this in officially, but I don't want him to say any more.

I don't want him to tell . . . them . . . any more.

Bad enough that they know about Ben.

I don't want them to know what happened back in the summer. That other *shock*.

I close my eyes and for a moment I see it all again. The colour red. The blood all over my hands . . .

CHAPTER 7
BEFORE

That first and terrible shock came from nowhere. Like an explosion.
Bang.

The impact so brutal, and so very physical too, like running around the corner, smiling in the sunshine, before smashing right into a wall.

One day we were talking about the deli plan on the beach; one day my life was normal and so much happier and busier and more fun thanks to Emma . . . and then?

Suddenly it was all smashed; broken like a glass, smooth and glinting one second, then slipping through the fingers to lie threatening on the floor with angry, jagged edges. Just a blink – and suddenly there was this policewoman in my kitchen staring at me. Wanting me to *go over it again.*

But the thing is I didn't want to. Not again.

I closed my eyes and could see it. Red. And I didn't want to feel this tightening in my chest; this strange, out-of-body sensation as if I were not quite there at all, in the room, in the scene, in this story.

DI Melanie Sanders was clearing her throat and I opened my eyes to catch her glancing across to the window seat. She was waiting but still I said nothing.

Instead I was thinking, *So is this what real shock feels like? Hovering just outside your own body? Watching it, not living it.*

'I really am very sorry to trouble you again so soon, Mrs Edwards, but there were a couple of things I just wanted to go over.'

Next she asked a series of questions and I realised what she actually wanted was for me to go over every single detail from the very beginning. And so finally this was what I did. I drifted slowly back into the room, into the present, and I told the whole wretched story all over again.

◆ ◆ ◆

How we had woken, all of us, ridiculously early because of the flags. Six a.m. blinking on the dressing table clock and Ben standing by our bed. 'There's a man outside my window, Mummy, with a ladder.'

I turned to the kitchen window and could picture the very moment of opening the curtains upstairs.

Turned out to be Alan – parish council chair. Some of the fair bunting had come down in the night. I remembered waving in my dressing gown, yawning and worrying that he had no one holding the bottom of the ladder; then deciding to get going early myself. So that by nine I was marching around the village, ticking boxes on my little black-and-white chequered clipboard, relieved that the weather, though a touch breezy for the tents, was at least dry.

I was happy. I was calm. I made them write that down in the first statement. *I was fine.*

I told DI Sanders again that the fair starts every year at 2 p.m. and my only concern had been the piano demolition competition – a hazard-assessment nightmare. Our insurers had been unhappy about it and so I made everyone set the safety barriers further back, but apart from that one niggle, everything else was fine.

'So was it your idea for Miss Carter to be the fortune teller?' DI Sanders had taken out a notebook from her bag and was flipping through the pages. It was not the small, tidy police notebook you see in films, but a larger pad – the kind normally used by reporters.

'Yes. Look – I told your colleagues all of this last night. Though I don't understand all this interest in the stupid fortune teller's tent. For Christ's sake, it was a village fair. A bit of fun. A *joke* to raise money for the church.'

'So it wasn't Miss Carter's proposal? You're quite sure about that?'

Give me strength . . . What is the matter with these people?

'Absolutely not. In fact she took quite a bit of persuading. Look, Emma is new to the village and she was doing me a really big favour. She didn't want to do it at all so I really don't understand these questions.'

I looked the policewoman in the eye. 'It was just a silly thing. A bit of fun.'

If anything, I was understating Emma's reluctance. At first she'd point-blank refused, arguing that it would be embarrassing. That a bit of fun with palms and tea leaves among friends was one thing, but charging money?

She had only caved in when I turned the tables. *Oh, for heaven's sake, lighten up, Emma. No one will take it seriously. It's for the church roof.*

'And there was just one other thing.' DI Sanders was staring at her notepad again, but this time self-consciously, like an actor feigning hesitancy. I looked at the clock, wondering how long Mark would be, wishing now that I had not let him fetch the papers.

'It's just, going over the statements my colleagues and I took yesterday . . .'

I glanced at the playroom door. It was pushed to but had not quite clicked shut, and though I could hear the television up quite loud I was suddenly anxious about Ben hearing. I walked over to close it – holding the brass doorknob, conscious suddenly of its coldness. I found myself thinking of that other sensation, closing my eyes to it but unable to shake it off. The warmth of it on my hands. The smell of it. The thickness of it. Wanting so much to pull my hand away but knowing that I could not. Must not.

'It's just. Well, it must have been the most terrible thing for you, Mrs Edwards. Awful. But one of the things which I didn't understand' – the police officer paused – 'from the statements, it doesn't appear that you called out. Shouted for help, I mean.'

I let go of the doorknob and wiped my hands down my jeans over and over.

'You have children, Inspector?'

'No.' She looked confused. Uncomfortable. 'Why do you ask?'

'I didn't call out, because my son was on the doorstep.' Still I was smoothing my hands down the sides of my legs. 'I had asked him to wait there a moment. He's a good boy. He normally does what I ask. But if I had shouted, he would have run in. He's four years old.'

DI Sanders twitched her head, glancing between my fidgeting and her notebook. 'Yes. Well, of course. I see. That's not explained properly in your statement.' She was running again through the notes in her book, tracing a pen down one page then the next. 'You did what you could. I'm not suggesting . . .' Her tone defensive but not unkind. 'Well – I think that's just about it.'

At last there was the sound of Mark's key in the door. We both glanced to the hall, and when he appeared in the room, his expression moved quickly from puzzlement to irritation.

'I was just going over a couple of things with Mrs Edwards.'

'But we went through all of this last night. Hours of it. My wife is absolutely exhausted. Look at her. She's hardly slept at all.'

'Yes, of course. I have everything I need now. I'm sorry to intrude again. Thank you.' The inspector stood, hurriedly replacing her notebook in her bag and then headed for the hall, followed closely by Mark.

I heard them whispering and waited for the click of the front door and for Mark to reappear in the kitchen.

'She's a DI. That's CID, isn't it? Why do you think CID are involved, Mark?'

'I've no idea.'

And then we both watched in silence through the kitchen window as the woman walked not to the police car on the square, not towards the police cordons beside the church, but along the lane which leads to Emma's house.

'Do you think I should ring Emma? Warn her she's on her way again?'

'Absolutely not. I think you should do what I've been suggesting all morning and go straight back to bed.'

This I did and immediately regretted it because, just like last night, it was most vivid when I lay down, as if stamped behind my eyelids and waiting for me to close them.

I'd thought I was good about blood. There was a spell when Ben suffered nosebleeds and some nights it would just pour from him. That had not troubled me but this was entirely different, and not at all as it was on television, either. Not when you knew the face. The eyes.

Which is why I wondered if I would ever sleep properly again, knowing already that the quiet and the stillness is where it comes back strongest. The warmth of it. The smell of it. And yes – the feel of it all over my hands. I thought of last night, ending up twice in the en-suite bathroom, retching into the toilet bowl; Mark outside, calling to me through the door.

Are you all right, Sophie? Are you all right?

Of course I'm not all right, Mark.

I had seen the worst of what two people can do to each other. My neighbours and friends. How could I be all right?

I had walked into a room, happy and relaxed, with my son waiting for me on the doorstep. Unknowing. Innocent. Me. Sophie. The woman who allegedly had this chocolate-box life.

I had walked in smiling and been met with a scene which I never, ever want anyone to imagine. Not my son. Not my husband. Not even the police inspector with the wrong notebook and all the wrong ideas about all of us.

It was *unreal.* That is what it was.

Shocking and unreal.

◆　◆　◆

Seven p.m. last night, we were behind. The evening competitions for the fair were running late because Antony Hartley was a no-show, and I remember being cross at him because everyone else had turned up on time and the whole day had stuck pretty much to its schedule.

Antony is a strange fish. Dear God – *was* a strange fish.

But I liked him, you know? I liked him a lot.

An attractive man – long fair hair, and deep brown eyes like a child's. That was his main appeal: he had the air of never quite letting go of childhood.

When they came to dinner that night with Emma, I could see that she liked them both too. They had charmed her as they charmed me with their alternative life.

Gill and Antony lived modestly but happily in their tiny two-up two-down that had an extension housing the bathroom downstairs which meant you couldn't use the loo without everyone in the house hearing.

I remember the first time I went round there for supper, dreading needing a wee – imagining everyone listening. But Gill and Antony had this trick, this way of making you relax. Laugh at yourself.

Well, I suppose Gill had – *had to*, rather. She had long been the sole breadwinner while Antony worked on his dreams. Forever taking up some new course, he was going to be a poet or a playwright or something. Creative Writing MA.

So Gill paid the rent while Antony paid *homage* to his dreams with enormous stacks of books bearing witness all over the house so that some weeks you could hardly manoeuvre around them.

Not that Gill seemed to mind. 'One day he will pay me back,' she would say. 'When he has his *bestseller*.' And then they would laugh conspiratorially, eyes locked on each other – a gesture so intense and so overtly sexual that it was, to any outsider, borderline embarrassing.

Meantime, she seemed to work all hours while Antony worked his charm. Every time we went round there, there would be some new philosophy or writer to discuss and Mark would come home tutting and sighing. *In his bloody dreams.*

But – the truth? I envied them their dreaming and the simplicity of their lives. Two-up. Two-down.

And so when I set off for their house yesterday evening, I was smiling to myself – thinking of Antony, who was bound to win the skittles as he always did, and how Gill would wink in the background as he accepted the cup, her eyes shining with pride. I was thinking that they were lucky not to be chasing the same dream as me and Mark, with the huge mortgage and the business loans and Mark working away. Me stuck at home. *Drowning* at home. In my perfect life.

And so I left Ben on the doorstep, to hurry Antony up. 'Just stay here a minute, Ben, darling. I won't be long.'

When they didn't answer the door, I didn't think anything of it because the Hartleys insisted on an open-door policy and I often went straight in. No doorbell. *Just come in*, they would say. So that's what I did, calling out as I went.

To be absolutely honest with you, I was never comfortable with the whole open-door thing. I was always worried that I'd catch them having a row – or worse, making up. That's why I left Ben on the doorstep.

So I walked through the study at the front to their hall, calling out quite loudly, 'Antony? Gill? Hello? Are you there? We need to start the skittles. And everyone is wondering—'

And then there it was. The colour red.

Vivid and angry . . . *everywhere.*

A spray of droplets right up the wall like an abstract painting not yet dry.

And him lying in a great and terrible puddle of it, eyes staring at the ceiling. Gone.

The inspector was probably right. Any normal person would have called out for help. Screamed.

But all I could think was that Ben must not see this. Clamping my mouth closed and shouting only in my head.

I did not even check his pulse.

I just went through to the kitchen – I don't know why I didn't think of my mobile, picturing instead the phone on their kitchen wall. That's all I was thinking. *Get to the phone, Sophie. Get to the phone . . .*

And then – there *she* was. Sitting on the floor with her back to the cupboards. Staring also.

There was blood pouring from her stomach and also down her hair. She turned her eyes towards me. Nothing else. Just her eyes.

And still it poured from her. Thick. Warm. Bright red.

And I put my hand over the stomach wound, pressing as hard as I could, trying to stem it. To stop it. *Please, dear God, stop this.*

I was too afraid to touch the wound on her head because it was gaping so wide – white and dreadful underneath as if some of her brain was coming through her skull – and because I couldn't now reach the phone, I finally remembered the mobile in my jacket pocket. I didn't know the number of the house so I had to describe the pots of petunias outside – *hurry, you must hurry* – before I hung up to phone Mark.

'Ben is on the doorstep. Of Antony and Gill's. You need to come now, Mark. *Now.* It's dreadful. Take him away. Don't bring him inside. Whatever you do, don't let him come inside.'

And then a complete blur.

The phone records say I rang the emergency services twice more and someone talked me through what to do to help Gill, but I don't recall any of that. All I remember is this surreal mix of colours. The familiar and the shocking; noticing the little orange espresso cups all lined up neatly on a shelf while I felt the warmth and the horrible wetness of the red on my hands. Pressing and pressing as hard as I could on the wound.

And waiting.

All the while, Gill staring into my eyes.

A large knife in her other hand.

And yes.

Blood all over my own hands.

CHAPTER 8

BEFORE

'So what do you think? Do you still want to go ahead today?' Nathan's voice on the line was hesitant, and Emma realised – as she glanced across at Theo sorting tractors and cars from a bright green box – that something else needed to be said between them.

'Look – about Friday, Emma.'

'It's OK, Nathan. You know me. I don't do *needy*. So please don't feel that—'

'No. It's the police, Emma. I had to tell the police about Friday night. I'm really sorry. I mean – it's private. Clearly none of their business, but they put me on the spot and I didn't know what else to do.'

'I see. No, it's fine, Nathan. Really.' And then there was the doorbell. 'Look, I'm sorry but there's someone at the door. It's probably Sophie. I'd best call you back.'

'OK. But you'll let me know by lunchtime? About Theo's robin, I mean. And I really hope, well, me saying anything won't make it any worse with the police.'

'Yes, yes. Of course. And please don't worry. About talking to the police. It's not your fault.'

Emma badly needed to talk all this through with Sophie – to find out what they were saying – and was entirely unprepared for the woman in civilian clothes who held up her badge before even speaking and was then very soon prowling around her kitchen, blatantly reading things on the noticeboard as if a badge allowed this behaviour without further explanation. Rude. Intrusive. Offensive. This woman, this DI Melanie Sanders – prying with absolutely no justification at all. Question after question not just about Friday, about Nathan staying overnight after dinner – as if that had anything to do with anything – but making her walk through every scene at the stupid fair again. Over and over. Every person she saw and spoke to throughout the day. And in the tent.

Jeez – why did I let Sophie talk me into it?

'Look, I don't remember exactly what I said to everyone in that tent. It was just a bit of fun, like I said yesterday. People were relaxed and played along. Most had had a couple of drinks so we had a laugh. They knew it wasn't for real. I made stuff up. You know: lucky numbers, lucky colours, tall dark strangers. I explained all of this to the policeman who called round yesterday. It was just a favour for my friend. To raise some money.'

'And you don't remember what you said to Gill Hartley?'

'Not exactly.'

'And she seemed OK to you?'

'She'd had a couple of Pimms from one of the stalls like everyone else. Apart from that she was fine. Enjoying herself.'

'It's just it seems you may have been the last person to see her.'

'I'm sorry?' And now the air stilled.

'Well, putting all the statements together now, it looks very much as if she went straight home after speaking to you.'

For a moment Emma said nothing, glancing at the floor and then back at the police officer.

Damn.

'But Gill was fine when I saw her. Absolutely fine.'

'So you said.'

'So, do you have any idea yet what happened? Was there a break-in?'

'No. That's why we're trying to piece together exactly what happened.'

'And she's still in a coma? Gill?'

'Look – I'm afraid I'm not able to discuss Mrs Hartley's condition.' And the policewoman was now standing, putting her card on the table. 'Right. I'll leave you in peace. Though if you remember anything. Anything at all.'

'Of course.'

◆ ◆ ◆

Two hours later, and pulling her coat tight around her against the wind, Emma was replaying the conversation in her head.

'Nathan. The police seem to think I was the last person to see Gill. Before she went home.' Emma had lowered her voice, though looking up she realised there was no real need, for Theo was way ahead of them already, eager and impatient – the lights on the heels of his trainers flashing as he skipped along, kicking a large stone in front of him.

Nathan carried on walking, his arm extended awkwardly so that the cage with the robin would not swing too much.

'Right. Well. *Christ.*' A pause, during which he frowned, biting into his lip. 'Explains why the police have been poking around so much. But you mustn't feel bad. I mean – it's nothing to do with you. You said she was fine when you saw her.'

'She was. No different from anyone else. Tiny bit squiffy on Pimms, that's all.'

'Well, there you are. Nothing else you can tell them. Terrible, terrible thing but they're saying there was no break-in so it's clearly a domestic. I suppose if Gill recovers, they'll have to decide about charging her. That's what this is about.'

'So what on earth do you reckon happened?'

He raised an eyebrow.

'What?'

Nathan stared at the ground.

'If you know something, Nathan, you seriously need to tell me. This is doing my head in.'

'Well. The usual, don't you think?'

'The *usual*? Oh right, so mayhem and murder is usual for Tedbury, is it?'

'Oh, come on, Em. You know what I mean. Never in a million years would I have thought Gill capable of something like this but it's not rocket science. He was very obviously a player. I guess she must have found out and flipped.'

'You're kidding me? You really think—'

'Come on, slowcoaches.' Theo was frowning, his tone impatient – turning to walk backwards up the hill ahead of them.

'Best concentrate on the robin.' Nathan lowered his voice and surprised Emma by linking his arm through her own.

They had agreed, the three of them, to release the robin in exactly the same spot they'd found him. For a time the poor bird wasn't expected to make it. Despite hand-feeding and a serious dose of TLC in Tom's aviary, it had not done at all well initially. And then very suddenly there had been what Tom called a Lazarus moment. He had gone out one morning to find the robin hopping around the base of the cage, eating and drinking independently – staring at him as if to say *what the hell am I doing in here?* From there, the recovery was swift, the robin soon testing its wings – flying between perches. Tom's reckoning was they needed to move fast; that its best chance for survival was to get back out in the wild before it became too dependent on, and also depressed by, the care they were providing.

Interestingly, Theo had not even once suggested that they keep him, which had surprised Nathan though not Emma. Just like Granny

Apple, she had preached the doctrine of freedom. The glory of wide-open spaces. The outdoors. Maybe Theo had actually been listening.

'Here. I think it was here.' Theo stamped his foot by the hedge and Emma checked around her. Yes. The stile where the dog and Nathan had appeared was just a stroll along the lane.

'OK, young man. Well – I reckon you should do the honours. Are you ready?' Nathan set the cage on the floor.

'The bird might be a bit nervous, Theo.' Emma crouched to her son's level, conscious that Nathan was watching.

Theo opened the door and they waited. At first, disconcertingly, the robin did nothing at all. The three glanced one to another. They waited some more. Emma was just beginning to shift with impatience when very suddenly the bird hopped on to the wire base of the open door. From there he moved down to the ground. Again there was a worrying impasse – the robin seemingly reluctant to move further.

'Keep very still, everyone,' Theo whispered. 'I think he's just saying goodbye.'

And then, in a flash, the bird was gone: up to the top of the nearest hedge briefly – seconds only – and onward to a telegraph pole.

'Do you think he will visit us?' Theo's face was tilted up to the sky, his hand shielding his eyes in the sunlight.

But Emma wasn't listening and instead could feel Nathan's gaze, his expression concerned.

'They're going to Cornwall,' she said suddenly.

'I'm sorry?'

'Sophie and Mark. They're going to Cornwall. That's a good thing, don't you think? After what she's been through, I mean. The shock of finding them like that.'

Nathan's expression was now puzzlement.

'Means we can crack on with the deli plans. Surprise her. Give her something to focus on.' Emma's tone was steady, but now Nathan was frowning.

'You're not serious, Emma? I rather imagined you'd put all that on hold. I mean, I can't think that anyone in Tedbury, least of all Sophie, would have an appetite for—'

'No, no. We need to go right ahead, Nathan. Trust me on this. It's the *very* best thing for Sophie. It's exactly what she needs.'

TODAY – 6.00 P.M.

I refuse to look out of the window for this part of the journey for it is too beautiful – my favourite section once, past the sea wall at Dawlish where, for a time, it feels like flying, as if the train is skimming the surface of the water.

Beautiful, yes, but today just a worry. Say Dawlish now and everyone thinks of *those* TV pictures – the railway line washed away in that terrible storm. And so I am thinking, *Will it be OK? Or will the wind whip up even more? Will we be delayed yet again?*

In the end we were stuck back there between stations for thirty minutes because of the wretched signal problem. They still haven't told us exactly what caused it. But I am on my best behaviour now. I am trying to stay calm and have apologised to the guard for getting off the train. For a time I was worried he was going to insist on me leaving at the next station for a medical check. I rather fear everyone thinks I am some kind of loon, but the guard seems to have put all that down to stress and now that he knows the whole story about Ben, he has given us a quiet spot at the very front of first class. Me and Mark and the doctor who I strongly suspect has been tasked with keeping a quiet eye on me, as he keeps giving his wife this little apologetic smile while looking up from his book.

'Are you feeling OK, Sophie?' he says.

'Yes, fine. Thank you. Please don't feel you have to stay and mind me. I'm perfectly OK now.'

'No trouble. I have my book. Just shout if you feel at all unwell.'

And so I force a small smile, catching Mark's eye, and I try to pretend that this is just another journey – *ta-tum, ta-tum* – and that I am just another passenger, whiling away the time when in truth I am chanting a mantra in my head, pleading with a god I am not sure I believe in, to just keep this train moving. *Please.*

Nathan has just phoned Mark. He was in Somerset on business but is now en route to the hospital to try to sort out this identity nonsense with the boys. I mean, for Christ's sake, they're not *that* alike. If you put their pictures side by side, you would have no trouble. I'm losing my patience but the medical staff are apparently very stretched and there are protocols. They couldn't delay the surgery for identification because it was way too urgent but they want someone to positively ID the boys as soon as possible afterwards. It is all such a terrifying muddle still. From the snippets the ward nurse shared before everyone clammed up, it seems one child has a collapsed lung and the other the more serious spleen damage. But the staff are now sticking rigidly to the rules and won't share any more specific information until the boys' names are sorted.

It's such agony. Do I want my child to be the one with the collapsed lung? Or the damaged spleen? Both sound completely terrible but the spleen sounds so much worse somehow and I feel like some monster, willing the more serious injury on someone else, but I just don't want it to be Ben. The spleen. I don't want it to be Ben . . .

So – yes, we just have to wait. Nathan is on his way to Durndale and has promised to phone if there is any news once they are both out of theatre.

Mark held the phone out for me and I tried to thank Nathan, but no words would come out of my mouth and so I had to just hand it back. It is as if any gesture of kindness is simply too much. Like the beauty of this stretch of coastline. Which is why I am keeping my eyes down, trying to tune out the doctor glancing at me and the blur of pictures which are much too pretty. Seagulls overhead. The white foam of the rolling waves.

Instead I am looking at the floor which has some kind of stain – coffee? – making promises that everything in my life will be different from this point, that I will change and learn and be a better person and a much better mother *if you will just grant me this one thing.*

CHAPTER 9

BEFORE

Detective Inspector Melanie Sanders stared at her housemate across the kitchen table and poured coffee from a large cafetière into two bright pink mugs.

'You been up all night *dye-ing* again?' Melanie was rather pleased with the pun so early in the morning, though Cynthia was patently not, groaning and then holding out her hands to confirm palms which alarmingly matched the mugs. 'I'm supposed to get six rugs finished by Friday. I will never do it.'

Melanie smiled. Cynthia, like so many artists, seemed to live in a permanent state of self-imposed bipolar chaos. Up or down. Broke or buying all the drinks. Too little work or too much. Never the even keel. Despite all protestations, which Melanie had learned to ignore, this was precisely the way Cynthia liked it; she was addicted to the drama, which matched her outfits – today an interesting choice of lime green boiler suit with black Doc Martins.

In the early days of their friendship Melanie had made the mistake of challenging her. *Why don't you just get yourself a job, Cynthia? You know – novel concept – you turn up every day and they pay you at the end of the month?* But Cynthia's expression had been so painfully disdainful that Melanie had learned to keep quiet.

Today she glanced into the utility annex, where three clothes horses were covered in long strips of cotton dyed various shades of pink. Cynthia must have been up most of the night working – her current 'signature product' being rag rugs which she made in the traditional style, hand-dyeing cotton which she then wove strand by strand into bright, contemporary patterns. The finished effect was very striking and the current order from a boutique hotel that intended to use them as wall hangings was impressive. The problem was the expanse of wall involved. Two dozen rugs had been ordered, and given Cynthia rarely made more than two or three at a time, the commission was proving problematic.

'Do you think you could help me, Mel?' She was tilting her head and using the whiny voice of a small child.

'Ooooh nooo. We've been here before, Cynthia. You *say* you want help. You may even believe you want help, but the reality, as I have discovered to my cost, is you cannot bear anyone near any of your work. Anyway, I've got this new Tedbury case. I'm going to be busy.' Melanie tried to make this sound challenging. She was not ready to admit, even to Cynthia, that this first case since her much-longed-for promotion was clearly a wind-up in the department. A domestic.

'But I thought we already know who did it?'

'Yes, well. We can't assume it's that simple.' Melanie's defensive tone gave her away. 'I'm still waiting on the forensics. And the phone records. Also we haven't confirmed motive.'

'Er, excuse me. I saw his picture.'

'Well, the word is they were devoted.'

'Yeah right.'

'I thought it was *my* job to be cynical.'

'So is she going to make it, then? The wife? Otherwise there doesn't seem to be a whole lot of point.'

'I don't know. I'm going to the hospital now, actually. Do you want anything in town?'

'Homity pie.'

'I'm sorry?'

'Homity pie.'

'And what, in God's name, is homity pie?'

'You really are a lost cause, Melanie. I blame all that canteen food.'

'Sorry.'

'No, you're not. And for your information, homity pie is a delicate fusion of potato, onions and garlic in a light shortcrust pastry.'

'A pasty.'

'I give up.'

And now Melanie was grinning. She had found the house share in the small ads when she first moved to Plymouth. She hadn't expected to stay – especially once she confirmed Cynthia actually owned the Victorian terrace overlooking Peverell Park, though clearly with no spare funds for upgrades. No central heating in the bedrooms. No power shower. And yet Melanie had very quickly grown fond of the contrast: the lentil-soaking, cotton-dyeing craziness which could not be further from her own working life, with its drunks and its violence, its prostitutes and its seedy, nasty and – on this patch – mostly petty crimes. Murders were, in truth, pretty rare, which was why she was so peeved to be assigned the Tedbury job. Cynthia was right. It wasn't a proper murder inquiry at all. If Gill died, there would be no one to charge.

'I'll see you this evening, then.'

'Drowned in a vat of beetroot dye, most likely.'

Durndale Hospital, like many of its high-rise contemporaries, was externally as depressing as the misery it contained. Just outside the main entrance, overweight patients in cheap dressing gowns were hiding from staff, choking on cigarettes – their expressions, to Melanie at least, showing no acknowledgement of the irony of their behaviour. Inside was little better. She stopped momentarily at the snack bar and glanced at the offerings. There was talk of it being replaced by a salad bar, but meantime she was confronted by more irony in the form of cream cakes, doughnuts and sausage rolls.

'Do you have homity pie?' The server, a middle-aged woman of rotund proportions and cheeks rosy from proximity to the grills, shrugged blankly. Melanie eyed the pastries and the pasties and made her excuses.

Gill Hartley remained in intensive care on the fourth floor. There was, in truth, no need for this visit, but Melanie wanted to take another look at the woman who was at the centre of the first inquiry she had been allowed to head up since her promotion and transfer to Devon. Also, she had been promised a chat with the consultant in charge of Gill's care, who should be doing his rounds very shortly. Melanie badly needed this woman to wake up, otherwise Cynthia was absolutely right. The preliminary forensics did not suggest a third party.

Gill's coma, Melanie had learned, had nothing to do with the knife wound and everything to do with the popularity of marble worktops. She had smashed the back of her head quite spectacularly as she collapsed to the floor. Apparently a piece of her brain was exposed – hence the medically induced coma to try to give the swelling time to reduce. Heaven knows what real damage had been done. The stomach wound also involved heavy blood loss but major organs had been missed. She had been lucky in that respect.

Or perhaps not, Melanie was thinking as she stared through the blinds into the room, imagining what the wretched woman had to wake up to. Possible brain damage? Prison, almost certainly. She could hear nothing from the corridor but could imagine perfectly the eerie sounds of the ventilator and the profusion of other machinery. Alongside the bed was a grey-haired woman, wearing a black cardigan to match the circles under her eyes.

Melanie watched the woman's face change as she walked over to show her badge. There were times when her job and her duty made her feel important, all the intrusion justified . . .

'We still can't believe it.'

. . . but not today. Always toughest with the mothers.

'No. It must have been a terrible shock for you – Mrs . . . ?'

'Baines.'

'Mrs Baines.'

'They were so happy.'

Melanie did not reply.

'At least they always *seemed* so happy.' Gill's mother shifted in her seat.

'Look – we don't have to do this now but if you feel well enough to answer a few more questions?'

'Sorry? Oh, right. Yes, of course.' And then she was agitated, glancing at her daughter. 'Though not here, please. They say she may be able to hear.'

They stood awkwardly in the corridor for a time with visitors brushing past, many of them appearing entirely lost. *Excuse me, but do you know the way to the cafeteria?*

'So you didn't pick up on any problems, Mrs Baines? Anything worrying your daughter recently?'

Sorry. Is this the same floor as X-ray?

Look. We're having a private conversation, OK?

So that in the end they had to move into a little alcove by the lifts.

'You think one of them was cheating, don't you? Or up to something illegal. Affairs. Drugs. Gambling. That's what everyone's whispering back in Tedbury, isn't it?'

'I don't think it helps to speculate, Mrs Baines. We're just trying to find out what happened.'

No reply, and so Melanie decided to quietly withdraw, allowing Mrs Baines to return to her daughter's side and to pick up a book from beside the bed.

She watched the familiar and comforting sight of a mother reading to her child, remembering how her own mother used to climb right into bed for their story time; the echo of her many ridiculous voices. Seeing it made her feel embarrassed. An intruder. As Mrs Baines turned the page, Melanie turned away also, grateful for the flurry of activity along the corridor – the consultant, complete with student entourage.

She was just preparing to approach him, fumbling for her notebook – still using a large one because she couldn't find her glasses – when, looking up from her handbag, she caught a flash of something else way back along the same corridor. Red coat. A glimpse of long, dark hair. Enough. The woman, carrying a child on her hip, spun through 180 degrees and turned the corner, but something in Melanie's stomach, something which she had never been able to define but in her job had learned never to ignore, made her bolt along the corridor.

'Excuse me?'

The woman turned, feigning surprise. The child tilted his head, apparently shy.

'Miss Carter, isn't it?'

Emma stood rigid, clutching a small basket of mixed fruit with her free hand.

'Inspector. I was just . . .' She looked about her then, at the signposts for the different wards and departments as if for inspiration, and finally back at Melanie who noted again what peculiar eyes she had. Strange streaks of different colours. 'I was just bringing something for Gill. To see how she's doing.'

'That's very nice of you. Her mother's with her. I didn't realise you two were close. You didn't mention that when we spoke before.'

And then Melanie adopted the expression and the silence which had served her so well during her time in uniform – and did so now, out of it. She waited, keeping her face neutral. Waiting for Emma Carter to speak again.

To say something which might explain the decidedly odd expression this strange and striking woman was now wearing on her own face.

CHAPTER 10

BEFORE

I was unsure at first about coming here. Mark felt it would be the best place – our favourite part of Cornwall – to try to somehow process what had happened. But . . . me?

I was worried it might spoil this place forever.

Ask me last week about the Lizard, I would have beamed and bored you; I would have said that driving here always made my shoulders relax, like unbuttoning a shirt too tight at the neck. Like a secret; a discovery best kept quiet from the hordes who trek further north to the more familiar and obvious destinations of Rock and Padstow.

To know the Lizard is to drive past the flat and unpromising landscape of the RNAS base, smiling inwardly at the trick of it. For, just a few miles in any of several directions from the neatly fenced but unlovely facility, there is this feast of the unexpected and unspoilt. The breathtaking Helford River, best explored by boat; the pale sands of umpteen perfect coves with space for cricket even in the summer months; and all around the coast, communities with proud, whitewashed cottages tumbling down steep hills to tiny working harbours.

For me this place smells always of the past, too; of the days when a holiday bedroom reeked not of playdough and nappies and Sudocrem, but of croissants, good coffee. And sex. Yes. The days of that different Sophie, before we were married, when me and Mark worked hard – *both* of us – and played hard too. Daytime sex. Imagine that. Coffee and toast, naked in bed with butter licked from fingers. The days when holidays and weekends away from London had that almost desperate edge of being so deserved. Necessary. *Precious.*

And yet there I sat, on the front step of this familiar cottage, hands clenched tight between my thighs, worrying that this was the year the spell would be broken. The magic ruined.

In the car this time I came close to a panic attack – a sudden urge to turn around and hole up at home, but then in the mirror I could see Ben sitting in the back, his new fishing rod across his lap, so I wound down the window instead, feigning a coughing fit to choke in the air, to try to calm myself.

I have no idea how much you are supposed to tell a small child when something terrible happens. Ideally nothing, but the trouble is they pick up vibes and they notice whispering – and they certainly notice police cars and blue-and-white tape. All we have told Ben so far is that something very sad happened in the village but he was not to worry and we were having a surprise holiday while it was all sorted out.

What happened, Mummy?

An accident. Antony died in an accident which is very, very sad. But it is nothing for you to worry about, Ben.

Are we going to die in an accident?

No. Of course not.

He was certainly pleased to be here. A rare treat at such short notice and one of the few places we truly relax as a family. Holidays are always a challenge for Mark as he has to juggle time off around his staff, who always want the peak summer months. That's why July and August have always stretched so very long and hard in Tedbury since I had Ben. How shameful to admit that, until Emma arrived with Theo, I had rather come to dread the summers in Devon. Crowds of tourists everywhere and the paradox of me feeling lonely with Mark always overloaded at work.

So this was unusual – to make it here during peak season. We normally come in the spring or autumn. Mark only managed to swing this late booking because we know the owners so well. A relative was supposed to be here this week but bailed at the eleventh hour; we got lucky.

Lucky?

No. *Surreal* was how it felt to be here – everything so shockingly different at home, and yet in this place?

I looked up.

Completely unchanged. The same old view from the cottage. The same trees climbing in giant strides up the hill opposite. The smell of the hedgerow flowers, sweeter than at home and mingled with the salt on the wind.

Yes. I closed my eyes to take it in properly. It was what we always noticed and appreciated most when we arrived, and missed more than anything when we returned home.

The smell of the sea.

'You OK?' I could hear clinking as Mark placed a glass of wine on the step beside me, and so opened my eyes and raised my left hand to shield them from the evening sun.

'Think so. Still shell-shocked but I think you were right.' I stretched out my right hand, which he took and held tightly. 'It's not a fix, coming away. I mean, I keep seeing it all every time I close my eyes . . . but you're right; if we'd stayed at home, it would probably have been worse. I would have gone completely mad back there.'

He sat alongside me, still squeezing my fingers but picking moss from the stone step with his other hand. 'Look – Sophie. I know I can be a bit, well, a bit hopeless, never really knowing what to say. But you do know you *can* talk to me? Or at least try.'

I tilted my head. I hadn't shared much detail. That's what he meant. His face revealed he was out of his comfort zone; he looked afraid and I wondered if he was worried this could tip me back to that awful place after Ben was born. I held his stare and tried to find a small smile.

'And I want to listen. To help. No rush and no pressure. When you're ready to talk a bit more – properly about this, I mean.'

'Thank you. And I will try but I just need to, I don't know, process it first? It still feels so . . .' I paused. 'I can't find the right words, Mark.'

'P45.'

'Sorry?'

'Copywriter who can't find the right words. Always said it was a good job you refused to work for me.' He was trying to make me smile and I was grateful for the effort, but then there was this shift, a strange sensation in my stomach.

He was looking right into my eyes still and I was sad that I was the one who had to look away first.

Copywriter? Another thing that felt surreal. It was still on my LinkedIn profile but felt fraudulent. Some days I found it hard to believe I ever did it. Held my own in that world; no – better than that, I was good, actually. Pitches. Slogans. One-liners. Sometimes now it felt as if it all happened in some parallel world.

At first when we moved to Devon, I shared all the stories with Caroline and Heather. The outrageous all-nighters when we were up against a deadline. The parties when we landed a big new contract. Once, after way too much wine, I showed them some clips from a campaign which went viral.

'You wrote those ads? But I remember those. They were every-where . . . You really wrote those, Sophie?'

Both Caroline and Heather had sat wide-eyed and incredulous.

'So why the hell did you give it up, Sophie?'

I tweaked the script. Played down how much I missed it.

'Ridiculous hours. Very macho culture. Half the people were on drugs to hold it all together. Completely impossible to combine it with children. Not if you want to be any kind of mother.'

◆ ◆ ◆

'Are you sure you don't want to lie down, Sophie?' Mark was still brushing moss from his fingers.

'Yeah. Yeah. Fine. Sorry. Miles away.'

'It's just our son and heir wants a barbeque. And none of your fancy sea bass.' His tone was still feigned brightness and I tilted my head, touched again by this effort. The patience, also. 'The boy wants burgers. I'm taking him to the supermarket. We'll probably try to find some frozen bait for fishing as well, if they're still open. Do you want to come?'

'No. If you don't mind, I think I'll just sit, actually. I'm hoping Helen will be home soon.' I glanced at the only cottage visible from the front step – a larger, double-fronted affair, consumed in a bear hug of wisteria just a few minutes along the lane.

I willed her to come quickly and it worked – I was just pouring a second glass of wine when the familiar battered Volvo crunched over the gravel of the unmade road and swung into the little parking bay opposite.

Bill and Ben – a springer and a Highland terrier – leapt from the back seat and bypassed the gate to sneak through a gap in our hedge. All slobber and tails almost knocking my glass over.

'Oh – it's you at last. Thank *heavens*!' Helen's voice boomed – her hearing one of the few things to betray her age. 'We've had some absolute shockers in that place so far this summer.' Helen's hair was mostly white now but her skin was still translucent. Ridiculously unlined.

By the time she was through the gate herself for a hug, I couldn't help myself, clinging on just a tad too long. Too tight. 'I can't tell you how good it is to see you, Helen.' Voice breaking. Which of course made her pull back to check my face at arm's length.

'So what's all this, then?'

◆ ◆ ◆

We met Helen the very first year we discovered the Lizard. You might say we owe her for falling so quickly in love with it. She is certainly the reason we return to this same cottage.

Helen knows everyone. From the very start she was so incredibly generous with her time and her contacts – directing us to the best pasties in Porthleven, the best cream tea at a tiny café overlooking the Helford River. Our very first visit she fixed for one of her sailing friends to take us to tiny beaches which could only be reached by water, and she pointed out the best boats to buy fish and crabs at knock-down prices at the various local quays. She taught us to shuck oysters – shocked and amused in equal measure at my initial squeamishness. And she provided the champagne when, like giggling teenagers, we told her first when we got engaged on our third visit. Mark proposed at Kynance Cove – swept along by the magic of the place, though entirely unprepared.

Helen had been horrified. *So where's the ring? You're kidding me? No ring? And no champagne. What are you, Mark – a bloody amateur?* And then she disappeared into her house, returning with a chilled bottle of Pol Roger, explaining that decent champagne was one of her few pleasures *now that sex is off the agenda.*

Helen had been widowed in her fifties, moving to the Lizard soon afterwards, and we supposed that she was like this with everyone – extrovert, entertaining and eager in her loneliness for company of any kind. But no. The years taught us, with surprise, that this was not so. Comments in the visitor book of our cottage revealed Helen was regarded by many as an irritable recluse, evidently sharing her favours, her company and her contacts with a chosen few.

'You look white as a sheet, Sophie. What on earth is the matter?'

I was fighting tears but was not embarrassed. I always knew I would talk to Helen – practical, sensible Helen who would not gush and gasp as others back in the village had, too many feigning sympathy but in truth keen for the lurid details. *So was there a great deal of blood?*

'You heard about the guy who was killed in our village. In Tedbury?'

'Yes. I read about it in the papers. Saw it on the telly too. Awful.'

'Well – I was the one who found him, Helen. And his wife. They were my friends.'

'Oh my God.' And then Helen, true to form, wasted no time with all the platitudes which were driving me insane at home, but instead stood to announce a temporary pause for supplies. 'Forget the wine. We need something stronger. And ice. I'll be back in a minute. Mind the dogs.'

She returned not only with vodka but a tray of oysters also. 'I see Mark's got the barbeque out, which means he'll be feeding you some burnt offering later. So here – we need fortification for this.'

And now, for the first time since Saturday, I heard myself laugh – the shock of which made me pause, holding myself rigid.

'Don't fight it, Sophie. Delayed shock. Crying is good . . . but not over the oysters, please.' She was passing a tissue from her pocket. 'It will dilute the liquor.'

To my surprise I cried for quite a long time but Helen at no point tried to shush me. And when I stopped, she encouraged me to describe it. Share it. *Let it out, Sophie.* And this was not like the policewoman prying; this felt different. So I told her about all the blood and how shocked I was at the bit of Gill's brain showing. And how I felt guilty for noticing the orange espresso cups. That I was still in that strange zone, as if I were remembering and relating something from a book or a film, not something that was truly happening in my own life.

Helen, in return, did not tell me to stop talking or to put it out of my mind, but seemed to understand instead that I needed now to rerun the film to accept it. She walked through it with me and she said that I would need to do this many times in order to get used to it. These reruns.

She told me, quite matter-of-factly, that for the first two years after her husband's heart attack, she relived finding him time and time again until she knew every beat of the scene; as if she needed to be sure of every single gasp of pain and every second of what had happened in order to accept it and learn to live with it.

'People tell you to try not to think about it. Your own instinct is not to think about it. But that doesn't work,' she said. 'The trick is to learn to *cope* with thinking about it. To accept how truly awful it was. Am I making any sense?'

I nodded and I cried and ate more oysters and drank more vodka and thanked my stars that I had her in my life, so that by the time Mark and Ben returned, they told me that I looked better.

'You look smiley again, Mummy.'

Mark looked relieved, and I held Helen's hand while the two dogs chased a Frisbee which Ben threw over and over.

◆　◆　◆

For the next two days Helen gave us space, as was our custom – exchanging morning and evening pleasantries only. I spent time with the boys. Outings. Cards. Monopoly. And then when Ben and Mark set off for a day's fishing, I was on her doorstep early. Our cue.

'Ah. Crab sandwiches? I've been looking forward to this.' Helen was smiling broadly.

We set off in the Volvo for Coverack, parking in the official car park at the top of the hill and walking slowly down to the seafront to a favourite café. Another little secret – from the outside an unpromising affair with plastic chairs and tables and wasps playing havoc around a huge bin awaiting collection by the council, but to those in the know a blissful little haven offering the best coffee locally and sandwiches packed with the sweetest, freshest crab straight off the local boats.

We queued for our treat and took the brunch on to the rocks opposite, watching the children on the beach.

'So, how are you doing really, then?'

'Quite a lot better – thank you, Helen. Mark was right. This place is just what I needed. I only wish Ben wasn't starting school next week. Truth be told, I don't want to go home.'

'Well, you know you can always stay on with me. You're welcome any time; I've told you that before.'

I looped my arm through hers. 'That's very kind but I have to think of Ben. Also – I rather think we take enough advantage as it is.'

'Don't be silly. Like I said – we get some real shockers in that place. Last week there was a couple who complained about the noise from the seagulls. Imagine that, eh? Seagulls by the coast. Oh, and they didn't like the smell from the oil-fired Rayburn. Or the downstairs shower. And they couldn't come to terms with a barbeque without an on-off switch. Complete bloody nightmare. If it was my place, I'd have turned them out.'

I was smiling, and pushed my hair behind my ear before starting on my sandwich – a chunk of crab spilling on to my jeans which I scooped straight into my mouth.

'Actually, I have something else I want to talk to you about,' I said.

'I'm listening.'

'It's just. This is going to sound very selfish . . .'

There was a pause as Helen finished a mouthful of food before swigging at her coffee. 'I said I'm listening, Sophie.'

'I mean, I feel terrible for Antony and Gill. Shocked rigid.'

'Of course.'

'Like I said, this sounds terrible – but I'm surprised at how angry I feel.'

'That you were the one to find them?'

'That. Yes, I suppose, but also . . . Oh, Helen – it's the *timing*. I mean, for the first time in so long, I was just beginning to feel more like my old self. Stepping back a bit. Thinking things through. This new friend I've been telling you about.'

'Emma?'

'Yes. I know I've been going on about her a bit, but if you met her you would understand. You'd really like her, Helen. She has this incredible energy; it's like she's breathed new life into the whole place and it's been so good for me. I honestly had no idea how bad a rut I was in. She's really got me thinking about my future. Before this awful business with Gill and Antony, we were even talking of resurrecting my deli plan.'

'You are kidding, I hope? After what happened with Caroline?'

'I know, I know. And don't worry, Mark's done all the lectures. And to be honest, I see his point. Start-ups are going to the wall left, right and centre, and I think it would be a small return for a bucketload of work. But it at least got me thinking properly about going back to work – with Ben about to start school, I mean. And I know I blow hot and cold on this, Helen. You must be sick of all these U-turns, but I realise now that I can't just sit doing nothing while I wait for the next baby. So I was starting to gee myself up, work through some options in my head – and I was feeling really good about that. And then . . .' I had been gabbling but now my voice faltered. I coughed. Paused.

'Look, you've had a big shock, Sophie. You're bound to feel knocked back. We always think these things happen somewhere else. On the news. Not in our own lives. But places and people do recover from these things. They have to. I know it doesn't feel that way right now but you just need to give it time. The great thing from my point of view is to hear you talking like this. About getting out there again. It's good, Sophie. Really good.'

'You think so?'

'I know so.'

'A joke, though – that we moved here, to the south-west, because I thought it would be safer.'

'Yes – but it's a domestic, Sophie. And domestics happen everywhere and anywhere. You moved for the best of reasons. For Ben.'

'You're right. I know you're right.' I took in a long, deep breath. 'And you're not to worry. I haven't agreed to anything. Over the deli, I mean. I don't like to disappoint Emma, but just between us I'm thinking more along the lines of a part-time job. PR agency maybe? Something to stop me bonking the postman once Ben's in school.'

And now Helen was smiling.

'Sounds like a plan. Just give yourself time to get over the shock with your friends. To let things in Tedbury settle down again.'

'Oh, and that's the other spanner. Mark is now talking about us moving. A fresh start. The dreaded suburbs.'

'Well, he's probably just panicking. Feeling protective. I mean it can't be easy for him. All the commuting.'

'Oh God – I know. To be honest I feel terrible about him doing all that driving. But I just don't think it's the right time for major decisions. I'd still prefer him to relocate the company at some point, especially if I can get some work going to balance the income. I mean, that is what we originally agreed. Him moving the company nearer.'

'So tell him that. Buy time. Say you sympathise but it's not the right time for such big decisions . . .'

'You're right.' And then I turned my head to glance up to the coastal path in the distance, and that's when I suddenly saw her.

Helen frowned and turned her head to follow my gaze. 'You all right, Sophie? You look as if you've seen a ghost.'

I didn't answer, instead blinking to reset my vision. The flash of red linen coat disappeared as the woman turned and strode out of sight.

'What is it, Sophie? Seriously? You're white as a sheet.'

CHAPTER 11

BEFORE

'I need you to come out from there right now, Theo!'

Emma's knees were hurting as she crouched to peer under the bed again. It had been a long day and she was tired. There was no response – Theo, in his hideous dressing-up outfit, was now wedged into the far corner, wrapped in a blanket with his hands over his ears. His exposed arm confirmed that again he had drawn a small robin in felt pen on his skin. His new craze. *Damn him.* Another fight at bath time.

'I mean it, Theo. You need to come downstairs and see what you've done. Also I have some more questions. About Ben and his mummy.'

'I haven't done anything wrong. I'm Superman and I have special powers. I can fly out of this room right this minute if I want to. I can go find my robin and we can both fly to Cornwall to be with Ben.'

Emma sat back on her heels. She was wishing that Granny Apple were still alive. Yes. If Granny Apple were still around Emma would drive Theo to Kent right this minute and leave him there.

She had done this more than once – left Theo for weeks at a time when he was really small and especially difficult. Granny Apple always complained that it was not a good idea, not good for the child, but she never actually refused; always gave in.

These days Theo was becoming more and more impossible. He wouldn't answer any of her questions about Emma and Ben. He just pulled this ridiculous face and challenged her. *Why do you keep asking about Ben and his mummy?*

'Did you hear the smashing noise earlier this evening, Theo? Just after we got back from Heather's?' Emma had shifted position again to stretch her sore knees, still leaning down to stare at her son.

'Is it like in France? Because I didn't do anything. I didn't break Granny's plates in France. And I haven't done anything bad today. I promise. I was a good boy for Heather. Ask her.' Theo was curled into a ball on his side now, with his knees up to his chest.

'Well, how about you come and see, Theo, because I'm not imagining it. I mean it. Downstairs in two minutes or you'll be sorry.'

The phone was now ringing. Emma glanced through the open bedroom door and across the hall to the extension on her bedside table, but decided to ignore it. After a minute her mobile started up. *Damn.* She guessed it would be Nathan again, wondering where she had been, and so she stood and headed downstairs, out of earshot.

Nathan's mood was at first hesitant and apologetic; he was clearly still baffled over her pressing on with the deli work. The last couple of days he had been trying to get her to slow down. Seemed to think it was upsetting people in the village, her pushing ahead with the builders with Gill in her coma and Antony barely cold in the morgue.

'Look, I do get that people are in shock and I understand that village life is different. Tight-knit and all that. But I didn't really know Gill and Antony very well so I don't understand. I can't put my life on hold and I really don't see why it's anyone's business what I do.'

'OK. Here's the truth. Tom had a bit of a go at me in the pub last night. Seems there's some stupid gossip flying around.'

'Gossip? What gossip, Nathan?'

There was a long pause as Emma made it to the sitting room to again survey the damage.

She listened to Nathan explaining that the village crones were bad-mouthing her. Had entirely the wrong end of the stick.

'Well, I wouldn't normally give a damn, Nathan, but that might explain something.' Emma stared at the brick on the floor. 'In fact I was hoping you could come over urgently and help me out. I've just got in and something horrible has happened.'

After she explained further, Nathan changed his tone completely and agreed to stop by in half an hour. Emma hung up and picked up the brick as Theo appeared in the doorway.

'At last, Superman puts in an appearance.'

'I've packed my rucksack. I am going to Cornwall to stay with Ben.'

'Well, good luck with that, buddy, because it's a long walk. See this, Theo?' Emma held out the muddy brick and tilted her head to the broken window looking out on to the back garden. 'This is all your fault.'

'I didn't do it.'

'I beg to differ, Theo. Do you know what has happened here?'

Theo shook his head and Emma could see tears welling in his eyes as he stared at the glass all over the floor.

'Because you are a wicked boy and bit Mummy in the bath again last night.' She let out a long sigh. It had happened while she was scrubbing off one of his stupid felt-tip robins. Theo had taken to secretly doodling robins on his upper arm and hated her removing them. 'Because it is very, very bad to bite and people always find out about these things, Theo – you have made everyone here in Tedbury *hate* us.'

Emma turned over the brick so that her hands were now covered in wet mud.

'You make everyone cross, Theo, wherever we go. That's the truth. You made Nanny Lucy cross when we lived in Manchester. You made Granny cross when we lived in France. And now you have made everyone cross in Tedbury. Well done, Theo. Excellent work.'

Theo was now crying properly and Emma took a deep breath. She looked at her watch, working out if there was time for a shower before Nathan turned up. No. Probably not.

'Do you know that you ruin everything for me, Theo? Wherever we go and however hard I try, you ruin absolutely everything.'

CHAPTER 12

BEFORE

Matthew Hill was chopping a large banana into small chunks, staring at his daughter in her high chair.

Four years out of the police force and just one as a father. He could not quite believe how dramatically his life had changed.

'You want banana with your toast, sweetie?' He already knew what her response would be. His daughter so far had only one word in her vocabulary.

'*No.*' She was smiling.

Matthew tried to smile too, but through gritted teeth. After months wondering whether Amelie's first word would be Mamma or Dadda, the reality for Matthew and his wife had been a blow.

'You mean *yes*, don't you? You like banana. Say *yes, Dadda*.'

'No.'

He put the banana on his daughter's bright pink princess plate, alongside her fingers of toast. Amelie tucked in immediately, still beaming.

'You see. You meant *yes*. Amelie loves bananas. *Yes.*'

Amelie continued to smile as she munched her breakfast, holding out a chunk of squashed banana for her father to examine. Matthew leant forward and feigned exaggerated munching noises, pretending to nibble at the squashed mess before pouring himself another coffee. Five minutes later, as Sally arrived back from filling up the car, he greeted her with his new theory on their daughter's contrary vocabulary while flicking on the kettle switch.

'Do you think we say no to Amelie too often? Is that the problem here?'

'No, Matt. The problem here is that she has half your genes.'

He bumped his shoulder playfully into his wife's and poked out his tongue before moving to the sink to rinse the cafetière and refill it with fresh coffee grains.

Matthew watched as his wife moved forward to kiss their daughter ever so gently on the forehead. It still got to him. The little punch of disbelief.

His two beautiful girls.

He checked his phone for today's notes while making the fresh drinks. Life as a private investigator was not what he had expected but there were some distinct advantages now. At least he could control his hours, work around Sal's plans. He had been running his agency just long enough to pick and choose jobs a bit. Security-consultancy gigs were on the increase, which meant – *hallelujah* – he could wind down the dreaded divorce snooping. Today? He had a couple of missing person cases. Good. He liked those.

'Any cruising this morning?' Sal was hanging her coat on the back of a chair. Walking was the other milestone their daughter was withholding, apparently keen to keep the upper hand.

'No. Just bum-shuffling. My theory is she is going to leapfrog straight to running. Aren't you, Amelie?'

'*No.*'

They both let out a little huff – a half-laugh of love, exasperation and worry all wound up into the same parental knot.

Matthew put away his phone and grabbed the remote for a news update. He flicked channels on the small kitchen television to see the familiar village scene. A reporter with an update on the Tedbury case. Matthew felt an uncomfortable surge inside and turned up the volume.

'Isn't that the place you had a case?' Sal was adding milk to their fresh coffees.

'Shhh.' Matthew listened more closely as the reporter confirmed the identity of the man who had been killed. 'Sugar. That's not good.'

'Why . . . *sugar*? What's up?' They had both been training themselves not to swear around their daughter, terrified that she would learn to curse before she deigned to say Mummy or Daddy.

Matthew was trying to process this new information. *Antony Hartley?* He felt his frown deepen and took in a long, slow breath. Must be a coincidence. Had to be . . .

'I thought it was just some planning case you were working on. Research.' His wife was now seated next to their daughter, who offered her a share of the banana mush.

'It was.'

'So not linked with this case. I mean – you're not in any kind of trouble, Matt?'

'Certainly hope not. Unlucky coincidence most likely, but I might have to make a few more inquiries. Just to make sure I don't need to disclose some stuff. To the murder team, I mean.'

Matthew twisted his mouth to the side and narrowed his eyes. He had a mate still working in forensics; he would just need to check that it was a straightforward domestic. No third party . . .

'Sure there isn't something you're not telling me?' His wife sounded a little more worried now, and so Matthew brightened his tone and deliberately calmed his expression.

Since Amelie had arrived, Matthew had tried to downplay work worries. In the force he had watched too many marriages dissolve.

Though it wasn't why he left the police; Matthew Hill had left the force for reasons he preferred not to think about.

These days he tried to count his blessings and to keep work and home entirely separate. He looked again at his lovely daughter, a squelch of mashed banana in each of her little fists. Then he turned to his wife, who still looked worried.

'I promise that if there's anything to worry about, I will tell you.'

Sal tilted her head and looked unconvinced, so Matthew turned to their daughter.

'Tell Mummy that she is to stop worrying, Amelie.'

'*No!*'

CHAPTER 13

BEFORE

I stared at the two puzzles on the large coffee table. Paw Patrol for Ben and a coastal scene for me and Mark.

We hadn't got too far with ours. The sky, as always, was proving infuriating. I knelt on the floor, then sat back on my heels, scanning the scores of seemingly identical blue pieces which Mark had set to one side.

Why don't they put in more clouds, Sophie? This is ridiculous . . .

It was the Lizard that got us into puzzles; a holiday cottage cliché but a welcome one. It had become a ritual, even before we had Ben. During our early visits, Helen would sometimes join us for an evening, bringing good wine and an eagle eye. To Mark's astonishment, she could quickly place a tricky piece that had been baffling us for hours. *How do you do that? Seriously. How do you do that, Helen?*

I tried a few of the contenders for a space in the top right-hand corner of the puzzle.

'You're rubbish, Mum.' Ben was suddenly standing beside me.

'Thank you very much, darling.'

'I've nearly finished mine.'

I glanced at the second puzzle, about seventy-five per cent complete, and pulled him to my side, kissing my congratulations on his forehead.

'Theo's rubbish at puzzles too. I always beat him.'

'Well. Theo's a bit younger, remember.'

'Anyway. It doesn't matter. Puzzles are dead boring. We like it when you let us play on your phones . . .'

'Shhh.' I put my finger up to my lips, pulling a face at our 'bad mother' secret as Mark appeared in the doorway with two rucksacks and the beach cricket set.

'Did I hear something about phone games?'

'No.' Ben pulled a face.

'So – you still too tired to join us?' Mark was grinning, staring right at me before picking up his sunglasses from the kitchen surface.

I sighed. I'd tried my best not to disturb him last night but the insomnia was so bad that in the end I got up to make tea and read for a couple of hours. He assumed it was flashbacks over Gill and Antony, and it was. Partly. But I couldn't tell him the extra thing now troubling me. *Daren't . . .*

'Yeah. Do you mind if I pass? Sorry, Ben, but Mummy is going to be lazy this morning. I'll make a picnic lunch and join you on the beach later. I'll text when I'm on my way and we can all play some more cricket this afternoon.'

'OK, love. Take it easy and we'll see you later.' Mark crossed the room to lean down for a kiss, whispering that I was *busted over the phone games*. I smiled.

I was genuinely sorry to disappoint them but I was suffering that shell-shocked fuzziness of true tiredness. Also my vision was a little blurry around the edges, though I wasn't going to share that either; I didn't want to worry Mark. I would just sit tight until it passed. Rest.

Once I heard the click of the door, I moved back to the sofa, tucking my legs up to the side and picking at a piece of stray cotton on the cuff of my dressing gown.

No surprise that the scene with Gill and Antony was still disturbing my sleep; I had accepted it was going to take time to come to terms with it. But the problem now? I felt disorientated that it was no longer just the flashbacks from Gill's cottage that were troubling me. I glanced at the cliff section of the puzzle – about a third completed – and felt my frown deepen.

The simple fact was it *couldn't* have been her I saw yesterday. So – either her doppelganger and hence just a very weird coincidence with the coat, or I had to have been imagining it. It made no sense otherwise. I thought of my tiredness and all the stress. Yes. Most probably my mind playing tricks.

Yet oddly I couldn't let it go; wanted to share this. To sort it out properly in my head somehow.

I tried Emma's phone again but it was still going to voicemail. I'd already sent two texts and didn't want to seem paranoid. Pestering.

I twisted my mouth to the side and then pinched my bottom lip several times. Finally I scrolled the contacts for Heather, putting the phone up to my ear as, through the window, the sun emerged suddenly from behind a cloud to light up the whole room.

'Hi there, Sophie. You OK?' Heather sounded as if she was walking, slightly out of breath. 'I thought you were supposed to be having a complete break from us?'

'Sorry. Just checking if there is any news on Gill. The hospital won't say anything as I'm not a relative.' I felt guilty at the half-truth. I did badly want to know how Gill was doing but it wasn't why I was ringing.

'Her mother says no change. Still in an induced coma. But honestly, darling. You need to put all this out of your mind. Have a proper break. *Rest.*'

'I know and I am trying. I was just wondering if you knew what Emma was up to? Can't seem to get hold of her.'

There was a pause.

'Not urgent or anything, Heather. It's just she's not answering her mobile. I wanted to run something past her.'

I now remembered it more vividly. The flash of red coat and dark hair up on the cliff top as I glanced up while eating my crab sandwich with Helen. I knew it *couldn't* be her. I knew that my mind was probably simply in terrible turmoil. Tired. Playing tricks. But the problem is it really did look like her, even from the distance . . . I'd even fancied I saw the light catching on the distinctive large buckle on her belt.

'No idea, darling. She was off chasing some business contact yesterday. I had Theo for her for the day but no idea where she is now. You want me to tell her you rang? Chase her up?'

A strange frisson of confusion right through me . . .

'No. No. It can wait. She'll be cross if she knows I'm fussing. I promised her I'd rest. Zone out. Please don't mention it.'

'OK then. Listen, I'm actually in the garden and need to run. You sure you're OK, Sophie?'

'Yeah. The rest is doing me good. Just what I need. See you when I get back.'

I put the phone down at my side and found myself staring at a knot in the wood of the stripped floor until my eyes were smarting. The call had made things worse, not better; I just didn't know what to think . . .

Then the doorbell rang; I was delighted to find Helen had spotted the guys leaving and she was soon in the kitchen, depositing a bag of mussels and two crabs in the top of the fridge.

'Excuse me, still in my dressing gown. Didn't sleep very well.'

'Flashbacks?' She turned with a look of real concern.

I nodded, and made her coffee and myself lemon in hot water as I toyed with whether I should tell her what else was troubling me. I couldn't share this with Mark. He felt my friendship with Emma was coming between us quite enough already, without adding hallucinations into the mix.

'Actually, I have a confession, Sophie. I called round because I was worried about you. At the beach yesterday . . . I've never seen you so disorientated.'

I looked her in the eyes. I didn't want to sound delusional. Paranoid. Oh hell. What did I have to lose? Helen wouldn't judge me.

'I think I'm going a bit mad, Helen. I honestly thought yesterday that I saw my friend Emma. On the cliff, watching us. Completely ridiculous. A mistake, obviously. It *couldn't* have been her, but it really threw me because my brain in the moment was saying that it *was* her . . . Like a hallucination almost.'

Helen looked really concerned. 'So why did you feel so convinced it was her? From that distance, lots of people can look alike. I don't understand . . .'

I paused. I knew it would sound odd and I wished I could be rational and dismiss it for what it was. A harmless and inconsequential mistake.

'She has this striking red coat. She's very arty, always dresses beautifully, and she changed the belt on the coat to add this big, beautiful buckle and I thought . . .' I glanced away, embarrassed. I felt torn and even more confused suddenly, because out loud it somehow sounded disloyal to Emma to even discuss this. 'Oh, it doesn't matter. Ignore me; I'm really worried I'm going completely nuts. *Seeing* things.'

I stood up from my chair quickly, intending to nip to the bedroom to throw on some clothes before continuing this, and then, to my horror, all was a blur.

The next thing I felt was this strange ache to the side of my cheek and also my leg. Somehow I was now on the floor with Helen's voice alongside me. 'Right. Keep still, Sophie. You're all right. You just fainted. I managed to hold you as you fell so I don't think you hurt yourself but you need to keep still, honey. You understand? Take slow breaths . . .'

TODAY – 6.15 P.M.

We have made it past Dawlish. No waves. No landslide. All this is good but there are still miles and miles to go and no further news from Nathan.

I have borrowed Mark's phone – mine is absolutely useless – to message Helen, but the signal has been patchy; no reply from her either. She said something about visiting Truro today and I have been wondering if she would drive to the hospital, just in case she could make it there ahead of Nathan . . . and us. Ben would like that.

Ben.

I keep picturing him waking up all alone and frightened, calling out for me. All confused on morphine or whatever it is they give children after surgery.

I asked the nurse if they could rig up a phone call from me the moment one of the boys comes round but she said this could be disorientating for a child. And I read between the lines: they don't want me accidentally talking on the phone to Theo until they can carefully share what has happened with his mother's surgery.

What a godawful mess.

I keep thinking about this feature I read once in a Sunday supplement; it was written by a mother who had to sit for three nights by her child in the high dependency unit of a hospital. She didn't know if he was going to live or die and had to just sit there, listening to all the machines bleeping and watching the numbers registering his oxygen levels and his heart rate. She said she was afraid to sleep or even go to the loo in case the worst happened while she was away. She wrote that, although her child had eventually recovered, she never has.

I remember so clearly that when I read that article I thought it must be the worst thing in the world to have to sit by your child, watching them go through all that. Helpless. And now, of course, I realise that there is something much worse.

Which is not being able to sit by your child as they go through all that.

Maybe all this is my payback. For all the bad sex and for taking Ben for granted; for failing to be satisfied with one child and for longing so badly and so selfishly for another.

I think of all the time I could have spent being happy and satisfied instead of obsessing over ovulation charts. I think of all the good sex Mark and I used to have long, long ago. And yes – all the bad sex and the rows, trying to make a baby according to the calendar and my temperature.

Mark has been gone from his seat for ages but is suddenly back in the aisle, holding another set of drinks. Coffee for me and him, and tea for the doctor and his wife as a thank you.

I take the coffee but know I will not drink it. All I can think of is Ben.

I close my eyes, coffee cup warm in my hands, and listen to the beat of the train. *Ta-tum. Ta-tum.* I get it now . . .

All this is my payback for moving us to Devon, for digging in so selfishly, but most of all for taking motherhood so completely for granted.

CHAPTER 14

BEFORE

LIBRA
Be careful. Sometimes when we read back what we have
written, we read what we intended to write, not what
is on the page. And sometimes when we listen, we hear
what we expected to hear and not what is being said . . .

The first thing I noticed when we pulled back into Tedbury was that
the police cordon was gone. At Gill and Antony's pale pink cottage, the
curtains remained drawn, like eyes closed against the daylight – but at
least the horrid flash of blue-and-white ribbon was no more. I noticed
also that someone had thought to water the tubs which stood either
side of the deep blue door – Gill's petunias thriving, faces upturned to
the afternoon sun. I didn't understand why this bothered me but I was
wondering who had thought to do this and felt oddly troubled over
whether they would have done it openly, watering them in daylight, or
crept out quietly after dark.

They stayed in my head, the petunias, as I unpacked the cases, hurl-
ing piles of dirty clothes on to the bedroom floor. *It's tough but life goes*

on. Be strong. That's what Helen had said when we hugged goodbye, and she was right.

The doctor was right too. Before the shock of the Hartleys, I had allowed myself to spiral into a world of waiting. Pinning everything on the next baby. Small wonder I coped so badly; made such a spectacle of myself in Cornwall. Started imagining things . . . Fainted.

'Enough, Sophie.'

'I'm sorry?'

Mark was standing in the doorway. He was wearing a favourite shirt in this soft turquoise colour which so suited him. I looked at him properly and was struck by how handsome he still was. Why did I dwell so often on his little flaws? Cause arguments over nothing? Why did I do all that? Was this how all couples ended up or was it because of the wait for the second child? All the time apart.

'Oh, nothing. Just thinking aloud.' I tilted my head. 'You do know I hate that you're still doing all this driving.' It was true. I really had hoped he would have been able to move the business by now. That we could have found some compromise on the geography.

As he walked into the room I began sorting the clothes into piles: darks, mids and whites.

'Yeah, I know.' A pause. 'You look much better, by the way.'

'I am. Helen gave me a good talking to. I need to try to put this behind me; also I'm going to get my act together, Mark. About work.'

And now he pulled a face.

'Don't worry. I won't rush into anything, but when the dust settles I'm going to get myself back to work. It's been long enough. And if I could contribute again maybe you could scale back a bit? Afford to move the business out of London?'

'I thought we both agreed the deli's the last thing you need. And to be frank, I doubt it would make much money, Sophie.'

'I didn't mean the deli. I haven't decided about that. Although I rather think you're only dead set against it because Emma's involved.'

'That's not fair.'

'Isn't it?' I checked myself. 'Look. I don't want to argue and I don't want you to worry either. The truth is I'm beginning to agree that the deli probably isn't the right way forward but I need to do *something*, Mark. Especially after what's happened here. I need to get out of the village a bit. Get a different routine.'

'And Ben?'

'Ben is starting school. Ben has a big enough slice of Mummy and is going to be just fine. I need to do something for myself. At least until—'

Another slip. I needed to stop automatically assuming this default position, linking everything with my ovaries. Bumping every decision, where we lived and what I did, until I knew if our family would be four.

'OK. I see what you mean. But you won't rush into anything? I was rather hoping we might talk some more – about moving. At least considering it before Ben gets too settled in the village school.'

I sat down on the edge of the bed and looked at him really carefully. How I hated this stalemate of the geography. I was torn. I felt disorientated now in Tedbury because of what had happened with Gill and Antony but I couldn't face a move anytime soon and I hoped the feeling of unease would pass. Most important? I simply loved having Emma's support and didn't want to lose her friendship or having her close by. Hell – maybe that was why I conjured her up in Cornwall. It was almost like a girl crush back in school. I had started to feel so *differently* about Devon with Emma around and I hoped I could build on that; at the same time I did feel terribly guilty over the price Mark was still paying.

'Could we just give ourselves some time to regroup, eh, Mark? Not make any big decisions just now.' I was remembering what Helen had said. 'I know you can't keep up this commuting forever. I just need to press pause. *Please.* Maybe down the line we could consider Exeter or Bristol?'

'My clients need me in London.'

117

'So why didn't you say that when we bought this place? I thought the whole plan was to relocate the business.'

There was a long pause and Mark looked at the floor. 'I miscalculated, Sophie. I took on too many clients who want me in London.'

'But lots of media companies thrive outside of London.' Mark's admission was really worrying. His office lease had run out only recently and he had moved the business to slightly bigger premises. He had still implied it was a phase, staying in London. Just for a couple more years . . . Now I wasn't so sure.

Mark held his hands up in mock surrender.

'OK. First things first . . .' I really didn't want this to spiral into another argument. 'I'm going to get this wash on and call into the shop. Find out if anyone knows any more about how Gill is doing.' I babbled on that I'd tried phoning the hospital several times from Cornwall but they would only share details with relatives, so this was my first real chance for a full update.

I headed downstairs to the utility room, loaded the machine quickly and unhooked a string bag from the back of the door, checking my watch. Ten minutes till closing. Just milk and bread, then. Oh – and chocolate for Ben for being so good in the car.

◆ ◆ ◆

In front of me in the queue, Mrs Richards had her arm linked through her neighbour's. I couldn't remember the other woman's name.

'Well, from what I hear, she's cold as ice, that Emma. And the police have been sniffing about again. Checking out her inheritance . . .' Mrs Richards didn't even attempt to lower her voice.

'Who told you that?' The neighbour at least had the decency to whisper.

'Bloke up the garage knows someone in the coroner's office. Reckon they're going to dig the mother up. In *France*.'

I could feel the shock on my face.

'Can they do that?'

'Oh yes. The word is there was a very big inheritance. That's how she afforded Priory House. And you know she was the last one to see Gill?' Mrs Richard's head was making little jerky movements. 'Didn't I always say there was something a bit odd there . . .' And then suddenly she was prodded hard in the back by Alice Small who was standing close by. Both women then turned and blushed.

'Ah, Sophie. You're back.'

'Yes.'

'So how are you bearing up, dear? Terrible, terrible business.'

'I'm doing OK, thank you. Is there any more news from the hospital? On Gill?'

'Still no change, I'm afraid.'

The two women turned back. All was suddenly stillness and quiet, only the ping of the electronic till piercing this new awkwardness. I waited for what felt like an eternity to be served.

Once back home at last, I continued with the unpacking but all the time my mind was back in that shop. I normally ignore the tittle-tattle of Tedbury tongues. But what the hell was going on?

I texted Emma.

Back. Feeling better. You OK? S x

'Did you get my chocolate, Mummy?'

Damn.

'I'm just going to the garage, honey.'

'But Daddy said you were getting it from the shop.'

'I forgot – all right? I'm really sorry. I'm going now. Right this minute.'

Twenty minutes this second trip took – the shop now closed and a tractor blocking the B road to the nearest garage. And then – with two bars of Cadbury on the passenger seat – I pulled the car up on to the little verge outside Priory House, en route home. Yet again, there had been no reply from Emma. I left the engine running and tried the bell. No response, so I peered around the side of the house where, to my astonishment, the large window to the kitchen-cum-family-room was boarded up with a patchwork of crudely fitted MDF sheets. Inside, all was dark and silent. I tried Emma's mobile but it went straight to voicemail.

I got back in the car and parked on the village square, hurrying across to Heather's, relieved to see a light on in her kitchen.

She didn't look at all surprised to see me as she answered the door. 'Good to see you. You'd better come in. So you've spoken to Emma?'

'No. I didn't manage to get hold of her. Why – what's been happening, Heather? I've just seen her window. And I heard the most bizarre nonsense in the shop.'

'Someone put a brick through her window, Sophie, with a rather unpleasant message attached.'

'You're kidding me.'

'I wish. Happened yesterday.'

'But why on earth? I don't understand.'

'Yes, well. Feels like the whole world's gone a little crazy while you were away. Do you want a drink?'

'No. Look, I haven't really got time. So where is she?'

'She's at Nathan's, I think. Until they get the window fixed properly.'

I felt this sinking feeling in my stomach; guilt for all the stupid overthinking in Cornwall while poor Emma was so up against it. 'So – have the police been?' I started to pace while Heather sat ashen-faced at the kitchen table.

'She doesn't want the police involved.'

'But that's ridiculous. You can't have someone throw a brick through your window and just leave it.' I could feel myself shaking my head, not understanding this. 'And you said there was a message? With the brick?'

'Yes. Suggesting that she leaves the village.'

'*Leave?* But why on earth would anyone be so unpleasant?'

'Oh, there's plenty of unpleasantness, Sophie. It's getting quite ugly.'

'But I just don't understand. What's Emma supposed to have done? I don't get it.'

Heather took a deep breath. 'The police are saying that Emma was the last person to see Gill before it all happened. In the fortune teller's tent at the fair. People have put two and two together and made five – decided she was the one having a fling with Antony.'

'Oh, but that's completely ridiculous. She's only just got here.'

'Yes, well. People aren't exactly being rational at the moment.'

'Jeez.'

'And there's another rumour.'

I sat down, feeling just a little bit giddy with it all.

'I'm embarrassed even to repeat it. But better you hear it from me.'

'What?'

'That the police are looking into how Emma's mother died. While she was in France. Questions about her inheritance before she came here. Apparently the police always look into bank accounts.'

My face must have given me away.

'So you didn't know either? That her mother died while she was over there?' Heather was watching me very closely.

'Of course I knew. She just doesn't like to talk about it.' Later I would ask myself over and over why I lied; also why I minded so much that I felt I *needed* to.

'Yes – well, I guessed it was something like that. She never mentioned her mother dying to me. But like I say – people round here have gone a bit over the top. You know what they can be like. It doesn't help, of course, that she's seeing Nathan. People can be—'

'I'd better get out to see her. This is my fault.'

'Your fault?'

121

'Yes. If I hadn't made her do that stupid turn in the tent – people wouldn't have jumped to the wrong conclusion.'

'Yes, well. I guess everyone's still in shock.'

'I'd better go. See how she's doing.'

'Look – why not leave it until tomorrow, Sophie? You look done in. Do you want me to ring Mark?'

'No, no. I'm fine. Really.' And then back at the front door, a long sigh as I reached for the handle, turning suddenly. 'Heather. My friend in Cornwall – Helen. She was saying that places eventually recover from this kind of thing. That, in the end, they simply have no choice. Do you think she's right? I mean – I don't want to sound callous and I'm not saying we won't always remember him. Antony. But I just can't bear to think that Tedbury will always feel *like this*. Sort of ruined.'

'I don't know, Sophie.' Heather's eyes were fixed on the floor. 'I just don't know anything any more.'

Out at Nathan's barn there was just the dog barking furiously as I tried the bell, and then I waited for a time in the car, sending another text to Emma just as my phone chirruped. Not her. Mark's voice.

'Sophie. Thank heavens. I've been worried. Also, I have a child here point-blank refusing to have his bath until he gets chocolate.'

CHAPTER 15

BEFORE

Later, in bed, I had the familiar dream about the deli. I was serving customers in my crisp, striped apron, happy and humming until I retreated to the back area to fetch more bread, where on the floor – *dear God* – Gill Hartley sat staring and bleeding with the bread knife lolling from her hand and her head gaping with the white matter pulsing and dreadful . . .

My gasp was so loud that it woke me. I felt the sweat on my forehead and under my arms, but turned to find, to my surprise, Mark still asleep. I wondered if I had made the noise out loud at all, or just in my head, and very carefully lay back down to allow my mind and body to find each other.

I tried to calm myself but other images began to swirl around my brain then. That day Ben fell into the swimming pool and Mark had to dive in to haul him out, gasping and coughing. Me fainting in Cornwall. That woman on the cliff in Cornwall with the same coat as Emma. The brick through Emma's window. I closed my eyes and felt another headache coming. *Enough . . .*

Quietly I slipped from the bed, grabbing my dressing gown from the chair, and meandered carefully through the darkness, keen not to wake Mark or Ben.

Downstairs, out of habit not thirst, I put the kettle on the stove and sat at the table. The deli dream had completely winded me. So vivid. I looked across to the window seat. Just a few months ago, Emma was kneeling right there, looking at her furniture van, the parsnips overflowing from the split bag on the floor. I couldn't believe so much had happened.

I thought again of the dream and of Emma's plans. I lost out to the tune of ten, maybe eleven thousand pounds over the deli disaster with Caroline, and though I hated to disappoint Emma, I really couldn't afford to lose any more money. Also I wanted to help balance the finances so that it might seem more viable for Mark to move the company. Wind down the pressure on him so that he could afford to lose a few clients.

Next I got that prickling sensation of being watched and turned to see Mark standing in the doorway. So odd, isn't it, how you know when someone is looking. His hair was sticking up in little horns, his pyjama bottoms hung low on his hips. I found myself looking at his body, noticing that he had lost a little weight. The stomach more toned. All that golf.

'Was I a complete idiot over the Caroline business?'

Mark's face softened. 'Sophie. It's three o'clock in the morning.'

'I know that. But I can't sleep. You think I'm a bad judge of character, don't you?'

'You married me.' He was yawning. Tired eyes. Cute little spikes of hair. 'Come back to bed. Please, Sophie. We'll talk about it in the morning.'

'You're wrong about Emma, Mark. She's OK. And the thing is I don't want to become this really cynical, glass-half-empty person. I don't want to stop trying new things just because of what happened with

Caroline. Don't you think that would be a horrible way to live your life? To always think the worst of people just because—'

'Sophie. It is the middle of the night. Will you please just come back to bed?'

I stared again at his torso, thinking how he had turned down ice cream and cake a couple of times in Cornwall. Was he trying to lose weight because I'd teased him a while ago? I felt guilty, then touched, and then a stirring. So that I smiled. He smiled back. I went back to bed. To surprise him. Myself also.

And then, when he was once more asleep, naked now, I stewed some more. Four a.m. Five a.m. Until Ben was suddenly standing by the bed in his school uniform.

'What are you doing, Ben? It's Sunday. You don't start school until tomorrow.'

'I'm practising.'

Slowly I opened my eyes properly. He looked so cute, but the olive green sweatshirt was too large. I should have gone for the smaller size. The white polo shirt was all twisted at the neck. The grey trousers – too long and with the zip undone.

'You look great, darling.' I would have to get the sewing basket out. *Damn.* Not my forte, hemming trousers. 'Now put it all back on the hangers and go back to bed.'

'I can't. I'm too excited.' He moved over to the mirror on the double wardrobe, chest plumped up proud. 'Can I have school dinners?'

'I thought we agreed on sandwiches.'

'Theo says you get puddings with school dinners.'

'Theo doesn't start school until next year.'

'I like puddings.'

At that moment my handbag buzzed on the floor. Well practised, Ben walked across the room, removed my mobile and handed it to me in bed as Mark opened his eyes.

At last. Emma.

Sorry AWOL – loads to tell. Meet Hobbs Lane 11 am.

I put the mobile on the bedside table as Mark stirred fully along-side, swung my legs out of bed and wriggled my toes into the carpet. I wandered over to pull back the curtain slightly, intending to check the weather, but instead noticed something odd. A tall man with white-blond curly hair over by the church, taking pictures. Initially he seemed captivated by the church itself. This was not surprising. It is a splendid church – the original section dating from the thirteenth century, with magnificent stained-glass windows. But the man, wearing a dark parka-style jacket, then turned his camera around and seemed to be taking pictures of other houses. And cars . . . including ours.

I felt a strange sensation. A feather touching the skin. And the more I looked, the more the feather teased the flesh for there was something familiar about this moment. About the camera. And also the man.

'So can I have school dinners, then, Mum?'

I let go of the curtains, convinced now that I had seen this man before.

CHAPTER 16

BEFORE

Melanie woke with a start – her right hand touching a lump of dead flesh in the bed. Eyes immediately wide, it took just a couple of seconds to confirm that the dead flesh was actually her left arm. Entirely unfeeling.

She waited some more. Sometimes she had layered dreams in which she thought she was awake, only to discover, through some subsequent horror, that she was still in the midst of a nightmare. She used her right hand to lift the 'dead' one – a horrible, entirely detached sensation, the left limb dropping to the pillow the moment she let go.

Melanie breathed slowly and felt the familiar terror that the sensation in the arm would not return at all. Her heart thumped, but then ever so slowly there were tantalising tingles and prickles – the pins and needles that signalled she had probably just lain awkwardly on the arm for too long.

She sat up, but though the immediate panic was subsiding, her heart was still pounding. One by one she ran through her other tests, stretching the right hand before circling both feet under the duvet. Clockwise then anticlockwise.

'You all right, Melanie?' The voice – right outside her door – made her start again. Melanie looked about her, eyes wide, as the room and its shadows slowly revealed their familiar forms. Her desk with a pile of books. Her dressing gown thrown across a chair.

'It's OK, Cynthia. Just a dream.'

'Oh, right.'

'Sorry, did I wake you up, Cynth?'

'No, no. I've been up all night again so I heard you calling out in your sleep. I've just finished the final rug. Are you sure you're OK? Want a coffee or something?'

Melanie slumped back on the pillow – still examining her left arm, which was feeling hot and uncomfortable now. Briefly she checked the alarm clock on the bedside cabinet – 6.30 a.m. – for a moment unable to remember the day.

'Coffee would be fabulous.'

Monday. *Damn.* She had promised her boss an update on the Tedbury case. The forensics were now so conclusive that she was under pressure to stall further inquiries in order to spare resources and file her report. If Gill Hartley woke, there was enough already to charge her – whether they got a murder or manslaughter conviction was not Melanie's call.

But the various routine financial checks were proving a bit of a puzzle, especially regarding Emma Carter. Melanie's application to investigate Emma further, in particular her recent history in France, had been laughed out of the office. There appeared to have been a leak – probably by someone trying to undermine her – which had reached Tedbury and was causing wild gossip. This in turn had somehow made its way back to her boss, who had not minced his words.

You think we have the money to fund holidays to France over a domestic? I'll see you Monday, Melanie. The forensics are clear enough so I want this one tidied up, you hear me? No more wild fishing trips. No more talk of international jaunts. Monday. Latest.

Downstairs, the final rug was laid out on the dining table alongside a pink cotton case Cynthia had run up to keep each rug in pristine condition during transit. The rug and the case were set at a casual angle but Melanie realised they were actually on deliberate display for her evaluation. She smiled. There would be no need to be false.

This last creation was a complete surprise – a tropical scene of vibrant foliage in various shades of green, with a bewitching centrepiece of a parrot in glorious turquoise, yellow and azure. It must have taken hours of dyeing to achieve the clarity of colour.

'Can't we keep this one, Cynth? It's gorgeous.'

'You think so?'

'Absolutely. Your best yet. I love it.'

Cynthia appeared from the kitchen, her wide smile in stark contrast to the deep, dark circles under her eyes.

'Though you look terrible.'

Cynthia held out a mug, poking out her tongue.

'It's quite different from the others.' Melanie was stroking the woven cotton.

'Yeah. I couldn't decide on the design. It got to one o'clock in the morning and then it suddenly came to me. I'm sick as a bloody—'

'Parrot.'

'Exactly. Just finished it when you started groaning in your sleep. So what's all that about, then? Nightmare?'

'No. Must have slept funny. Woke up with a completely dead arm. Gave me a fright.'

'What kind of fright?'

Melanie sipped her coffee.

'It's not hereditary, Mel. Your mum's condition. We've been over this.'

'I know.' Melanie continued to stare at the hot liquid, blowing on the surface. She was thinking of all the complex new research. The cause of her mother's illness remained a scientific puzzle and technically Melanie's risk factor was tiny.

Technically . . .

'So how's she doing – your mum?'

'OK, I think. I spoke to her last week. She's spending all my dad's money trying out some new therapy abroad. Portugal, I think.'

Cynthia smiled encouragement. 'So how's her mobility at the moment?'

'I tell you what. I'll commission one for my room.'

'I'm sorry?'

'A rug. Exactly like this one.'

'Don't be ridiculous.'

'I'm not. I like it a lot, Cynthia. It's really good.'

On the phone, Melanie's father had raved about a new folding wheelchair that was compact and light. Which meant that her mother's mobility was not good at all.

Cynthia's face softened. 'You'd really like one? A rug?'

'Yes. Though I'll want mates' rates. None of your fancy hotel prices.'

'You are not going to get multiple sclerosis, Melanie.'

A pause.

'I know that.'

And now they both quietly sipped at their drinks.

'Right – so what's happening with your first murder inquiry, then?'

'Don't ask.' Melanie put the mug down and stretched. 'All sewn up by forensics really. Conclusive evidence from the blood-splatter patterns, etc., that the husband was trying to defend himself. He was left-handed, apparently – put both hands up, walking backwards to try to fend her off. All knife blows were from the wife – right-handed, including the wound to her own stomach.' Melanie began walking through the scene, waving her hands to demonstrate the tussle.

'Yuk. She actually gouged her own stomach?'

'Yep. Killed him in one room then went into the kitchen to stab herself. Pretty gruesome, though her most severe injuries were from banging her head on the way down. I shouldn't be telling you all this, by the way.'

'And the motive? Was I right?'

'Yeah. Word around college – a very naughty boy. Same old story – everyone knew except the wife – though I haven't been able to confirm his latest conquest. Personally I've got my money on someone in the village. A strange woman. Very attractive. Phone records say he rang her home number the day it happened but she didn't pick up. Unfortunately there's no appetite at work to take that lead any further.'

'Why not?'

'Doesn't add value. We've got enough evidence already for a charge, no forensics on any third party, and we don't even know if our attacker will wake up to bring the whole thing to court. We're very short-staffed right now so I'm under pressure to move on to another case.'

'But something's niggling you?'

'Yes, it's this woman in Tedbury. There's something I can't quite put my finger on. Something not right there. The bank records don't make sense either – though I'm waiting on some more to come in.'

'Go on.'

'Oh, I don't exactly know, Cynth. Instinct. Completely unscientific but she was in France for a bit and no one seems to know much about that. Word in the village is she bought her house with an inheritance but that's not what her bank records are saying. It's all a bit odd and I just wish I could dig a bit further.'

'So dig.'

'I honestly can't spare the time – at least not officially. According to my boss we have enough unsolved crimes on the books without going abroad looking for new ones.'

'So you might dig on the quiet?'

'Really nice parrot, Cynth.'

Cynthia smiled.

Two hours later, Melanie called again at Durndale Hospital on the way to work. To her relief, Mrs Baines was still in the accommodation provided for patients' relatives nearby, and Melanie was able to sit alongside Gill Hartley undisturbed for the first time. There was a suite of three separate rooms with a nurse checking each at regular intervals from a central station – a bank of monitors, wired to sound alarms if anything changed in-between these checks. Most of the time relatives and friends kept their loved ones company, so Gill was rarely alone like this.

As Melanie moved two magazines to take up a seat alongside the bed, a text buzzed up on her phone. Melanie checked it quickly. To her surprise, it was from Matthew Hill, a good friend. She'd trained with him, and in the early days in the force they were best buddies; pretty much inseparable. But Matthew had suffered a crisis some years later and left the force disillusioned – working now on the 'dark side' as a private investigator.

Coffee? Have something to share.

Melanie shook her head at the text and smiled, knowing this normally meant Matthew was after a favour. She took a deep breath. It still made her sad to think of him in civvy street. He was good; one of the best she'd worked with. He had this trick of seeing things that others didn't; should definitely have stayed in the force. Selfishly she would rather have liked him on her own new team and could certainly do with his support right now.

Melanie decided to contact Matthew later and put the phone away to watch the rise and fall of Gill Hartley's chest, controlled by the ventilator. She tried to imagine how a woman who looked so harmless, who in this bed and in every statement taken seemed so very ordinary and who had no record of any violence, could become so suddenly and overwhelmingly angry at someone that she would shake off her character like some temporary cloak and reach for a knife.

Sure – Melanie had known fury herself. After her mother's diagnosis she had thrown china at the wall. Plate after plate, picturing her mother and her father dancing around the room to show off their outfits when she was a child – the swish of her mother's lemon silk dress brushing against her leg as they waltzed and waltzed, laughing.

Yes. She had screamed. Ranted. Raved that it was unfair.

But violence against a *person*? Someone that you loved. How could anything make you so angry that you would suddenly cross all the lines?

'What happened?' Melanie leant in closer to the bed, whispering the question, remembering what Mrs Baines had said. That maybe Gill could hear.

The nurse reappeared to glance across from the central station, her expression one of unease, but Melanie did not care and whispered again.

'What really happened, Gill? You need to wake up and tell me.'

CHAPTER 17

BEFORE

First day back into work after Cornwall and Mark could not concentrate. He stared out of the window, then glanced back at the two cups of cold coffee on his desk. He badly needed caffeine but was reluctant to ring through to Polly for a third, well aware that the same thing would happen again. He was so snowed under, trying to catch up after the holiday. This was the very reason he never took a break in the summer.

Mark had 728 unread emails and knew that the moment a new drink arrived, he would end up swinging his chair through 180 degrees to give a client on the phone his full attention, and then his mind would meander back to the mess that was their life in Devon. And another coffee would go cold.

Why oh why had he ever let Sophie persuade him? He so regretted saying that he would try to move the business. When they bought in Tedbury, he had agreed to relocate the company within three years. At the time he'd meant it but he got cold feet, and with Sophie so unwell after Ben was born, he didn't have the heart to tell her. So he fibbed and fudged about just how many new London-centric clients he had taken on, and now it was all proving *impossible*. Oh, to hell with it. He glanced at the wall clock and decided to take ten.

Mark stood, grabbing his jacket from the back of the spare chair, and marched through the door, struggling to push his arm through the twisted right sleeve as he passed Polly's desk. 'Hold my calls, will you?' Feeling a twinge in his shoulder. *Bloody stupid jacket.* 'Look, I'll be half an hour tops. Only message if an A-list client or lawyer is getting arsy. Or if it's Malcolm, get him to ring my private mobile. I *really* need to speak to Malcolm.'

Polly smiled. 'And when you get back, will you *please* look at the pictures I had framed for the corridor, Mark?'

'Do I look as if I have time for decor deliberation?'

Polly poked out her tongue and Mark did the same back, aware he had been a complete pain so far today and needed to keep his staff on side.

At Starbucks, he sipped at his macchiato and finally closed his eyes. Ten minutes to think, please God . . .

There was a rattling noise from just next to his table. An annoying vibration. Mark kept his eyes closed and tried very hard to ignore it – only giving in finally to a crescendo of tutting from a neighbouring table. He opened his eyes to see a couple staring at him.

Next, the echo of Sophie's voice:

You don't even realise that you're doing it, Mark – do you?

What?

Jiggling your foot up and down like that. You do it completely subconsciously – in a world of your own – whenever you're wound up.

I don't.

You do.

Mark followed the couple's stare to the source of the rattle – his phone and set of keys in the centre of his own table. He put them back in his pocket and uncrossed his legs, placing both feet firmly on the floor. He smiled an apology and the couple at last turned back to their newspapers.

The truth?

135

Mark was sick and tired of thinking, dreaming, worrying and scheming. He couldn't talk to Sophie about the problem – *the money* – because he was terrified it would all be too much. The last straw. After Gill and Antony, he was seriously concerned her depression might return.

Bad enough that, even before this awful business, they spent most weekends arguing over whether to consider IVF. Mark was more and more alarmed by how desperate Sophie was for this second child. He loved Ben to bits and loved being a dad too, but did it really make him wicked to be content? Happy if another child came along, happy if one didn't? He wanted to let nature decide. He didn't want fertility treatment to bump up the risk of twins, and he was genuinely terrified that if Sophie got postnatal depression again, they would never cope with three.

It had crossed his mind that they could get a live-in nanny for a while, but Sophie was against that. And in the end it all came back to the new, underlying problem. Cash flow. Also the geography.

And now this terrible business with Gill and Antony. Life just seemed to throw one curve ball after another at them . . .

Mark sipped again at his coffee, then leant forward, elbows on his knees and head in his hands.

Dear God. Never mind past promises, he had to get them away from Devon and nearer his work. It was completely insane.

IVF was where they were clearly heading – no doubt in his mind – and Sophie had not the first clue what that might do to them. He, on the other hand, had walked through every detail with Alistair, a mate in HR. Week after week. Month after month. Injections. Hormone meltdown. Raised hopes. Dashed hopes. It would surely put them back – both of them – *right back* to that terrible place after Ben was born.

Mark felt his muscles tense as he thought of what Sophie went through back then. Crippling guilt as he remembered how long it took for him or anyone else to realise what it truly was.

If that's where they were going – God forbid – they needed at least to be living in the same house full-time.

So yes, Malcolm . . . He very badly needed to hear from Malcolm about the money. And then there was a loud buzz from his private phone. The couple at the adjoining table glanced over once more but Mark no longer cared what they thought.

He stared at his watch. Precisely eight minutes without interruption.

Mark took a final swig of coffee – at least it was still hot – before opening the message. It was from Polly. Lawyers chasing over an urgent contract.

Halle-bloody-lujah.

CHAPTER 18

BEFORE

Matthew placed the shape sorter on to Amelie's highchair tray. According to Sally, their daughter was now a little miracle, a mini Einstein. She might be playing stubborn with her language but, apparently months ahead of time, Amelie could put the square shape into the square hole.

Matthew placed the red square on the tray alongside the sorter.

'Now show Daddy what a clever girl you are.' Matthew handed Amelie the plastic cube and smiled.

'No.' Amelie threw the cube on to the floor and picked up her bright pink juice cup to suck away loudly.

Matthew moved across the kitchen to retrieve the cube and try again.

'Now, Mummy says you are a very clever girl and that you can do this already. Like a little Einstein.' Matthew held the red cube close to the red-coloured square hole by way of a clue, and then handed his daughter the cube for the second time. She looked at him as if he were mad, put the cube down on the tray and drank more juice.

Matthew moved a plate of toast fingers from the kitchen table to his daughter's tray, shook his head and took out his mobile. Just time to try his contact in the local planning office. 'Hi there – Samantha. It's Matt Hill here.'

'And what favour are you after this time?'

'Just an eensy-weensy tiny one. Nothing irregular.'

She laughed. Matthew had helped her out with her divorce evidence in the first year of working as a PI, and she had been forever grateful. And a very useful contact.

'OK. So I need some details on a planning application. A consortium looking for outline planning permission in Tedbury.' He could hear that she was writing this down, which was a good sign. Matthew paused to pull faces to make his daughter smile as she stuffed toast into her mouth.

'It's all in the public domain but it will take me forever to go through official channels. So I was hoping you might help me speed things up. Find out what's what and who's behind it all . . .'

'Can't help you out right away.' She had lowered her voice. 'Got the suits in.'

'Your boss?'

'Whole army of them.'

'Oh dear. Right. Look. Don't want to put you on the spot today then, but can I email you the full details? See what you can dig out when things are quieter?'

'Sure. So long as it's public information.'

'Course. Just looking to speed things up. You're a star. I'll message you straight away. Many thanks.'

Matthew put the phone back in his pocket. He would send the email soon as he could. Just at that moment, there was the key in the door, and father and daughter turned to see Sally appear, carrying two bags of shopping and a bunch of tulips, all of which she placed next to the fridge.

'How's she been?'

'Thirsty. But in no mood for genius shape-sorting. I think you might have imagined it, love.'

Matthew's wife glanced at the large shape sorter on Amelie's tray and narrowed her eyes. 'You have to look the other way. Did I not mention that?' She then carried the bunch of flowers to the draining board.

'Excuse me?'

'She won't do it if you're watching.'

Matthew could hardly believe it.

Sally walked over to hold up the red cube to hand to their daughter. 'Bet Amelie has no idea where *this* goes?' She turned her back on her daughter and grabbed at Matthew's shoulders to spin him around also.

'This surely can't be a good idea,' Matthew protested. 'We are creating a monster here, Sally. A little girl whose only vocabulary is *no* and who refuses to be cooperative unless you look away . . .'

'Shhh. Now, I wonder if Amelie has a surprise for us.' Sal had raised her voice to an excited pitch as they both turned back.

To Matthew's astonishment the small cube was gone. At first he looked around the floor, imagining she had thrown it again. But Sally picked up the shape sorter and rattled it to confirm the cube was inside.

'It's a poltergeist,' Matthew announced. 'She can't have done it. She's not supposed to be able to do that for *weeks*.'

Sally laughed, and moved back to the sink to take a vase from the windowsill which she filled from the tap.

'It's a poltergeist, isn't it, Amelie?'

'No!' Amelie picked up her juice cup again as Matthew leant forward to kiss her on the forehead.

And then it happened.

'Dadda.'

There was a pause; a freeze-frame of complete stillness. Matthew heard the echo of the word as if it was bouncing off all the walls but hardly dared imagine that it was real.

'What did you say?' He whispered the question as Sal turned, tulips in her hand.

'Dadda.'

Amelie was looking right into his eyes before sucking again on her juice. The moment of pure magic. The moment that suddenly surpassed all the ones that had gone before. The day she was born. The day she came home. The day she first smiled.

This day.

The day his stubborn and adorable little Amelie finally called him her *dadda*.

TODAY – 6.30 P.M.

And now – trance-like. Shallow breathing. Still. Staring.

Is this shock? I don't know.

Maybe this is what it takes to simply survive this journey. My own limbo land with the trees just a blur through the rain, streams of water tracing an angle down the train window. And somehow I sit now, staring and staring until my heartbeat matches the beat of the train and I travel with the trees and the rain back through time – much, much further back – watching how it all began. How simple and perfect and special it was that night I first met Mark. How safe I felt back then.

Love can do that. Make you feel safe . . .

I look across at him now. He has his eyes closed and I wonder what he is thinking; if he is trying, like me, to just zone out. To remember better times? Safer times.

We met at an awards do, me and Mark. We were both pretending not to mind that we had each come runner-up in our category; we were standing side by side at the hotel reception desk, in a queue to order a cab for an early exit as the winners sprayed Bollinger over their colleagues back in the awards hall.

Mark had only just set up his own company and had been pipped at the post by an arch-rival, PRO-motion. Oh God, I see it so clearly – how young I look. Young, and yes, quite pretty even though I was so cross and disappointed; smiling through gritted teeth too, as a fellow copywriter, prone to stealing clients (also husbands if rumours were to be believed) wiggled to the podium in a spray-on dress.

Half an hour. Those were his very first words to me. *The wait for a cab, I mean. Half an hour.*

I looked at him and I remember that I instantly liked what I saw. Nice jawline but ill-fitting suit. Too big, as if he had just lost a lot of weight.

But I was grumpy and so I shrugged and headed to the door of the hotel, where outside I discovered he had followed me.

'Can I help you?' I wasn't flirting at first, just puzzled. Disappointed and keen to leave.

'You're not going to try to hail one?'

'I'm sorry?'

'A cab – at this hour? No chance. Not here. I've already tried.'

This was before Uber and phone apps and my face must have betrayed what I was thinking, that I could not see how this was his business.

'It's just that I don't like to think—'

'Little girl out in London on her own? So late?' I widened my eyes as I spoke.

'I'm sorry.' He raised his hands in mock surrender. 'I didn't mean to cause offence.'

And that's when I pressed pause and felt this physical shame at my tone as he blushed.

'I'm sorry. I'm being a complete cow' – and then, holding out my hand – 'Sophie Hill. Copywriter for X-posure. Tipped, inaccurately, to win Slogan of the Year. I really didn't mean to be so pissy. I'm just a bad loser.'

He smiled then and held out his hand. Formal handshake, which I thought was quite sweet. 'Mark Edwards. Runner-up for New Agency Award. Bloody hate losing too, but I'm very pleased to meet you.'

And then he undid his bow tie and top button and we fell into step, failed to hail a cab as predicted, and instead took refuge in a corner bar, following the scent of decent coffee.

It was a really old-style bar. Faux Parisian. Dark cane furniture. We talked travel, mostly Paris, and I was pleased to discover he liked the same out-of-favour districts as me.

Two hours, three coffees and I knew the map of his life. Working-class boy made good. First in his family to make it to university, high-flyer in his first two agency jobs and now the owner of a terrifying business loan for his own start-up.

'So you needed to win tonight?'

'It would have helped, but hey – *c'est la vie.*'

His text the following morning was perfect:

Dinner – Paris. Two rooms. No strings . . .

I used the second room for the first night but not the second.

We made each other laugh so much back then.

Made love so much back then; as if the world were ending each time . . .

And yes.

He made me feel safe.

CHAPTER 19

BEFORE

Meeting Emma on Hobbs Lane was probably the moment I would come to revisit the most. Perhaps will for the rest of my life.

It came to feel like the turning point – more so, strangely, than the terrible and bloody scene with Gill and Antony because it was the moment I realised something had shifted between me and Emma.

So why did I not listen to the discord inside? Why did I not listen to Mark? Why did I not tell her right away about the woman on the cliff?

I don't know.

At the time I simply walked to Hobbs Lane, wondering why Emma had suggested this so soon after my return from Cornwall. I felt uneasy, unsure whether I should mention my disorientation over her doppelganger; also worried that she would be upset that I was still not ready to commit to the deli project – but I put these feelings aside, imagining she just wanted to show off the property, the potential. Make a stronger case? I expected also that she wanted to distract us both from the police inquiry and the cloud of shock and sadness hanging over Tedbury.

On the way there I rehearsed in my head my stalling tactics. I would be honest about why I was still undecided; that the terrible scene with the Hartleys had hit me harder than I realised – no lie. I was not saying a final *no* to the deli but it had to be a no for now. Emma would need to be patient.

The first thing I noticed on arrival was that the single-storey building had material up at all the windows so that you couldn't see inside. That was both new and odd. There was no bell or knocker so I tapped on the door with my knuckles. Immediately there was a scraping sound inside, like a chair being disturbed, and then the sound of a heavy bolt as the door was opened.

Emma's expression as she peeped around the door was at first difficult to read. 'You OK, Sophie? Did Cornwall help? Sorry I didn't reply to your texts. Phone was playing up.'

'It's fine. I had a good rest, thank you. But never mind me – what about this brick through your window? I spoke to Heather. I've been really worried about you.' I didn't add that I wished she had phoned rather than just a text.

'Well – stop right there and close your eyes, Sophie.'

'Excuse me?'

'I have a surprise.' Emma's face was more animated.

'Look, I'm not really in the mood. We should talk about the brick and about the message . . .'

'Do as you're told and close your eyes.' Her voice was all excitement.

And so, like a child, I did as I was told. I closed my eyes. I allowed Emma to lead me inside by the hand as she closed the door. And then I opened my eyes . . .

The shock of the image inside Hobbs Lane was still pounding in my head the next day as I stood with all the other first-time mothers in the playground as Ben prepared for his first day of school.

The teacher, a blonde gentle soul with a quiet voice, was admiring all the soft toys which the children were clutching – each animal sharing the same battered and grey evidence of tug-of-wars twixt child and mother and washing machine. Mrs Ellis was exactly what you would hope for in a reception teacher. Flowing skirt and comfortable shoes matching her flowing hair and comforting voice.

There had been a 'home visit' several weeks earlier, in which she did a puzzle with Ben at the kitchen table, explaining he could bring his favourite soft toy along for the first few weeks of school until he felt comfortable. There was to be a week-long induction period of mornings-only to help the children adjust, but they were encouraged to stay for lunch to get used to the routine in the dining hall.

I looked at Ben in his uniform, thinking of the picture shared earlier with his dad. Though the trousers looked better for the hem adjustments, he still looked much too small for this, clutching his towelling giraffe.

'What's his name?' Mrs Ellis crouched down to Ben's level.

'Mr Giraffe.'

And now came the spasm to my stomach, realising that I could too easily grab his hand, explain that there had been the most terrible mistake, and take him home to remove the uniform and replace it with his Robin Hood outfit. We could go to the park, then visit the garden shop to gawp at the lizard and tarantulas before large slices of cake in the cafeteria.

'Nice to meet you, Mr Giraffe.' Mrs Ellis was nodding her head as I fought the ridiculous stabbing of tears, realising that I had no idea how teachers managed their job. The patience. The energy. All those young faces staring at you. It was hard enough when you loved them.

Inside the cloakroom there followed the collective chaos of coat hooks and cuddles and then much too quickly all the children were gone – ushered seamlessly by the very clever and evidently well-practised Mrs Ellis into the bright distractions of toys already laid out in the reception classroom. Buckets of Lego and bricks and counting beads and puzzles. I barely caught Ben for the swiftest of kisses before he was working his way through the rails of dressing-up outfits. 'OK, children. Why don't you all have a good look around for a bit. See what we have here and then we'll sit down for circle time and do our register.' Mrs Ellis was making exaggerated shooing signals with her hands at all of us mothers peering through the window from the corridor.

Secretly, I was deflated. I had expected many things of this moment but it had not occurred to me that Ben would be absolutely fine.

Back at home I was soon sitting stunned on the sofa. In the hole of silence I again saw the scene at Hobbs Lane. I felt anxious. Confused. And so I did what I always do by way of distraction – I hoovered. Not a general sweep around the furniture, you understand, but a veritable assault – moving all the sofas and chairs, the sets of pine drawers, the heavy coffee table and even the dark mahogany tallboy in the bedroom upstairs, regretting this latter struggle as the phone went.

'So how did he get off? The picture looked great.' Mark's tone was buoyant.

'Fine.' I was twisting my hair around my finger, unable to find the right tone.

'Sophie – has something happened?'

A pause.

'He was *too fine*, Mark.'

'How can someone be . . . *too fine*?' I could hear the smile in his voice.

'You're laughing at me, aren't you?'

'I'm not—'

'He hardly looked back, Mark. No wave. Nothing. It was all so hurried; not what I expected at all – I'm worried that it was all bravado. That he could be in a complete state by now and I won't know.'

'Look, Sophie. He's a really confident little boy. He's been looking forward to this. It just means you've done a good job.'

And now I had to cover the receiver with my left hand.

'Oh, Sophie, you're not crying?'

'Of course I'm not crying. I just thought he would miss me, that's all.' I was fishing in my sleeve for a tissue, ridiculous tears running into my mouth. 'I'm fine, honestly.'

'So how's the hoovering going?'

And now I let out this huff of air, wondering when we reached this point, knowing each other this well.

'Look, I've got to go. Meeting. I'm serious – don't overdo the distraction cleaning. I love you. And text me when he gets home, yes?'

'OK. Love you too.'

I put the phone down, whereupon it rang again instantly.

'Thought you had a meeting.'

'Pardon?'

'Oh – sorry. Emma. Thought it was someone else.' I felt my heartbeat immediately quicken. *Hobbs Lane.* Thank Christ I didn't tell Mark. 'So how did Theo get off? At playgroup?'

'Not a backward glance. I'm feeling completely redundant and unloved. How about Ben?'

'Same.'

'Fancy a walk?'

I was aghast. 'Oh, I don't know. No, look, I'm in the middle—'

'Come on, Sophie. I need to talk to you about yesterday. And we'll only mope.'

I looked at my watch; I had until 1.30 p.m. tops.

'I was thinking a bit of the coastal path, while we're free of the boys.'

'You have got to be kidding.'

'Deadly serious. I've checked the map. There's plenty of time to do Bantham to Thurlestone and back if we leave straight away. It'll stop us worrying.'

'But what if the car breaks down? We can't just—'

'I'll toot outside your house in ten minutes. See you in a bit. We need to talk.'

I didn't remember saying yes, but as I scrambled to lock up, I felt a creeping unease which had nothing to do with Ben. I closed my eyes and pictured it again. The woman on the cliff in the red coat. The shock of seeing Hobbs Lane; not the empty ruin I expected but fully painted with a shiny new floor and all my equipment installed. The oven. The refrigeration unit. The grills. The counter. The coffee machine. All of it.

My equipment.

'What have you done, Emma?'

'It's my surprise – to cheer you up!' Emma had clapped her hands like a child and moved over to the coffee machine to demonstrate that it was already connected. 'Best coffee you will have ever tasted. I promise you.'

'But I didn't agree to this. I haven't even said yes, Emma . . .' I was reeling. 'This is my stuff.'

And then Emma's face had fallen. 'You're not pleased?'

I was so disorientated – so utterly winded – that I honestly had no idea what to say.

'But I did this for you, Sophie. I've worked day and night at it. I thought you would be pleased.'

Our exchange over the next ten minutes was something I will pick over for the rest of my life.

I challenged her. Not a full-on row, not that, but I did say that she should have waited. Had absolutely no right. And in the stress of the moment, I brought up the gossip over France, wondering why on earth she hadn't told me about her time there, about her loss.

OK, OK, so I should have told you. About my mother. At least mentioned it. It's just I didn't want to start life here as an emotional leech. Bringing all my baggage. I wanted a fresh start.

I didn't say what I was really thinking. That the explanation was fine to a point. Privacy – sure, I could understand that. But not to mention it at all – not even in *passing*? Quietly I also felt uneasy about Emma's dogged refusal to report the brick through the window to the police.

And to install my equipment – to have it all transferred from storage without even asking . . .

◆　◆　◆

'You're still cross with me.' Emma was wiping the inside of the windscreen with an old rag as I threw my small grey rucksack through the gap between us on to the back seat.

'Not cross exactly.'

'Yes, you are.'

We fidgeted as she pulled out of the village – me with my seatbelt and Emma rewiping the windscreen, both in turn stealing a glance sideways at each other.

'So Ben was fine, then?'

'Yes. Too relaxed. It sounds crazy but I felt hurt.'

'Theo was the same. I guess it just means we've done OK by them.'

'That's what Mark said.'

'So – I've checked this route on the map and we'll have bags of time. We can either circle back via Thurlestone—'

'I am cross with you, actually.'

'Oh, thank heavens.'

'Excuse me?' I turned to see she was frowning. 'You're saying you're pleased that I'm pissed off?'

'No – of course not. I'm just saying it's such a bloody relief to get this over with.'

'What?'

'Our first row.'

'Oh – don't be so childish, Emma. We're not going to have a row.'

'Yes we are. It's precisely what we need.'

'*Need?*'

'Yes, Sophie. It's what people do. Say what they really think and feel. Have a row. Clear the air. Move on.'

'I don't see your point.'

'Well, you wouldn't, would you? Because you don't do rows, do you?'

'And now you're being ridiculous.'

'I'm not. It's the truth, isn't it? That you bottle things up. Do anything – say anything to keep the peace. To avoid conflict.'

'Rubbish.'

'Is it? OK. So when was the last time you had a fight? With Mark? With anyone? Not just a passive-aggressive niggle but a proper, let-it-all-hang-out ding dong. You know, where you say what you *really* think about something instead of eggshells and martyrdom.'

'Look, I have no idea where this is coming from. But if you're going to be like this, I think you'd best just turn round and take me home.'

'See. That's exactly what I mean. Sometimes I wonder how you ever held your own in advertising.'

There was a pause and I felt this strong tightening in my chest, my left hand clasped into a fist so that the nails were digging uncomfortably into the flesh – turning away to look out of the window because I didn't want Emma to see my face.

'Look – I shouldn't have mentioned work. Or Mark,' Emma said suddenly. 'I'm sorry. But the point I'm trying to make is that you always go with whatever will make for the easy life. In all the time I've known you, you always let me pick what we do. Where we go. What we eat. What we drink. It's a nice quality, Sophie. I admire it to a point, but in the end it's dishonest. Because the problem is you sometimes get this little look on your face, which you're wearing right this moment, which means that you're thinking something entirely different from what is coming out of your mouth. And it gets to the point where I just wish you would *spit it out* for once, for Christ's sake.'

'Why? So we can shout at each other?'

'No. Because I want things to be OK between us again.'

'They are OK.'

'Oh, I give up.'

'All right, then.' I turned to stare at her as she indicated to turn left, glancing at me when she could. 'I can't believe you would start work on the deli without my say-so.'

'But I thought you were on board? I wanted to surprise you. Cheer you up. I did it for you, Sophie. I thought it would give you something to look forward to.'

'But you should have waited, Emma. Until I said yes. And it's . . . well, it's not just that. I mean – I know it hasn't been long but I thought we were pretty good friends. Getting close. And then I hear from other people that your mother died while you were in France. And I know you say you didn't want to talk about it, but it just feels a bit odd not to have mentioned it at all. I mean – it's a pretty big thing. Your *mother*.'

And now Emma looked away momentarily through her side window, then back to the road ahead, fumbling once more with the little cloth to wipe the windscreen. We had reached one of my favourite stretches of road – closer to the coast. A snake of a road through the swollen, billowy hills which earn the South Hams its brown tourist label. An Area of Outstanding Natural Beauty.

In the ensuing silence, I watched a group of sheep huddled together near a fence at the far side of a field adjoining the road. There was just one ewe standing apart from them, near a large oak tree, and I stared at it, this strange sensation sweeping over me as if I knew precisely what the sheep was thinking. That to outsiders it looked lonely. Set apart. But that was not what the sheep was thinking at all. No. The sheep was thinking, *I'm quite happy here, thank you very much. The grass is nice here.*

'I needed a fresh start here, Sophie. No baggage. Not just for me but for Theo.' Emma's voice was flat. 'Look – it was cancer and it was ugly. I wasn't very good at it and I'm not proud of that. We never had a good relationship, me and my mum, and I just couldn't handle it. She was like a child again. Needing to be carried to the toilet. Her arse wiped. And I hated it. All of it.'

I had no idea what to say.

'You're right. I should have at least mentioned it, but when something big goes unsaid and you leave it too long, it becomes too late. Like a lie. I just wanted a clean slate here, Sophie. It seemed easier. The thing is, I've never really clicked with someone like I've clicked with you and I didn't want to spoil it. For you to think badly of me.'

Still I stared at the fields, taking in the various shades of green. Pale. Deep. Some of the patches closest to the trees almost brown. 'So how long were you in France?'

'Three months. She had a private nurse who did most of the real work. I just went out of guilt. She was leaving me quite a lot of money so I suppose I had hoped to make some kind of peace with her, but it had gone beyond that.'

'So why didn't you two get on?'

'Look – please don't take this the wrong way. I will talk to you about this – if it's important to you – but not now, please. Not in the car. Not today. Not like this.'

I turned to examine Emma's crumpled face. 'I'm sorry. I was over-reacting. It's a weakness. Overthinking things. Not my business what you decide to share with me.'

'So we can still walk today, Sophie? Yes?'

I nodded, though I was aware something had fundamentally changed between us and we said nothing more for the rest of the journey – me fumbling with the radio until I found a classical channel. Rossini. Which I turned up loud.

I also felt ridiculous that I couldn't put the stupid woman on the cliff in Cornwall out of my mind. For here we were. Another coastal path . . .

There were just four other cars in the car park – Emma pulled up alongside a dark blue Volvo. A couple were seated on the rim of the open boot, readjusting their walking boots – the woman, with a shock of white hair, was skinny with bare, muscular arms but the paradox of an enormous walking stick. For some reason I remembered a promise me and Mark had made years back, to walk the whole South West Coast Path when we retire. Six hundred and thirty miles. Don't know why the statistic stuck in my head. Would I need a stick by then myself?

It had been years since I walked this stretch – west from Bantham. We had to give up the coastal routes once Ben was too big for slotting in a rucksack carrier – a free-range toddler proving too stressful near the cliff edge.

The first section was a gentle climb, fenced and wide. Emma strode ahead, and then as we turned further west, the path rose more steeply to take in magnificent views across to Burgh Island to our right. I had forgotten how fabulous this felt. Majestic. Magical. The wind stronger against my face now. The white horses far below, smashing on to the rocks. I started to relax.

The spectacular view of the Burgh Island Hotel made my mood soften, thinking of our first visit to that beach and of the effort Emma had made over the summer. How good she was at getting me out, not just physically but out of myself too. Also how relaxed she was around Theo and how she had taught me to stop fussing over Ben.

I was a worrier. She was not. *Oh, just let them play, Sophie. They'll be fine.*

I stared at her back, and she turned to hold my gaze just long enough for her face to soften with apparent relief.

And then we picked up the pace, our breathing rising with the effort of the climb. I remembered there was a bench at the top where me and Mark would sit to eat our sandwiches in that former life, Ben's head peeking out of the rucksack carrier to receive crisps and a drink like a little bird in a nest, eager to be fed.

I stared again, this time at the back of Emma's head. I was glad of the noise from the wind. I was just beginning to feel that it was going to be OK between us again, though I did not want to break this silence – not yet. I needed to take in the unexpected relief that I was feeling – a recognition also that at least some of what Emma said earlier was true. In work I have always been happy to take anyone on. But in my private life I hate confrontation. Mark expressed the same frustration as Emma when we first met.

Not that I feel they are entirely right. Some rows are best avoided; things said that cannot be taken back. I can hear the echo of my mother's voice from when I was a child. Seven years old. Maybe eight . . .

If I hadn't been bloody pregnant, you think I would have lumbered myself with this life?

She was shouting at my father and he turned, startled, as I appeared in the doorway. I remember looking down at my fluffy rabbit slippers and then back up to see my father's face, panic-stricken across the room. 'We thought you were asleep, Sophie.'

Suddenly Emma stopped on an especially narrow stretch and stood with her back towards the cliff. 'Goodness. Look at me striding out. Why don't you go past, Sophie, and set the pace. Selfish of me, I wasn't thinking.'

I'm good with heights. Coastal paths don't worry me. But the path was only just wide enough for me to pass safely, and for some reason I paused. Inexplicably I felt uncomfortable. I didn't want to admit to this and I didn't want to tell her that I was thinking about the woman up on the cliff in Cornwall either, but I also didn't want to step past her. It was odd, ridiculous even.

And then, just as Emma was tilting her head and frowning, clearly waiting for my response, there was a burst of the 'Ride of the Valkyries' – a terrible, tinny version pulsating from her bag.

'Damn – my phone. I'm surprised we're still in range.'

Emma carefully swung the small rucksack from her left shoulder, unzipped the front pocket, trying to shield the phone and her ear from the wind.

'I'm sorry?' Her face was screwed up as she struggled to hear. 'You're kidding me. *Theo?* A pause then, as she listened intently.

'Yes. I'll come straight away . . . Of course. I understand. Policy . . . Yes. Yes. Whatever you say. Of course . . . No, I'm not at home so I'll be . . .' She checked her watch. 'Look, I'm sorry – it'll be half an hour at least. Is that all right?'

She snapped the phone case shut. 'I'm sorry, Sophie, but we're going to have to go straight back. It's Theo.'

'Oh my God. Is he OK? Has he been hurt?'

'No. Not him. He's bitten someone in playgroup. There's a real meltdown going on.'

'You're kidding me.'

'I wish. Bad enough to draw blood. The other mother's been called in and is making a complete meal of it. Apparently it's policy to ask the biter to go home.'

Instinctively I then leant back into the cliff edge so that Emma was the one to pass me to lead the way back.

'That's not like your Theo.' I didn't know what else to say; he was such a sweet child.

'I know. I don't get it. He's never bitten anyone before, Sophie. *Never.* I just don't understand it.'

CHAPTER 20

BEFORE

Mark wasn't hungry but knew that Malcolm would be.

Malcolm was always hungry – one of those infuriating people with a skinny gene. *Lucky metabolism*, Malc called it, though Sophie's theory was he was using cocaine, like too many of the creative crowd they used to hang out with in town.

Mark stared at the menu. Christ. Some days he wished he was the type to use drugs. No, he didn't mean that. A punch of guilt as he pictured Ben with tangled kite strings on the beach last weekend. No. Absolutely not.

Right. Steak and salad. He would resist Malcolm's insistence on fries and go for a run this evening. He smoothed his hand down his shirt as if straightening the fabric, while secretly feeling his stomach. Time was, Mark could also eat precisely what he wanted – but not any more.

Good God, Mark, you're getting a tummy, Sophie had teased last year in Cornwall. He had pretended to be amused but was secretly mortified, confirming in the bathroom mirror later that she was absolutely right – golf no longer apparently enough.

Mark stared at the cutlery until the glint of steel began to blur. Cornwall. He was thinking how much it meant to Sophie – that tiny haven where a million years ago they had both seemed so different. God. It was scary how much he still loved her. How some days . . .

He was aware of his stupid foot jiggling and set his legs further apart, rearranging the cutlery on the table.

'Cheer up, mate. Might never happen!' And now Malcolm, full beam of capped teeth, was towering over him – all Hugo Boss suit and salmon pink silk shirt. Infuriatingly thin.

'Jesus. You startled me, Malc. Sorry. Miles away. Good to see you, mate.'

They shook hands briefly, Malcolm pulling back to grab the menu, still standing. 'God. I'm famished. You ordered yet?'

Mark smiled. 'No, not yet. I'm thinking just a steak and salad. Dinner with a client later.'

'Anyone I know?'

'No.'

Mark then, by way of distraction from the lie, winced and winked his way through the minutiae of Malcolm's chaotic week – also his love life, which had taken an unexpected turn with 'the one' suddenly breaking things off to take up a new post in New York.

'God, why do women have to be so unpredictable? You got so lucky with Sophie.'

'You think I don't know that?'

They ordered red wine, which Mark knew he would regret, though for now it served a purpose, settling his nerves.

'So then, Malcolm. Where are we at on the money?'

'And do you want the answer from your accountant or your friend?' Malcolm was buttering bread now – two large pats on to one small slice.

'Would both hats be too tricky?'

'It's like I said on the phone, Mark. Now is the worst possible time to talk about taking money out of the business. You've only just expanded. When we worked through all the figures for the new offices last year, I thought you understood that. It's a solid five-year plan. You're pretty much on target. Nothing at all to worry about but there's not a great deal of wriggle room just at the moment.'

'Look, I know that. And I appreciate everything you put in place, Malcolm. But I couldn't see this coming. All this upset for Sophie in Devon. It's knocked her really badly.'

'So take her on holiday. Long haul. Mauritius . . .' His voice distorted by munching the bread now. 'Darn sight cheaper than rethinking your whole bloody cash flow.'

'OK, Malc. Cards on the table. I'm finished with this long-distance commuting. It isn't working. Living apart midweek. Sophie needs me around more. She won't even contemplate selling the place in Devon. Between you and me, she's fallen in with some new friend. Not a good influence, though Sophie doesn't want to hear that. She wants to stall; still thinks I can move the business, which I can't. So I'm thinking we hang on to the place in Devon as a second home – for holidays, rental income and somewhere to move back to down the line. And in the meantime I need to raise the cash for a decent place nearer London.'

Malcolm took a sharp intake of breath. 'So rent somewhere.'

'No, Malcolm. I want you to crunch the numbers. Big numbers. See how much I can raise against the business. Dividend. Loan. I don't care how you do it.'

'And Sophie thinks this is a good idea?'

'I told you. She's not seeing things clearly, Malc. I need to keep her out of the loop for a bit, otherwise she'll worry and say no. You know what she went through after Ben. I don't want to do anything which might put us both back there. That's why I need to do this.'

Malcolm pulled a face. Paused. The friends locked eyes and Mark wondered if his buddy was remembering the worst of it. The two weeks when Sophie's postnatal depression was so bad, Mark had to take Ben to his mother's while trying to juggle everything. The business in London.

Sophie. The baby. Malcolm was a rock. On the phone pretty much every night with support.

'OK, mate. Understood. But I wouldn't be doing my job if I didn't at least warn you – accountant hat on – that this isn't the wisest move. Not for the company.'

'I do hear you, Malcolm. But I'm big enough and ugly enough to do the worrying on my own. I need you to at least see what you can come up with. Yes?'

'All right then, but the interest rates will be punishing. Give me a few days.' Malcolm began to spread butter on a second piece of bread, narrowing his eyes. 'Of course, a better investment option would be to buy a flat in London, rather than that shoebox you rent. You know that.'

'She won't move Ben to London.'

'Friend hat on?'

Mark shrugged, fiddling with his napkin.

'You and Sophie were always the ones we all envied. You know that. Out of the whole gang, you were the ones who had it sorted. It doesn't sound to me like a brilliant plan, Mark, to be playing at reinvention without Sophie on side.'

'I hear you. And I wish she would listen. But believe me, I'm doing this *for* Sophie. She's not herself right now; not thinking straight. She's buddied up big time with this new friend; there's gossip all over the village about the woman but Sophie just won't see it. Won't listen. She needs me around, Malcolm. And this is the only way I can achieve that and keep the business afloat.'

And now Malcolm's expression changed – his head tilted to the side before he placed both hands up in mock surrender. 'Right. Lecture over. Your business; your call. But now my turn. Food. No arguments, buddy; we are having steak and chips. And dessert.'

'Oh, I don't think I could, Malcolm. Really, like I said, I'm having dinner later.'

'Nonsense, my good man. They've got sticky toffee pudding.'

CHAPTER 21

BEFORE

When I was little, I would often sneak a book into the bathroom, and instead of washing my face and neck as instructed before bed, I would sit on the floor reading. The result, through *Little Women* and the Pippi Longstocking series one summer, was a tidemark around my neck which I tried to explain away as a tan line. But then autumn came, and with it a scene with my mother which bubbled back up to the surface as I sat on our bathroom floor in Tedbury . . .

My mother had shown little interest in my bedtime routine past the toddler years, and then all of a sudden she was fetching her glasses one evening to lift one of my plaits and examine my neck more closely.

Grime. This isn't tan, it's grime.

At first I wasn't bothered to be found out. It was inevitable and I was surprised to have got away with it for so long. But I was marched to the bathroom, where my mother began to scrub my neck so furiously with a rough flannel and soap that the skin was soon pulling and burning.

You're hurting me.

She ignored me. I said I would do it myself properly but this seemed to make things worse, until my mother's eyes were wide and wild with a frustration which I realised later had nothing at all to do with my neck and everything to do with Martini.

There were tears. My neck really hurt. I tried to grab the flannel from my mother's hand to stop her. And then there was the shock of my bottom being smacked very, very hard – first with my mother's hand and then with the large wooden backscratcher which had been balanced on the edge of the bath. Screaming followed – my mother's voice as well as my own as I ran along the hallway to my bedroom and slammed the door, pushing a chair against the inside and sitting on it, panting. Petrified. Her banging and banging and shouting at me.

And then, in the morning, the strangest thing – for it was as if the whole scene had been imagined. I crept down as late as I dared for breakfast to find porridge – my favourite – on the stove and fresh orange juice in a sparkling glass jug on the table. We crept around each other in silence – as if a page had been turned to a new chapter which neither of us wanted to read. That evening there was no mention of washing and my mother never checked my bath time again.

But the Jekyll and Hyde behaviour continued. Out of doors and ahead of her lunchtime tipple, my mother could be a different woman. She was excellent at picnics, and in the summer would sit by the river while I swam with friends. Sometimes on these outings she would even brush my hair and whisper in my ear that she was sorry. But indoors everything changed, especially in winter. She was like a trapped animal. Stifled. Suffocated. And permanently cross.

My father had to travel a lot for work and so I became a very lonely only child. I watched jealously as my friends feuded with and then ferociously defended their siblings. For a time I even invented a sister of my own.

I called her Laura, inspired by *Little House on the Prairie*. My Laura was tough and funny and brave – standing up for me against teasing, and stroking my hair to soothe me at night after scenes with my mother.

And now, all grown, I wondered if my mother also suffered post-natal depression – undiagnosed. Was that it? I would very much like to have discussed it with her, but sadly it was too late. Our adult relation-ship too fractured. My mother eventually left my father when I was thirteen, moving abroad with a heavy-drinking solicitor called Gordon. I visited them only occasionally during the school holidays. They had a small villa in Spain with a pool, but for all the sunshine and swim-ming, I found these visits lonely and distressing. Most of the time my mother and Gordon went out, leaving me to my own devices. When home they enjoyed long, boozy lunches and took even longer siestas which seemed to roll day right into night. I could not speak Spanish and there were only cursory efforts to introduce me to other children. In the end, I mostly opted to stay with my father for the holidays. He would invite my grandmother to help and it was during these years that the love affair with Devon began.

During the six-week summer break we would rent a little cottage on the south Devon coast, visiting local beaches daily. The climate was no match for Spain. There was no private pool. But there was always a large crowd of children on the beach to play cricket with and to make huge sandcastles with moats which we would struggle to fill, running with a chain of buckets to the water's edge. My grandmother made picnics of egg and cress sandwiches and homemade lemonade in a huge thermos flask, and my father would bowl for the cricket wearing a white floppy sunhat and a terribly serious expression.

I was sitting now on the bathroom floor, remembering all of this as I tried desperately to recover – my head still spinning. I stared at the bathmat – a cream affair with a host of rope-like spikes, some of which had a strange, orange stain like rust which I had never been able to get out. I should throw it away. *Why do I still wash it and put it back out?*

I found myself putting my hand up to stroke the skin on the side of my neck before trying to stand, realising very quickly that I was not ready – my legs still weak and my head still woozy. I couldn't remember exactly what had happened here. Did I pass out *again*? Did I? And then, looking around as if in slow motion, a new thought suddenly fluttered into the room. I tilted up my head, my vision still slightly blurred as the idea seemed to hover above me before settling itself very calmly within.

I waited, putting my head down towards my knees, and thought back to the last time this happened, in Cornwall with Helen. I concentrated for a time on steadying my breathing and then, feeling a little calmer, looked up at the bathroom cabinet, trying to picture its contents and what time the chemist would shut, when my mobile buzzed in my pocket.

'Sophie?'

'Emma? What is it? You sound dreadful.'

'Listen. I need to see you. I think I'm going to have to leave the village.'

'Leave the village? What are you talking about? You've hardly unpacked.' I tried to heave myself up, holding on to the towel rail; still feeling giddy, I decided against the gesture and sat back down.

'It's Theo, Sophie.'

'Look. I'm sorry. I meant to ring. So how is he doing now?'

'Still in a complete state. Some kid was goading him and now he's refusing to go back to playgroup.' Emma had lowered her voice to a whisper.

'Oh – poor love, but these things blow over. He's probably just more nervous than he was letting on and is feeling a bit overwhelmed.'

'No. It's not just that. This other kid said something truly horrible. About me.'

'*You?*'

'Yes. To do with all this rubbish which is going round. It must have come from the mother.'

'Oh, God – poor Theo. So what exactly did the child say?'

'Look. Can you come over? After you've picked Ben up from school? I don't like to ask but I just don't know what to do for the best, and I don't know who else to turn to.'

I looked up again at the medicine cabinet and then at my watch.

'Of course. I'll come as soon as I get Ben. I just have to pop out very briefly first. Will you be OK?'

There was no reply.

'Look. I'm really sorry I got so upset over Hobbs Lane. Christ. I know you meant well. And you're right, it's not my business – your time in France with your mother. I was being completely silly.' I paused, feeling guilty also over my stupid upset regarding Emma's doppelganger in Cornwall. How could I have got myself into such a tizz? Poor Emma had enough people questioning her.

Just yesterday evening, on top of everything, DI Melanie Sanders had turned up at her house yet again – a whole hour grilling her about her finances, apparently. How she afforded Priory House. Her mother's will. Nathan had shared all this with Mark on the phone and was incandescent; he wanted Emma to make a formal complaint about police harassment but she was determined to keep the police hassle quiet – afraid of the Tedbury gossips. I couldn't help but increasingly feel it was all because of me, for persuading her to do that stupid turn in the first place. If she hadn't been the blessed fortune teller, she wouldn't have been the last person to see Gill. It was just bad luck, bad timing, but it was also *my fault*.

'Please, Emma, just try to stay calm and wait right there, OK?'

After I hung up, I stood very slowly, moving first on to my knees and then holding on to the edge of the bath for support. I stared in the mirror. Pale. Blotchy skin. The beginnings of a spot on my chin. I opened the cabinet and checked the top shelf.

I glanced at my watch again.

Three ovulation kits were stacked one on top of the other. I moved them to the side and checked behind, reaching for the pregnancy test, then sat on the toilet and turned to the back of the packet for the date.

It had been a while and I would need to hurry now. The last time was at Caroline's, not long before the deli plan imploded. I was two weeks overdue that time, and did two home tests for good measure. The first was positive – a faint blue line – but the second did nothing. A subsequent test at the doctor's came back negative also. Whether it had been a false alarm, a faulty test stick – or worse, some kind of early miscarriage – I had never known.

This time I peed straight on to the stick and put down the toilet seat lid to sit and wait. I stared again at the bathmat, deliberately allowing my eyes to smart and my vision to blur. I used to put Ben on that mat with his baby gym when I took a bath.

Where was it? The baby gym? In the loft? *No. Sophie. Do not start hoping . . .*

And then the phone again – this time flashing Helen's name. I held the stick in front of me, checking my watch for the umpteenth time to work out how quickly I could make it to Emma's after collecting Ben.

'Helen – what a lovely surprise. I hope this means you've been thinking about my suggestion?'

'Well, actually I have – if the offer's still there?'

'Absolutely. So when can you come?' I was struggling to keep my voice calm, watching a faint line appear, not wanting Helen to pick up on all this stress. So many thoughts competing and pounding through my head.

'Look, I know it's short notice, but I was thinking this week – as Ben's in school? I thought it might cheer you up. Help you adjust. But you must say if you have other plans.'

The line was darkening now. No mistake.

'I don't believe it.'

'Sorry?'

'No – not you. Something this end, Helen. Listen – I've got to ring off. I promise I'll ring you back later. But please – come as soon as you can. I really mean it. The sooner the better.'

CHAPTER 22

BEFORE

Emma was pacing. Things were not going to plan – not at all, damn it. Quite apart from Theo's spectacular playgroup outburst and DI Melanie Sanders poking her nose in again, an email from her lawyer early this morning had confirmed her worst fears.

Were there no limits to Theo's aggravation in her life? On top of everything else, she now had to find a way to persuade the playgroup staff to take him back. How the hell was she supposed to manage otherwise; to get everything done?

Emma felt in her pocket. No phone. She glanced around the kitchen and frowned, not remembering where she had put it. Irritation bubbled in her stomach as she moved across to her laptop. There was a second email from the lawyer – this time an invoice, pressing for settlement of all work to date. *Terrific*. She twisted her mouth to the side, ignored the wretched invoice and instead pinged a reply to the previous email.

There MUST be something we can do about the will. This isn't fair. An *outrage*. We need to challenge this. Please get on it immediately . . .

Emma then began moving magazines and papers from the kitchen worktops, searching for her phone. She was trying to remember when she had last used it . . . When she spoke to Sophie? She paused to conjure up where she had been standing at the time. Yes. Now she recalled: she was up in the bedroom.

Emma hurried upstairs to find her door ajar across the landing and Theo sitting on her bedroom floor. He was turned away from her, crouched over something. She moved forward more quietly, grateful for the thick carpets, and leant over to surprise him.

'What the hell do you think you're doing, Theo?!' Emma reached into his lap and grabbed her phone. She looked at the screen, which displayed the photograph she'd taken of Sophie in Cornwall. The zoom had made it a little grainy but it was clear enough . . .

'I just wanted to play my snakes game—'

'You know you're not allowed on my phone unless I say so. How *dare* you!'

Theo's face was white with shock but Emma didn't care. She looked again at the screen and thought very quickly.

'OK. So you were looking at my pictures. What did you see?'

'Nothing.'

'That's not true, is it, Theo? You need to tell me the truth. I know when you're lying to me.'

There was a long pause, Theo's eyes unblinking.

'Please don't be cross again. I just saw the picture of Ben's mummy. That's all. With her new friend on the beach. I didn't look at any others. It was on the screen when I picked up the phone. I didn't *mean* to look at your photos. I just wanted my snakes game . . .' He was starting to cry but again Emma didn't care. This was serious.

She crouched down in front of her son and pushed her face right up to his so that their noses were almost touching.

'Have you seen all the police in Tedbury lately, Theo?'

He just nodded, eyes wider.

'Well, taking someone else's property without their permission is *theft*, Theo. And theft is against the law. All I need to do is tell the police – that you bit another child, which is assault, and that you stole my phone . . . which is theft. And do you know what they'll do? They will come back to Tedbury and they will take you away and lock you up somewhere dark. *Understand me?*'

Theo was crying again properly, but Emma hadn't finished.

'If you tell a single soul in the world about that photograph of Ben's mummy, I will tell the police.'

No reply, just proper sobbing, his eyes now closed as Emma kept her face close to his.

'You do not . . . say . . . a . . . single . . . word, Theo. Do you understand me?'

CHAPTER 23

BEFORE

DI Melanie Sanders was skimming through the house particulars. There were a couple of really sweet cottages but the prices were a shock. One place had caught her eye, particularly because of a wisteria covering the front. She was just wondering if she was being too romantic – if climbers damaged the brickwork – when there was a knock at the door.

Damn. A glance at her watch. Early. Melanie called for the new witness to come in but was flustered, still gathering up the papers as a tall, slim man with piercing blue eyes was led in by someone from the front desk.

'Goodness. Not thinking of moving to Tedbury, are you, Inspector?' Her visitor was immediately staring at the paperwork, twisting his neck, apparently trying to read the top copy upside down.

Melanie, mortified to be wrong-footed, swept all the papers together and shuffled them into a pile.

'No. No. Just some research. Part of the inquiry.'

'Research? Because if you were seriously interested, there are a few properties I should warn you off. Structural problems. Is that Wisteria Cottage, because—'

'No. Honestly. Thank you. Just background inquiries. So, Mr, er . . .'

'Tom Fuller.'

'Mr Fuller. When you rang, you said you had some new information for me?' She was signalling for him to sit down and he smiled. Warm grin. Perfect teeth. He watched and waited as she put the little pile of particulars into the top drawer of her desk, struggling at first to close it. A nasty crunch so that she had to pull the drawer back out, press down on the contents and try again. 'So . . . this new information . . . ?'

'Yes. Well, your officer who called at the house said that if anything came to mind . . . And something has.'

She raised her eyebrows by way of encouragement.

'Look. It's probably not important but on the night of the fair – on the night that Antony died – I saw him having an argument with Emma Carter . . . the woman who was running the fortune teller's tent.'

'I see. So when exactly was this?' Melanie picked up a pen to start making notes. In truth, she had not expected anything useful. They'd had the usual round of time-wasters.

'It's hard to be precise. About six o'clock, I think.'

'OK.' Her tone was more considered now. 'So talk me through precisely what you saw and heard.'

'I was walking up towards the church to check on our stall. We run one for the RSPB each year.'

'You're into birds?' She did not mean to sound so surprised, to give so much of herself away again.

'Yes. We've been raising money for a cirl bunting project near the coast.' He was the one who was a tad flustered now, blushing.

'Not Labrador Bay?'

'You're kidding me – you *know* it, Inspector?'

'Not really, but I've just been googling local options for my parents. They're visiting soon and they're very into that sort of thing. My mother mentioned it. I think she saw something on Facebook.'

'Good grief. I was there just this morning.'

'No!' Melanie could not help herself; felt a warm smile spreading across her face at the coincidence. The pictures online looked terrific. She was thinking of how she hoped the access would be OK if her mother was still using the wheelchair; how much her mother would like to see it . . .

In turn, Tom Fuller was suddenly picking imaginary fluff from his sleeve and Melanie was rather pleased to pass the baton of embarrassment. Why was it birdwatchers were so often defensive? Her mother said people took the mickey a lot. It went with the territory, sadly.

'So you were saying. About the argument? I'm wondering why you didn't say anything before.'

'Well, it didn't seem important before. I mean – you get a good few frayed tempers on fair day, what with all the organisation. But now that there's all this gossip flying around.'

'Gossip?'

'Yes. About Emma Carter and Antony. Well, I thought I should mention it.'

'I see. So what exactly did you see?'

'Antony and Emma were on Green Lane, which is a short cut through to the village hall, and he seemed to be having quite a go at her about something.'

'You didn't hear what?'

'No. Not really. Just a few words. He said there was *no way he was going to pay*. Something like that.'

'You can't remember the exact words?'

'No. Sorry. At the time I assumed it was some aggro over the fair. But I do remember thinking it was a bit odd because she'd only just moved into the village. And it wasn't like him at all. He wasn't the confrontational type.'

'But not odd enough for you to mention this before?'

'No. I realise now I should have done, but I don't like to get sucked into things and I didn't want to be seen to be pointing fingers. But, as I say, there's a rumour going around now that they were having a fling. Is that right, then?'

Melanie did not reply. She was trying to stare Tom Fuller out, but was rather wishing that he did not have such striking eyes. It was making it difficult.

'There's another rumour that you're investigating her mother's death in France. The inheritance?'

And now Melanie leant back in her seat. 'So, Mr Fuller, did you really come here to tell me something or is this just a fishing trip on behalf of the Tedbury grapevine?'

'Sorry. Sorry.' He was blushing again. 'It's just I was fond of Antony. He was a bit of a lad – I guessed that. But he wasn't a bad bloke.'

'So you knew that he had affairs?'

'Not for sure. More an assumption. He and Gill were having a bit of a bad patch. She wanted a kid. He didn't. He was a bit like a kid himself still, to be honest.'

'And you didn't know who he might have been having an affair with?'

'He certainly never discussed it openly with me, but he may have said something to Nathan. Local architect. They were quite close; had a few lock-ins at the Church Inn.'

'OK. Anything else?'

'Yes, actually. I've seen a bloke hanging around the village. Seen him three or four times in the last few weeks. Taking pictures. I get up early – for the birdwatching – so I tend to notice people's movements.'

'OK. Can you describe him?' She had picked up her notepad and pen.

'Striking chap. Blond hair – almost white, actually. Very short and curly. And very tall too. Like I say – he's often taking pictures. I thought he was perhaps a freelance photographer. We get a lot of people taking pictures of the church because of the stained-glass windows, but again, I thought I'd mention it. Given what's happened.'

'Blond and curly, eh?' She paused. 'How tall?'

'A good six-three or four, I reckon.'

'And good-looking?'

He shrugged. 'You ladies would probably say so.'

And now she was frowning, her mind whirring. 'He wasn't by any chance wearing a long, dark green parka? Fur collar?'

'Yes. How on earth did you know that?'

'Never mind.' Still frowning, Melanie quickly changed the subject back to Labrador Bay. He told her that Tedbury had played a big part in the fundraising years. He was really proud of the support. The pub in Tedbury held quizzes. Darts nights. It was when the RSPB had been trying to buy the site – now a dedicated nature reserve for cirl buntings.

He gabbled some more about his hobby. Into his stride. Told how Antony would sometimes join him out at Labrador Bay. He would bring along notebooks for his writing – also tea in a large thermos, plus iced buns with hundreds and thousands. *I used to tease him about that. But he was all right, Antony. Hard to believe he's gone . . .*

Tom chattered on about his work locally with general RSPB fundraising; how he had recently helped with a robin rescued by Emma Carter's little boy.

He's a nice lad. Sweet boy . . .

And then finally a pause and Tom Fuller narrowed his eyes, and Melanie stood to signal it was time for him to leave. She walked over to the door and summoned one of the DCs from across the room to show Tom back to reception.

For a good few minutes after he had gone, Melanie sat entirely still at her desk. He really did have the most piercing blue eyes, Tom Fuller. She was not normally thrown but had found it quite disconcerting.

She thought of the man in the parka and began rummaging through the top drawer for her private phone, suffering a pang of embarrassment again at the house particulars – upset that Tom Fuller had seen them. She imagined him chuckling about it on his journey home. Telling everyone in the village?

The truth was Melanie had been thinking of getting herself on the property ladder for some time. The salary increase with her recent promotion made it complete nonsense to stay in rented accommodation, but she was reluctant to leave Cynthia. Lately she had been considering buying a place and letting it until she was ready to make the break and live alone.

Everyone told her the South Hams was a gold mine, at least in the good times, but the prices were a stretch. She stared again at the cottage with the wisteria. It would be hard to afford it but the estate agent had said it was a particularly good time to invest. Strictly off the record, he had tipped her off that a celebrity was negotiating to buy a large house on the outskirts of the village, which was bound to push the prices up.

TODAY – 7.00 P.M.

I stare out of the train window and can tell from the corner of my eye that the doctor is watching me.

There are just forty minutes of the journey left and still I fear that if I put a foot wrong, there is a chance they will put me off the train. Send for help. An ambulance?

Eventually, as Mark goes to use the loo, I cannot help myself.

'Has the guard asked you to keep an eye on me? *Unofficially.*'

The doctor looks at his wife. I wonder how long they have been married. He looks late forties to me, maybe early fifties; I can't tell. She is much younger and I am assuming a second marriage. Can they read each other's expression? Have they reached that stage?

'I'll get some more drinks from the buffet. Do you want something?' His wife is looking at me and I am thinking, *Yes. They can read each other. He wants to talk to me alone.*

Good? Bad? I don't know.

I ask for coffee for both me and Mark, and smile my thanks.

'The guard just has protocols to follow. When someone gets off a train. Is clearly under intense pressure as you are . . .' The doctor is looking at me very directly as his wife moves along the carriage, but his eyes are kind.

'So he did ask you? Officially, I mean?'

'Look – I simply offered to vouch for you. That's all. I hope you won't be offended by that. He was worried he would be blamed if you were taken ill or became—'

'Hysterical?'

'I didn't say that . . .' He smiles more broadly at me. 'You don't strike me as the hysterical type.'

'To be honest, I do feel a bit hysterical inside. Thinking of my son in that hospital bed without me. But you mustn't let them put me off the train.'

'I'm sure they won't do that.'

'So that's not something the guard mentioned?'

'Not as such. No. He's just watching his back; doesn't want to get it in the neck and he wants to make sure you're OK. As do I.'

'Thank you.' I feel better. Am glad I asked.

'It's not too long now.' He is looking at his watch.

'No. Not long.'

'So do you have other children?'

Of all the questions . . .

I want and need to stay calm, and so I look again through the window as the trees and the clouds and the green of the grass skim past like a sweep of paint across a canvas. The colours blurring together.

I took a watercolour course in the village hall soon after we moved to Tedbury, taking Ben along, asleep in his carry cot. Mark's idea. He'd seen a flyer. He was hoping it might gee me up out of the black moods, but it didn't. I enjoyed sweeping all the colours across the page, just like these colours sweeping past the train window. But the release was temporary. It didn't solve anything, and the minute I got home I would just sit on the sofa and cry.

I can feel my heart rate increasing again and I breathe in and out very carefully to try to counter this. I suppose I could tell the doctor the truth; what I increasingly think is the nub of it all.

My obsession with having another child.

You would think, after the bad time I had first time round, I would have been frightened, let it go. But somehow it had the opposite effect. Made me want it even more. To hope to get it right the second time, perhaps? I don't know . . .

Should I tell the doctor this? Any of this? That if I could have found a way to be happy with just Ben, maybe none of this would have happened.

CHAPTER 24

BEFORE

I looked out from the bedroom window just as the familiar Volvo with its battered bumper turned on to the square. Thank God . . .

Helen.

For the second time in as many weeks, I was very soon hugging her longer and tighter than I intended. And then I noticed the luggage – an enormous brown leather case and a plaid carpet bag.

'Heavens, Helen. Who do you think you are? Mary Poppins?'

'You are not to be rude. My husband bought me that.'

'And what on earth have you got in the case?' I tried the handle, but worried for my stomach muscles. 'A body?' I put it straight back down and closed my eyes to the flashback. The splatter marks up the wall. The blood oozing from Gill's head – knife in her hand . . .

'I put in some things for the boy. Books, mostly – oh, and a croquet set. So how's school going?'

I could hear Helen's voice but as if through fog, and she touched my arm ever so gently to steer me back.

'I was wondering how school's going, Sophie?'

'Sorry?'

'Ben? How's Ben getting on?'

'Oh, right. Yes. Sorry. Going really well, thank you.'

I led her through to the kitchen, followed by the two dogs – eager and panting. I wondered if it would always be like this. Feeling the punch of the wrong words and the wrong thought; triggered by a slip of the tongue. Thinking of Gill and Antony always. That scene. The colour red . . .

'He's absolutely exhausted but loving it. Not entirely sure how much they're learning – he seems to play, mostly. But – come through, come through, I'll make a drink.'

En route Helen paused, looking down. 'I had quite forgotten how gorgeous your floor is, Sophie.'

'Yes. Everyone says that. I'm afraid I rather take it for granted. I guess that's what we're programmed to do. Just leave the case in the hall. We'll do that later. I've got so much to tell you. But I must get a drink for the dogs. Did you bring their bowl? Oh, hang on. I might have an old ice cream tub out the back if Mark hasn't moved them. He's an absolute nightmare for turning things out without—'

'Sophie.' Helen put her hand on my arm again.

'What?'

'This is only me, darling.'

'Sorry. Yes. Christ. Listen to me, I'm babbling. Sounds silly but I feel really . . .' I wanted to say *nervous*. Not myself. Going mad. 'Oh, I don't know. I'm just so glad you're here. Everything's still so completely crazy . . .'

Helen tilted her head to the side affectionately. 'I'd rather gathered that from talking to Mark.'

'You spoke to Mark?'

'Yes. He phoned me. Didn't he say?'

And now I felt my expression change.

At the weekend we had had another terrible row – me and Mark. Over Tedbury; over the fact he was falling for all the grapevine gossip about Emma and Antony . . .

'Look, I was planning to come anyway so you're not to think this is some kind of conspiracy, Sophie. But – hold that thought, whatever it is. I very urgently need a pee. As do the dogs.'

Helen opened the French doors to let the dogs out before using the downstairs cloakroom. Then, five minutes later, we were both staring at my mug of raspberry and camomile tea as I poured her coffee.

'So – what's de rigueur here? Do you want me to pretend I haven't twigged?' Helen's eyes were wide with anticipation, her mouth breaking into a smile.

'What?'

'Oh, come on, Sophie. You practically mainline coffee normally.'

I'd guessed she'd guess. And I found as she examined my face very closely that I didn't mind at all; it was good for her to know. I certainly needed *someone* to know.

'Only *just*, Helen. Six weeks or so. Mark doesn't want us to tell anyone yet. He's really nervous.'

'Oh my God.' And now she was sweeping me once more into a tight bear hug, then pulling back to examine my face. 'This is quite simply the nicest news I've had in as long as I can remember' – tapping the table then with both hands like a drumbeat. 'Cross my heart, I promise I won't say a single word until you give me the all-clear. But I did wonder. The fainting in Cornwall. And I'm just so pleased I came now. You're tired – yes?'

'Exhausted.' Even my voice sounded tired, the word fading away and my shoulders slumping as if giving up on the effort of holding up my head. I looked away towards the window, thinking of everything beyond. 'It's still such a strange time here, Helen. In Tedbury. I mean, I've waited *so* long for this next baby and I thought it would feel so perfect but it doesn't. Mark – well, he seems more worried than pleased, and now I'm starting to feel guilty.' I glanced again through the front window on to the village square, where a white van was pulling up near Gill and Antony's cottage.

I thought again of the row with Mark and closed my eyes.

He had not reacted to the baby as I had hoped. There was this initial smile, a hug and a kiss, and then? Too quickly he was pacing and muttering about all the stress. Money. The Hartleys. The poisonous mood in Tedbury. Eventually, he sat sombre on the edge of the bed and advised we tell no one until we were through the dangerous early few weeks. And next – he was on his phone, googling estate agents; setting things in motion for a move. To Surrey.

Surrey?

Yes, Sophie. We can find a nice village with a good school and a good railway station. You know I can't leave the company in London, and with another child we're going to need the money. But you'll need me around more too. And with all that's happened here—

Oh no, no, no, Mark. This is not just your decision. I'm just starting to feel a lot happier. More settled here. With Emma, and with Ben and Theo getting on so well.

And that's something else I wanted to discuss . . . I think it would be a good idea to see less of Emma. With what's going on. I'm not liking what I'm hearing.

Oh, don't be ridiculous. That's all idle gossip and you know it.

From what I hear, it's getting nasty, Sophie.

Which is precisely why she needs me. She's a friend.

Oh, come on. You know what I think. You've hardly known her five minutes. She's very obviously—

Obviously what, Mark? Spit it out. You saying I have no judgement?

I opened my eyes and turned back to Helen. 'I mean – Gill's still in a coma, Helen. The cottage is still boarded up. My friend Emma that I told you about? She's having a really hard time.' I let out a huff of breath as Helen reached out for my hand. 'And to top it all, Mark is getting very much more determined about moving. We're arguing about it. Quite a lot, actually.'

'Right. That does it.'

'Sorry?'

'Come on. Get your coat. You need fresh air and the dogs have been cooped up too long.' Helen slurped the last of her coffee and stood, beaming. 'And then we can go to that nice butcher you showed me last time and get you some red meat.'

'Red meat?'

'Yes. I know what you stick insects are like. All steamed fish and braised chicken. That's why you're feeling a bit low. A good piece of steak or venison is what you need. Oh, and I hear ostrich is very good. Low in fat but you have to be careful how you cook it. You need more iron.'

I could feel the paradox of a smile and tears forming at the same time. I looked at Helen and I saw it. And she saw it. And I loved that as we held each other's gaze, neither of us had to say out loud just how much this moment meant.

'I am not eating an ostrich, Helen.'

CHAPTER 25

BEFORE

Emma was staring at a photograph of France. Theo beaming in front of yachts on the marina about fifteen minutes from her mother's home.

The photograph was on a noticeboard in the kitchen. It was fixed by a magnetic star, and Emma glanced from the yellow of the star to the brown of the boarding at the window. Nathan had arranged for someone to come and fix it properly soon. Some odd-jobber he knew from the pub.

Thinking of Nathan triggered a familiar contradiction in Emma. He was getting a little too clingy. It was a cycle she was all too used to. He kept telling her how unusual she was. How healthy and refreshing he found it that she was so laid-back around Theo – not overprotective and *fussy-fussy like so many mothers. I mean it. You are not like other women at all, Emma . . .*

Just as she was getting a little bored, in bed and out of it, so he was keener by the day – on the phone to her all the time . . .

It was Nathan who shared all the latest rumours on the Tedbury grapevine; he was livid the police were digging not only into her finances but seemingly interested in her time in France too. His tone was of outrage – *what is this, a bloody police state?* – and Emma had been careful not to give away the panic this had stirred in her, instead pacifying Nathan's curiosity about France as she had Sophie's, by sharing the headlines only. Her mother's cancer. Their troubled relationship.

Emma reached forward and took down the picture. Since the playgroup fiasco and the row over the picture on her phone, Theo had said not a single word to her. In fact, he wasn't saying anything to anyone, bar Ben – and then only the odd word occasionally. The silent treatment.

Emma was quite happy to sit this out, but other people were making the most godawful fuss. Nathan was all for calling in a doctor, which was quite obviously out of the question.

Forms. Questions.

No.

Emma examined the photograph in her hand more closely. She remembered very clearly the day she had taken it for Theo. He had been insistent that he wanted the boat with the yellow and white sails in the centre of the picture, and in the end she had capitulated, for people were watching. A little group of tourists, waiting to take their own pictures. The boat was Theo's favourite because the owner had tied a small teddy bear as a lucky mascot to the steering wheel, which was just visible through the glass window at the front. Theo liked to think it was the bear who sailed the boat.

She and Theo had walked down to the marina every day after lunch while the nurse was overseeing her mother's afternoon sleep. Emma recalled the flutter of panic she'd felt on arrival in France – assuming sole charge of Theo after eighteen months with Nanny Lucy.

She remembered too the greater surge of panic when she first found out about her mother's cancer. It was a friend of her mother's who had called her in Manchester. God knows how she found the number. Among her mother's things?

Stuff the past, Emma. You get yourself over to France before it's too late. You hear me? She's got no one else now and you two have things to resolve.

Emma had not seen her mother since her grandmother's funeral, when they had stood defiantly as far apart as possible outside the tiny church in Kent, as a small gathering of local farm labourers and a dozen or so Gypsies smoked and chatted as they awaited the arrival of the hearse.

Emma had arranged it all specifically to spite her mother, including a huge display of apples in a wicker basket on the coffin – the gesture evoking smiles and tears from those who had known her grandmother's love of the Kent orchards, but a small shaking of the head from her mother, as if in exasperation at this final finger to convention.

The story which shaped their conflict was as well documented as it was disputed. Emma favoured her grandmother's version, not least because she felt more naturally in tune with her anarchic attitude to life.

Growing up, Emma had been given only a brushstroke precis of the rift that was her unusual family history. Her mother Claire's version told of a harsh and difficult early childhood as part of a traditional group of Romany travellers. Emma's grandmother Dotia was painted as the villain – a stubborn and blinkered Gypsy, too nervous of outside influence to allow her daughter to attend school.

Emma's mother told how she'd begged to go to school, sick of the teasing from '*gorgios*' – non-Gypsy children – over her illiteracy. She told one story of standing outside a local sweet shop, waiting for it to open, as a gaggle of small boys roared with laughter at her – only later learning that there was an enormous 'Closed Today' sign right in front of her.

Claire claimed her relationship with her own mother had imploded when her father died in a road accident. Along with several other Gypsy families, they continued to tour farms in Kent for seasonal work, but despite repeated visits to the sites by local authority representatives, she was not allowed to go to school.

The work, though back-breaking, was enjoyed by Dotia, who had a particular affinity with the orchards and was able to name every apple variety they came across. But Emma's mother hated it.

Claire's version of her history was this: during one season in Mid Kent, she struck up a close friendship with the farmer's daughter, an only child called Lily who was secretly helping her with her reading. As the adults turned their attention to the hops, Claire begged to be allowed to go to school with Lily. After a series of terrible arguments, Dotia reluctantly agreed, firmly expecting the novelty to be short-lived. It was not. When the travellers packed up to move back to Essex for the winter, Claire refused to go. Physically carted off by two of her uncles, she remained defiant, and within twenty-four hours had run away back to the farm. This cycle was repeated twice until the farmer's family intervened – offering to allow Claire to board over the winter so that she could continue her schooling with Lily.

This compromise was where the story broke in two. Claire claimed her mother never came back for her, that the Ashford family allowed her to grow up on the farm, never formally adopting her but quietly allowing the situation to continue beneath the radar of social services. She worked hard, won a place at university and a job in the city, where she met her future husband Alan, Emma's father.

At first he was very successful and the marriage was happy. But when gambling became his weakness, Claire, remembering the poverty of her childhood, hired lawyers to freeze their accounts and filed for divorce. With the settlement, she and Emma lived irritably in Surrey – Emma blaming her mother for their diminished financial circumstances.

On moving later to France, Claire at first chose a chic resort in the south, within striking distance of Cannes. Emma left home as young as she dared for art college, and visited rarely. When her mother moved then to the north of France, finding the south too hot and expensive, Emma was persuaded to help her move. It was during this sorting of belongings that she came across a box of letters.

The shoebox was pink, and inside were more than two dozen envelopes, some unopened. A few were addressed to 'Sabina', care of a farm in Kent; others to Claire at her first flat in London. It took Emma a time to realise that Sabina must have been her mother's original Romany name.

The letters were all from Claire's mother Dotia – sad and persistent pleas, dictated to a friend whose handwriting was childlike and difficult to read.

I am writing again on behalf of your mother, whose heart is breaking. Please Sabina, will you just agree to meet her.

Emma hid the box in her room, delighted at the fresh ammunition against her mother. From the letters, which included some forwarded by the farming couple who had taken Claire in, it became clear that Dotia had returned many times begging her daughter to respect her heritage and rejoin her on the road. Claire, as she by then preferred to be called, not only refused to spend the holidays with her mother as originally agreed, but eventually refused all contact. The farming family clearly attempted to mediate, but Claire was having none of it – loving her new and more comfortable life and wanting no part of her old one.

Dotia's letters mentioned the farm work dwindling. Hard times. Emma had no way of knowing if her grandmother was even still alive, but the letters were clearly something which she could *use*. At breakfast she had confronted her mother by simply placing the box on the table.

I thought you said your mother turned her back on you.

There was a long pause in which Claire appeared visibly shaken. She stood then as if to leave the room, but Emma grabbed her arm, gripping the flesh so tightly that the tip of each of Emma's nails turned white.

So you lied. Mummy dearest who has always accused me of being the born liar in the family. What a bloody joke. All these years you say I'm the black sheep, the so-called nightmare daughter, and look at you.

Get off me. You're hurting me.

Oh, please. Spare me the drama. Emma's eyes were fixed on the white of her nails as she squeezed tighter. Tighter.

I mean it. Please. You're really hurting me, Emma . . .

It took Emma just two weeks to trace Dotia. A little googling led her to a smallholding in north Kent, where two old caravans were pitched in a field alongside a barn under conversion. She went out of mischief mostly, and a determination to wind up her mother further. But Dotia intrigued her, and Emma was impressed by her grandmother's lack of both sentiment and surprise when she found her. There was just a long holding of eye contact and a nod from her as if this were something she had foreseen.

Granny Apple, as she would very quickly become known to Emma, was evidently unwell, but despite this was brimming with stories and an engaging passion for her culture. Emma visited regularly, staying at a bed and breakfast just a few miles from the site. On long walks, often early in the morning, she would learn of the Romany ways. And history.

The artist, bohemian and rebel in Emma loved it all. The folklore. The tarot, the tea leaves – and yes, the finger to convention. So that when, two years on, she found that she was not only pregnant but too late for an abortion, she knew precisely where to turn.

From the very start Granny Apple not only adored Theo but had a special way with him. Emma took to leaving the baby regularly with her grandmother – sometimes for up to two weeks at a time. Dotia would chastise her but Emma could always charm Granny Apple into forgiving her.

Look, I'm sorry I couldn't get a message to you but something came up. And it's just you're so very good with him. He adores you . . .

Emma hoped this arrangement would continue, but her grand-mother's health suffered badly from her lifestyle. She became stubborn and refused to move on with other families in her community. Diabetes was diagnosed but went largely untreated due to Granny Apple's suspicion of local doctors. Emma, worried at the prospect of losing her babysitter, did her best to intervene but appointments were always conveniently 'forgotten', so that when news came that Dotia had suffered a fatal diabetic coma, her body lying in the cold caravan undetected for forty-eight hours, Emma was devastated.

So what, precisely, was she supposed to do about Theo now?

There was the sense of a draught from the boarded window, and Emma, folding the photograph of the boats into her pocket, checked first her watch and then her reflection in the mirror on the opposite wall.

It was not her fault, the way things were working out. All of this was her *mother's* doing. Emma looked into her own eyes and felt the familiar tightening in her chest as she recalled the latest phone call from the lawyer.

If things did not go forward in Tedbury as she had hoped? Well, she would not be to blame.

TODAY – 7.05 P.M.

'Any other children or just the one?' The doctor is leaning forward, repeating the question, his wife still away at the buffet.

I turn from the blur of fields passing the train window to answer him finally, calming my voice. 'Just the one.'

He smiles, and I turn away again because I do not want him to read too much from my expression, for I am thinking again about the nub of it all, of how much I enjoyed watching them together over the summer. Ben and Theo. How much easier it felt for Ben to have young company both at home and on outings.

There was one morning when Emma phoned with this terrible migraine and I took Theo for the whole day. The boys set up a camp under Ben's platform bed, with pillows and sleeping bags and a picnic lunch; later, I took them to the zoo. It was a shock to learn that Theo had never been to a zoo. He was a little nervous at first but then amazed at everything, especially the monkeys and also, to my surprise, the desert area. I bought them a toy monkey each from the gift shop as a reward for being so good – a black-and-white one for Theo and a marmalade-coloured one for Ben. Back home, I thought he might be fretting about getting back to his mother, maybe worrying about her too.

And now I feel a frown as I remember something really strange that he said. I asked him where he would go on an outing if he were able to choose anywhere at all. He said Krypton, which made me smile – Theo always so obsessed with Superman. But next he said something really odd.

'I want to go to Krypton so we can fix my mummy.'

'What? Her headache, you mean. You mustn't worry about that, Theo. It will be gone soon, I promise.'

'No. I don't mean the headache,' and he looked right into my face as if I was supposed to understand something important. He kept very still for a moment like a statue, and then he leaned forward, even closer to my face, and really widened his eyes as if asking me something. Yes. It was as if it were some special moment between us which I was supposed to understand, but the truth is I just didn't know what the hell he meant or what I was supposed to say.

So I just smiled, which I think was entirely the wrong response because he looked really sad suddenly before running off back to the little camp under Ben's bed.

CHAPTER 26

BEFORE

Mark knew that he drove too fast. He was driving too fast now. *Don't drive too fast*, Sophie said each week on the phone as he confirmed that he was setting out for Devon.

Driving fast was not just a necessary evil in this nigh-ridiculous geographical trap – *you live where?* people still gasped – but a pleasure which allowed the space for thinking and planning. Also, the opportunity to play the music he loved (and Sophie hated) at a volume which, along with his speed, she would consider irresponsible.

He had done a lot of driving this week – hence also thinking. Mark found himself squeezing the steering wheel as he conjured the most recent photograph of Gill and Antony featured in the local paper, his knuckles whitening. He thought next of the latest news from Malcolm about the money. *Not enough, Malcolm. Not enough.*

OK, so he would have to fudge it. He had found two Surrey properties, available to let but with the option to buy down the line. Perfect.

Mark glanced first at his watch and then at the passenger seat, where the estate agent's particulars lay fanned out so he could read each of the addresses. He would use the satnav to save time later but had arranged to briefly visit his mother first. This was one of the few advantages of his divided life – being able to make additional family visits without the strain of Sophie's involvement.

Mark was close to his mother, and since his father's death liked to keep a regular eye on things. Sophie, to her credit, had always made an effort with his family, but there was a sad undercurrent of friction since her period of depression which no amount of time would heal. Mark's mother, to his horror, had taken a dated and, to be frank, uncharitable approach to her daughter-in-law's condition – coming from a generation expected to 'get a grip'. Mark had tried very hard to soften her attitude once Sophie's depression was finally diagnosed. But his mother saw only the strain on her son during the terrible weeks when Mark was trying to run a business, parent a baby and care for a wife who walked in the shadows of life.

It's not Sophie's fault, Mum. It's an illness.

Yes, well. It's never easy with a new baby. In my day we just had to get on with it . . .

Despite all those past and terrible tensions, Mark loved his mother very much and could not deny the surge of pleasure these lone trips to his childhood home stirred in him, especially since his grandmother had now moved in with his mother. A thin, muscular woman with a mass of thick white hair and surprisingly good skin, she was as eccentric as she was endearing in her blissful ignorance of her declining mental prowess. Dementia had rendered her a bittersweet mix of sharp wit and intelligent observation on any subject from decades earlier, with a contrasting and often comic chaos in trying to deal with anything concerning the past five minutes.

Mark turned on to the street with the familiar and lovely ache of recognition. It was something Sophie, whose childhood had been so much more fragmented geographically and emotionally, had never quite understood. For Mark, driving past the newsagents on the corner evoked not just the memory but the actual scent of lemon sherbets and liquorice shoelaces.

The front gardens of the terraced homes had been open plan when he was a kid, and Mark and his friends would play football across the lawns, some of the mothers emerging to shake their fists and warn them off the grass. Most of the red-brick properties had long been sold to their tenants, who had years back advertised their new status by building proud little walls around their front gardens, with gates and chains or fancy wrought-iron railings.

Mark looked now along the row and remembered the day his own father, sleeves rolled up and red-faced with sweat, had toiled over the pile of bricks, which had been discounted at the builder's yard and sadly never quite matched the house. It had been Mark's job that day to check each row with the spirit level, smiling with a thumbs-up to his father as the yellow fluid settled between the lines.

What was so sweet and touching was how proud his mother remained of her little palace. The windows always polished to a shine. The net curtains regularly soaked in brightener, and an interior which smelled always of bleach and baking and beeswax polish.

Mark parked directly outside and swung open the front gate, which squeaked as it did the last time he called – the front door opening before he even touched the bell, his beaming mother frantically drying her hands on her apron.

'I must get that gate sorted for you.'

'You said that the last time.' She rolled her eyes in mock chastisement but then hugged him tight, hands still damp. 'Kettle's on. Come on in, love. I've made us a snack. Nothing much.'

Inside, the true extent of her preparations peeped beneath tea towels spread over three large plates on the kitchen worktop.

'It's just I know Sophie isn't one for baking.'

Mark smiled a half-smile, shaking his head in resigned exasperation. As his mother then waited for the kettle, he moved through to the back room to greet his gran, who was seated in a high-backed chair in the corner with a patchwork rug over her legs.

'Mark. How lovely – I didn't know you were coming. How's university?'

'Finished uni, Gran. Got a job now. I'm just in the area on business. The family are in Devon. Sophie and Ben? You remember? I work in advertising now.'

'Devon? What on earth have you been doing in Devon?'

His mother then appeared with a large tray bearing the best teapot and china cups. She paused to steady herself before lowering it on to the edge of the dining table, and Mark quickly returned to the kitchen to carry through the plates of cakes and sandwiches, carefully offering each in turn to his gran, who protested she had no appetite before tucking in heartily. Sandwich after sandwich. Cake after cake.

'So. How is university, then? Course going OK?'

'University was excellent, Gran. Would you like a cup of tea? I've brought some new pictures of Ben to show you. My little boy. They're on my phone. You'll need your glasses.'

'Oh, I don't need glasses, love. I have excellent eyesight.'

Mark frowned a question at his mother, who winked conspiratorially as he produced the phone from his pocket, turning back to find his grandmother holding an enormous magnifying glass up to her face, the single eye behind it enlarged to Cyclops proportions.

Like Sherlock Holmes, she then examined each photograph in turn as Mark scrolled through, barely able to contain his amusement.

Later in the car, roaring with laughter openly, Mark realised just how much good the visit had done him – the first time in so long that he had stepped outside of himself; outside of all the confusion and the gut-wrenching worry that was now Tedbury.

It made him so sad that his mother did not ask after Sophie more often. Why on earth did she have to feel threatened? Why could she not just accept that he loved them both with all his heart? But he had learned that pushing his mother over this just made things worse. And he knew too that, despite the terrible split loyalty these visits stirred, it was like recharging his battery to spend an hour with his mum and his gran – two women who would always put him at the very centre of their world.

As the satnav barked directions to his first appointment – a three-storey Georgian property on the edge of a much larger village, just forty minutes by train from London – he caught a glimpse of the flowerpots in the estate agent's photos on the passenger seat. He felt his face change at the thought of those other flowers now dying in the two large pots outside Gill and Antony's cottage. Someone had finally stopped watering them. He thought too of the pregnancy, wishing with all his heart that he had been able to answer Sophie's expectant eyes without the worry which gnawed inside him.

If only he could talk openly to his mother, his gran, to Malcolm, or to *someone* about just how torn he felt. How thrilled he was at the thought of a brother or sister for Ben. And yet? How terrified too he was of going back there, to those days four years ago when he would drive long hours through the dark to Devon, his stomach in knots with guilt and fear and dread, exhausted from work and the journey and yet knowing that the very moment he walked through the door, Sophie would immediately appear, to hand over Ben, her eyes entirely blank and dead.

He knew that second time around he would be looking out for it; he would know the signs and get help faster for Sophie. But back then, for a very long time, he'd had no idea it was depression. It was chilling and baffling and, yes, exhausting, because at the end of his working week it was as if Sophie were handing over a parcel.

It was not like he had imagined it would be; it was not like either of them had ever imagined it would be . . .

You need to take the baby from me, Mark. I just can't do this.

CHAPTER 27

BEFORE

I looked down at my feet. At least I was wearing the right shoes this year. Third time lucky? Twice before I had wandered around the South Devon charity craft fair in the wrong clothes and more especially the wrong shoes.

I had confused the event with the county contemporary craft fair, which sees a huge tented village descend on Dartmoor once a year, attracting stalls of exquisite ceramics, tapestries, silk work and every other imaginable artisan enterprise.

Turned out the local version was much lower-key, primarily a platform for artists – Heather included – who couldn't persuade galleries to take their work. A tented village was financially out of the question; instead, a humble-jumble of linked canopies and one single marquee left the event as vulnerable to the vagaries of the weather as the Tedbury fair.

That first visit, having so overestimated the occasion, I'd fancied being upstaged by colourful 'artistic types' wafting about in splendid hats, and I tried much too hard. Pink embroidered skirt, bright purple jacket and the biggest disaster – suede boots with kitten heels. Though it was dry on the day, it had been raining for most of the previous week, and I not only looked faintly ridiculous in my rainbow ensemble but sank in the soggy grass with every step, ruining the boots.

The second year I went too far the other way – a practical black jumper, jeans and trainers, which made me feel a complete frump when unexpected sunshine brought everyone else out in pretty floral skirts and jewelled sandals.

This year? I stared again at my feet. Rope wedges with cream ribbons tied around the ankle. Practical, but quite pretty too.

'I really don't know why we put ourselves through this.' I raised my voice to Helen, who was across the hall in the kitchen, as I rose again on to tiptoes to better check my reflection in the mirror next to the downstairs cloakroom.

'Stop worrying. You look lovely,' Helen replied, while helping herself to more coffee from the cafetière on the kitchen worktop. I turned left to right to check the length of my floral skirt.

Rather sweetly, Heather had telephoned to confirm that her stall was number sixteen, as if finding her at the event might somehow prove difficult.

In point of fact, she could be spotted immediately amidst the modest array of stalls, behind which eager artists smiled and swooped just a little too swiftly on every potential customer, so that the majority of visitors were already clinging to the central grassy area, sipping coffee while pointedly avoiding eye contact with the sellers.

'You realise we will have to buy something,' I whispered to Helen, squeezing her arm as I led her to Heather's stall.

And then, much louder, 'Heather, this is my lovely friend Helen from Cornwall who I've been telling you about. So, how's it going? The stall looks gorgeous.'

'Slow. Most of the customers are complete peasants.' She had lowered her voice. 'They keep trying to barter as if it's a bloody boot sale.'

'Oh, but this stuff is beautiful.' Helen picked up two bangles displayed on a wooden mug tree. 'Lacquer work, isn't it?'

'Yes. I've been having a lot of dreams about the sea. Marine inspiration. Sea urchins, mostly.'

'Right.'

Helen slipped on one of the bangles, rotating her arm to admire it while Heather was summoned away by a potential customer wishing to try on some earrings.

As Heather rummaged behind the stall for a mirror for her new prey, Helen suddenly turned back to me, eyes wide. 'Oh, sugar. That's not good.'

'What's the matter?'

'The bangle. I can't get it off.'

'But you must be able to. You got it on.' I tried to help. We pushed. We pulled. We twisted her wrist this way and that but all in vain. A complete biological mystery.

'I hate sea urchins, Sophie. Help me.'

But the more we continued to try to squeeze the thumb into the palm, the more the hand seemed to inexplicably swell, until Heather reappeared.

'So, how are we getting on, ladies?'

'I love it. In fact I think I'll wear it now.' Helen held her arm out triumphantly, pushing the bangle back on to the wrist.

'Thirty pounds. One of a pair, if you're interested?'

'*Thirty pounds?*'

'Yes. Hand-painted.' Heather tilted her chin up, eyes widening.

'Lovely. I'll just take the one, I think. I don't like to jangle.' Helen reached into her purse and began fumbling for notes as I bit away a smile and sorted through a range of pendants.

'I've been looking for something bold to wear with black.'

Heather, after producing change for Helen from a small blue cash box, immediately selected the largest pendant from the collection.

'This one is very striking. And there are earrings to match.'

'The budget's twenty quid tops, Heather.' I turned to wink at Helen.

'You're as bad as that lot, hiding on the grass. Oh – go on, then. Twenty quid for the set, seeing as it's you.'

It was as she again opened the cash box, and I noticed with a pang how little money there was inside, that I also caught a familiar flash of red linen coat out of the corner of my eye, over by the entrance to the main marquee. 'Oh great – Emma's here. I meant to ring her this morning.'

'Yes – she's here with Nathan. Also Tom from the village. He's doing his bird stall in the marquee – for the RSPB. But I'd better warn you who else is here.' Heather clamped the cash box shut and looked more serious. 'You'll never guess.'

'Who?'

'That woman police inspector. Or sergeant or whoever. The one investigating the Hartleys.'

'Here? Today? But whatever for?'

'Oh – not working. Word is she's with an artist friend – got some rug stall in the marquee. Very good work, actually.'

'So have you spoken to her?'

'The artist?'

'No, muppet. The *police officer*.'

'Oh no – just nodded. To be honest, I was a bit embarrassed. I mean, I assume she's off-duty so I didn't really know what to say. But I haven't had a chance to warn Emma.'

We both looked across to watch Emma and Nathan enter the marquee.

'It'll be fine.' I failed to make this sound convincing even to myself.

'Yeah.'

'Though I'd better just go and have a word. Moral support.'

'Good idea.'

En route, I quickly summed up for Helen the unfair hassle Emma was having with the police and the village gossips. The brick through the window. The tittle-tattle about an imagined affair with Antony. I explained that I had only recently managed to stop her throwing in the towel and leaving the village after Theo was upset in playgroup. But I didn't mention Hobbs Lane and Emma's continuing pressure to speed up the deli opening now that she had decided to stay; I knew Helen would worry for me.

There was a larger crowd inside the marquee and an impressive array of stalls along one side, and it was in this moment I realised, with another pang for Heather, that this was the prime spot. At the far end there was a group of smaller stands representing the charities which were to share some of the proceeds from the day, and to my surprise, it was here that Detective Inspector Melanie Sanders, looking relaxed and quite different with loose hair and a striking outfit of pale linen trousers and fitted aubergine top, was in animated discussion with Tom by the RSPB table. They were examining a map on a large display board, Tom pointing out different locations and both of them occasionally throwing back their heads to laugh.

'That's weird,' I whispered, turning to Helen. 'That woman in the cream trousers. She's the police officer investigating the couple I found. The Hartleys. And that man she's flirting with is the bird man of Tedbury.'

'I'm sorry?'

'They look awfully pally, wouldn't you say?' I was genuinely shocked.

Helen did not reply but instead moved across to a woodturning stall and picked up a fruit bowl.

'What are you doing, Helen?'

'I'm trying not to be so obvious, Sophie. You're staring.'

'Sorry.'

'And who's this bird man?'

'Wildlife campaigner. Tom – very nice guy, actually. He raised a packet a while back for that cirl bunting project. The one with all the pictures up on the stand.'

'Right. And so what exactly do you plan to do now? I should think all this is the last thing you need, Sophie.'

'It's OK. I'm fine. Really. But I just want to make sure Emma is OK. I've noticed that Theo's here too, which isn't good. Means he isn't back in playgroup yet.' I was frowning. 'Stay here, would you? I'll be back in a moment.'

I walked straight over to Theo, who was standing alongside another child in the corner of the tent, watching a basket-weaving display.

'Hi, Theo. You all right there?'

He nodded but said nothing, eyes uneasy, as the other child launched into a loud and highly animated running commentary on the basket-making.

I waited for the child to finish, then smiled at Theo. 'So what do you like best at the fair so far then, Theo?'

He shrugged, lips clamped tight, then looked across the tent to point out his mother, who was examining a display of silk scarves.

'Yes, thank you. I've seen her – I'm just going over. Now, you won't wander off? Promise me?'

Theo stared at me a little oddly, then shook his head and turned his attention back to the woman twisting the basket as she expertly wove the next row of straw into place.

By the time I reached Emma and Nathan, they had both just spotted the off-duty Melanie and Tom.

'Emma.' I kissed her on the cheek, trying to read her expression and resting my palm on her arm by way of reassurance. I took in the red coat and the large buckle and felt guilty for my stupid mistake in Cornwall, for letting it unsettle me. It was a Boden coat. There must be hundreds out there . . .

'I'm really sorry I've been so tied up the last few days. Are you two still OK for supper on Wednesday? We can catch up then. Helen's looking forward to meeting you.'

'Yes. It will be lovely.' Nathan was staring at his shoes, shuffling uncomfortably. I realised he was probably wondering why I had gone for a midweek invitation, while Mark was away. I half-opened my mouth to explain that I wanted a little social while Helen was staying, but changed my mind. I'd explain on the night.

'You've seen who's here?' Emma sounded wary.

'Yes. Heather says she's with an artist friend. A rug stall or something. Not an official visit.'

'Oh. Bit odd, don't you think? Seems she's quite friendly with Tom. I didn't realise—'

At that moment there was the sound of a motor from behind us and we turned to see a disability scooter moving through the middle of the tent. We all stepped aside as the very tanned woman driver, accompanied by a tall, grey-haired man, meandered her way past us to the RSPB stand, where to my continued surprise she was greeted with a warm hug by DI Sanders. Next there were introductions to Tom, who was soon shaking hands and leading them over to the map, where he pointed out two or three locations before handing them a selection of leaflets from the stall.

'So what's all that about?' Emma looked both puzzled and concerned.

'No idea.' I squeezed her arm and smiled, hating to see her this anxious; so unfair that some of the locals were being so small-minded. For a moment I took in how striking she looked; the contrast of the coat and her long dark hair. Jealousy. Yes. That was probably at the root of most people's problem with her.

'Look – I've been trying to persuade Em to leave. That police officer's caused enough trouble. And from what I hear, Tom isn't helping.' Nathan's voice was clipped and evidently angry.

'What do you mean by that?' I looked back across at Tom. 'I thought you two were mates?'

'We are. *Were.* Look – let's just leave it there. Things got a bit tricky while you were in Cornwall. Come on, Em.' He had his hand protectively on Emma's back, trying to steer her away, but she didn't move.

I waited before adding my own encouragement more softly. 'Come on, Emma. Nathan's right. You go on outside and I'll fetch Theo.'

Reluctantly Emma finally allowed herself to be led away while I returned to the basket-weaving display and took Theo's hand. He looked uneasy and withdrawn still, saying nothing at all as I led him off to join his mother.

'I really am sorry I haven't been over this week, Emma. With Helen staying, I mean.'

'It's OK. But I do need to talk to you again about Hobbs Lane . . .'

'Yes. I want to talk to you about that too. And so how's our lovely Theo?'

Emma paused to let Theo pull away again, wandering across the grass to watch a Great Dane being led a merry dance by its owner. 'Not good. I'll tell you Wednesday.' She was whispering now. 'He's stopped talking.'

'What? Shy spell suddenly, you mean? That's not like him.'

'No. He's stopped talking *completely*, Sophie. Nathan thinks I should take him to the doctor but I don't want a fuss.'

And now there was a truly uncomfortable sensation in my stomach. 'Oh, Emma. So he's not back in playgroup?'

'No. I've had to give up on that for now. He won't talk *at all*. Just points and mimes everything.'

'Christ, I didn't realise. Look, I feel terrible – I should have been in touch. We'll talk more on Wednesday, yes?' I glanced again at Theo as he stood on his own, very still, watching the dog. 'Kids have these wobbles but you must try not to worry. These phases always pass.' I didn't add, because I didn't want to alarm her, that I rather agreed with Nathan; if Theo had stopped talking *completely*, poor love, then maybe professional advice was a good idea.

'Yeah.'

It was only now that I noticed Nathan had disappeared back into the tent.

'So what's up between Nathan and Tom?'

'Oh, I don't know. He won't tell me. Some stupid row. You know what the village is like.'

And then from the tent there was suddenly the most deafening crash – the canvas wall taking the shape of something angular, rocking the whole structure as if something inside had collapsed. A number of people spilled from the main entrance, gasping and shaking their heads, and next Nathan appeared – marching towards us, face like thunder.

'Come on. We are leaving *now.*'

He took Emma's arm, steering her towards the exit sign across the grass, as I watched Tom appear at the tent entrance, clutching his jaw and followed closely by DI Melanie Sanders. Tom then held on to her shoulders, apparently to stop her pursuing Nathan.

I was just wondering whether to go after Nathan, Emma and Theo for an explanation when Helen emerged from the tent, her face white as she approached.

'So what on earth happened in there, then?'

'Nathan punched Tom and knocked over his stand in the process. But never mind that. We need to get you home.' Helen had her arm protectively around my shoulders. She then removed her cardigan and inexplicably tied it around my waist.

'What on earth are you doing?'

Helen steered me gently towards the exit. 'Come on, Sophie.'

Only alongside the car as she demanded the keys, insisting she would drive, did she finally explain. Ashen-faced.

'You're bleeding, Sophie.'

CHAPTER 28

BEFORE

Every day for the next fortnight I woke in the same transient fog. A sort of limbo where for a brief spell, numbed by sleep, I forgot the puddles of sadness I had to wade through as the day dragged on. Breakfast. Walking Ben to school. *Bye, darling.* A quick call to check on Emma. *How's Theo doing? Any better?* Lunch and supper with Helen.

You must try to eat something, Sophie. Just a little. Please.

Extraordinary that you can know so little about a subject one moment and become an expert the next. It felt as if I had read everything ever written about bleeding in early pregnancy. I quizzed the doctors at the hospital until their faces froze into the same strained expression as they repeated what they had already told me at the very beginning. That first horrible visit after the fair. That there really was nothing to be done now but wait.

The problem was I still felt pregnant. I still looked out on the world as if through a veil of detachment. I still couldn't touch coffee. I still peed every day on a stick which told me I was pregnant. And yet still most days I bled.

On that first emergency trip to the hospital with Helen, I was told that loss of blood early on was quite common and did not make a miscarriage inevitable. A jolly nurse on the maternity unit with plump hips and strangely arching eyebrows trotted out the statistics so calmly and easily that I came home genuinely reassured.

Bed rest at first. Mark rushed home and was wonderful. Kind and tender and yet terribly afraid – bringing me endless cups of camomile tea. I sat in our bed with the iPad, screenshotting every article I could find to support that initial reassurance.

I was no longer bleeding every day. And now that Mark had finally been persuaded to return to London, leaving Helen in charge, I picked up the iPad first thing every morning to skim through those articles, reading them over and over.

Around one in four women, according to the research, suffer bleeding in the first three months. For those whose subsequent scan confirms a heartbeat, ninety per cent go on to have a normal pregnancy.

So we just needed the heartbeat confirmed. *Rest, Sophie. Rest.*

The emergency session at the hospital was inconclusive. There was no evidence of an ectopic pregnancy, which had been the first fear, but the test for a heartbeat with an appalling internal probe did not go well. This was probably because it was so early, the doctor said. I'd been in something of a muddle over the dates.

By the time Mark first arrived from London, I was tucked up in bed at home, with the news that there was nothing to be done but wait another week then try the scan again, by which time the heartbeat should be clearer and stronger.

In complete contrast to his muted response when I told him about the pregnancy, Mark was in real shock at this setback. At first he would not talk about it properly, but then late that first night I found him in our bathroom, sitting in the dark weeping.

He was mumbling, almost incoherent, saying it was all his fault. For closing himself off. For worrying about money. For us still living apart; him unable to relocate the business . . .

Eventually I coaxed him to bed and we lay there just holding hands for hours. So sad and yet also the closest we'd felt for a while.

He stayed home the whole of the first week but there had been so many frantic calls from the office that Helen persuaded him to go back to London to catch up. The doctors had advised rest and 'normality', and I think secretly Helen felt Mark's anxious clucking was making me worse. Maybe she was right.

And now, as I slowly gained confidence – four whole days with no bleeding – she suggested resurrecting the supper plan. We had cancelled the dinner invitation to Emma and Nathan but Helen floated the idea of a quieter girls' night to lift my spirits – also a little platform for me to tell Emma what was going on. *If you want to, that is, Sophie.*

Truth is I didn't know. Emma had quite enough to deal with herself.

And so it was Thursday now, and with Mark staying another night in London, Helen and I drove to a favourite butcher for enormous lamb shanks, for a Moroccan dish to be served with couscous and homemade flatbread.

Helen made me sit at the breakfast bar while she chopped and fried and stirred and tasted until there was this intoxicating smell seeping from the Aga and through the whole house. Later I took a rest upstairs, still enjoying the delicious scent, so that I was feeling calmer and cared for as Helen arrived with a cup of tea.

'You'll like her, Helen.'

'Sorry?'

'Emma. She's unusual. Probably why people have taken against her.'

'Unusual is good.'

'That's what I think.'

'So what's the score with the real father, then? Is Theo's dad not around at all?'

'No. Another artist, apparently. Went travelling to Asia for "inspiration". Suggested an abortion, as did her mother.'

'Charming.'

'Exactly. She doesn't like to talk about it, mostly because she doesn't know what to tell Theo. There's this ludicrous rumour going round that Antony was the father. Complete nonsense, but small wonder Theo is so out of sorts. He was wound up by some other child in playgroup about it. The kid probably overheard his mother gossiping. Anyway. Poor Emma was all for leaving the village over it. Like I said, it took me a long time to calm her down and talk her into staying.'

'So are you going to tell Emma tonight? About the baby? Have you decided?'

'I'm still not sure, to be honest. Maybe. A big part of me doesn't want to add to her worries, but . . .' I paused. 'Also, it feels a bit silly telling you this, but she kept something from me when we first met.'

'Oh?'

'Yes. About her mother dying when she was in France. Just before she came here. It was to start with a blank page, she said. Understandable. But I was surprised how much I minded and I made a bit of a fool of myself over it. So I suppose it would hypocritical if I did the same thing myself. Kept something from her, I mean.'

There was a look of slight puzzlement on Helen's face which I found difficult to understand, but which reappeared later as she sat opposite Emma at the supper table.

It was not something I had foreseen. That Helen and Emma wouldn't get along. Nothing tangible at first, just an awkwardness in their body language which I put down to nerves. But sitting at the table, the three of us, with olives and bread and dips which Helen had put out on a wooden board in lieu of a starter, I found my eyes darting from one guest to the other, trying to make out what exactly was going on.

Helen was all politeness and good manners over the first gin and tonic, passing on her condolences regarding Emma's mother and then trying to lighten the mood by talking of the food and other delights of France. She seemed keen to know more of the area Emma had visited, whether she was fluent in French and whether Theo had managed to pick up much of the language during their stay. *Children learn so quickly. It's a marvel to behold.*

I wished I had warned her more openly that Emma didn't like to talk about France. And sure enough, Emma became very prickly, pointedly trying to change the subject while Helen seemed unwilling to take the hint. And now, as I poured us all water, Helen was off again.

'So which part of France did you say your mother lived in, Emma?'

'The south initially, then the north.'

'Oh, but my late husband and I loved the north. Underrated in my view, just as the Lizard is in Cornwall. We visited Brittany every year. I still do. Off there very soon, actually. So easy, of course, from here. Ferry from Plymouth, I mean. Cheap too – out of season. I visit my late husband's cousin in the most charming place. Landerneau. So where were you?'

'You wouldn't know it. A small place. So has Sophie been telling you about our deli plans?'

'Nearest town?'

'I'm sorry?'

'What was the nearest town to your mother's place? As I say, my late husband's cousin lives in Landerneau. The weather isn't always good, of course, but it has the sweetest bridge. And wonderful narrow streets.'

I stood up. 'I'll fetch the main course, shall I, Helen?'

'Near the coast or inland?'

'Near Carnac. It was La Trinité-sur-Mer, near Carnac.' Emma was clattering the starter plates together noisily.

'Oh, really? But I know the area quite well. Those amazing standing stones. Gorgeous marina, and an excellent market too. As I say – I'm due to visit again quite soon. Perhaps you could recommend some new restaurants?'

Emma's face was colouring deeply – unusual for her – as she adjusted her napkin. 'I didn't see it in the best of circumstances, of course.'

'No, I'm sorry, I wasn't thinking. Of course not. Forgive me.'

'Will you help me carry, Helen?'

'Of course, darling. Sorry. I'm talking too much.'

◆ ◆ ◆

In the kitchen I apologised, whispering to Helen that I should have warned her more keenly how sensitive Emma could be about France. The trauma over her mother, presumably? Also that she obviously wasn't quite herself just now – what with the police being such a pain in the arse.

'So when are you heading back to Cornwall, Helen?' Emma was topping up the wine glasses as we re-entered the room. I stared at the wine, which I would not touch. I would have to say something. Later . . .

'Sorry?'

'I was wondering when you're going back to the Lizard?'

'Oh gosh. I hadn't even thought. By the way, did Sophie tell you about seeing your doppelganger down there? Gave her quite a fright.'

I was mortified, mouth gaping.

'When was this? My double? How fabulous. I love the idea of having a doppelganger. Do share . . .' Emma began adding salad to her plate.

'Just a woman with a similar coat and the same hair. Up on a cliff. Looked really like you.'

And then Emma leaned forward to touch my hand. 'Sweet. You were missing me, weren't you? Conjured me up?'

'Probably. I feel a bit silly even mentioning it.'

Helen glanced from me to Emma and then, as if by way of penance, suddenly took a deep breath and steered the conversation via the story of Heather's bangle – which we had to remove in the end with warm oil – to Emma's ceramic work. And then the deli.

'Sophie is being very coy and insisting we keep a low profile but I reckon we can open any time soon. It's going to be just brilliant – don't you think, Helen?'

'Goodness. So you're ready to go? Everything set up? I had no idea you had made a decision about this, Sophie. Does Mark know?'

I stalled. Distracted. I talked about the butcher and the lamb shank recipe and the amazing flatbread. I joked about Helen trying to persuade me to try ostrich steaks. I laughed and it sounded false and I couldn't believe this was going so badly. And then as we finished our main course, I asked Helen if she would mind sorting the cheese, please, widening my eyes to signal for some time alone with Emma, until Helen nodded and retreated to the kitchen.

I stared at my wine – untouched. Emma stared at the wine and frowned, and so it was decided. I told her everything.

Only as Helen returned with the tray of cheese and biscuits and coffee were things finally easier between us all. The subject too worrying, I guess, for any more friction.

'The good thing is I still feel pregnant. Hormones all over the place. Swollen breasts. I did another test this morning and it's a solid line. I didn't bleed at all with Ben.'

'So when's this next scan?' Emma was holding my hand.

'Tuesday. It's an internal ultrasound so they can hear or see the heartbeat on the monitor. Mark's going with me.'

'Of course. Look, I don't really know what to say, Sophie. Except that if there is any justice in the world, it will be just fine. Trust what you feel.' Emma had lowered her voice so that I had to lean in to hear her.

'The doctors are very non-committal. I suppose they need you to prepare for all outcomes. We just have to wait. So what about you? How's Theo doing?'

'Oh, he's OK. Let's not talk about that.'

'Is he still not talking, little Theo?' Helen piped up suddenly.

'No.'

'So how long exactly has this been, Emma?' Helen smoothed her napkin.

'Since the rumpus in playgroup, pretty much.' Emma was still looking at me, blanking Helen. 'It's just a phase, I'm sure.'

'But that's quite a while now.' I was doing the sum in my head. 'You haven't tried the GP? Just to see what they think.'

'No. Look. I know people mean well; Nathan thinks he should see a specialist, but the thing is, once you start that ball rolling, it never stops. And I don't want him labelled.'

'Oh, I'm sure they wouldn't do that. I had a spell when Ben was supposedly potty training when he decided he wouldn't poo. A whole week he went.'

'A week?'

'Yeah. I was running a book on him exploding, but the doctor was lovely. They've seen *everything*, Emma. Why don't you at least consider a referral? Have a chat with the GP.'

'I suppose you're right.' Emma leant forward to kiss my cheek and then, to my surprise, was gathering up her things. Bag. Wrap. Phone. 'I'll see how this weekend goes.'

'Oh, you're not going already, Emma? Helen bought chocolates and it's so early still.'

'Thank you, but best I get back to the sitter. And anyway – you need to *rest*, Sophie.'

And then Emma, standing very upright, looked pointedly across at Helen. 'It was so lovely to meet you, Helen' – wrapping her pashmina around her shoulders – 'just lovely.'

CHAPTER 29

BEFORE

DI Melanie Sanders checked her watch and tried to catch the eye of the waitress to order a second coffee. She hated raising her hand or calling out; she'd worked in a restaurant herself one summer during her A levels and remembered how rude people could be.

After a few minutes the waitress finished delivering four full English breakfasts to a table by the window, and Melanie cleared her throat. The woman finally turned.

'Sorry. Did you want something?'

'No. Yes. I'm sorry, but if you're not busy, could I have another coffee?'

And then the waitress did a double take, tilting her head. 'Do I know you from somewhere?'

'I don't think so.' Melanie wiped her fingers on a paper napkin as two of the men at the other table turned around, one with a whole sausage paused on his fork.

'It's just your face looks familiar. Your hair. Hang on . . .' The woman's face confirmed a lightbulb moment. 'You've been on the telly. Over that Tedbury case.'

Melanie, mortified, signalled with her hand for the waitress to lower her voice.

'Sorry. Sorry. Are you undercover?'

'No, no.' Melanie glared at the spectators, who at last turned back to their breakfasts, sausage man biting into the huge piece of meat, spraying a burst of fat down his T-shirt. 'I'm just surprised you recognised me.'

'Well, I remember your hair. Thinking how nice it was. I was considering a change myself, see, and yours is just what I was thinking of. Layering but not too short. Also I think it's nice to see a woman police officer making the best of herself. Like that blonde woman, whatshername, in that serial killer thingy. That strangler bloke. You know. The good-looking one.'

'I'm sorry?'

'Oh – you're younger than her, of course. But she had great hair too, and it's just it's mostly men who get to do the TV interviews in real life. So did you work it all out, then? Horrid case. Though he had a bit of a look about him, I thought. The bloke that got killed. Too handsome by half. Like an actor or something.'

'I'm not allowed to discuss my cases.'

'Oh. Right. No. Of course. So are you on the telly very much, then? Do you get nervous?'

'No.' Melanie glanced at the door and began to stand, noticing that Matthew was just about to walk in. 'Actually, I'll forget the second coffee. It's later than I realised.'

'You sure?'

'Yes, thank you.' Melanie put coins from her pocket on to the table. 'Keep the change.'

'Thank you. And do you mind me asking where you get your hair done?'

'Er. A friend does it, actually.' A lie.

'Oh, right.'

In the doorway, Melanie grabbed Matthew's arm and turned him around, steering him right back on to the street.

'Excuse me? It's raining out there.'

'We can't stay here. Sorry.'

Back out on the pavement now, Matthew, in his trademark parka, pulled a face. 'What's up? Coffee not up to scratch?'

'Promise you won't laugh?'

'I promise.'

'I was recognised in there.'

'From court?'

'No. From the television coverage of the Tedbury case.'

He roared with laughter. 'Sorry. Sorry. Forgot you were a famous DI now.' His cheeks were wearing the dimples which had prompted so much teasing throughout their police training together.

Matthew had been the star recruit. Everyone thought he was a sure thing for the High Potential Development scheme. He was sharp, funny and distinctive, with his white-blond hair and tall, lanky frame. They had become close friends, and Melanie was gutted when they were immediately transferred to opposite ends of the region. They met up regularly for a drink, and emailed and phoned every week to swap notes. The highs. The lows. And then suddenly Melanie had a panic – worrying that she was sending the wrong signals, because Matthew had begun to look at her in a way which was unsettling. Even though she liked him, *really liked him*, she had never thought of him in *that* way. Not at all.

'You're going to give me the it's-not-you-it's-me speech,' he had said, clearly wounded at her reaction the one time he tried to kiss her, after a pub crawl in Exeter years back. She had been too drunk to travel home and he had given her his bed, changing the sheets and duvet cover and sleeping on the sofa downstairs, then making perfectly poached eggs on toast for their breakfast. Just runny – exactly the way she liked them.

I'm so sorry, Matthew. It's not that I don't think you're completely lovely. It's just—

Please, Mel. Don't make it any worse. We're fine. It's fine. Honestly.

They had stayed friends. They'd worked hard. They continued to swap notes and moans and then Matthew suddenly quit the force.

It took Melanie a good while to find out what had really happened. She did everything she could to try to change his mind, but it was no use. Matthew was too competent, too kind and too moral for his own good. He blamed himself for a child getting killed. Matthew had been chasing him after the boy was caught shoplifting. He ran straight on to a live line.

Nothing Melanie or anyone else said could dissuade Matthew from quitting. He set up his own PI agency in Exeter. Such a waste. She had told him so, furious that a man of his ability should go wasting his talent *snooping*.

Since then he had got lucky. Got married. A really lovely woman called Sally. Melanie liked her and was pleased for Matthew.

But . . .

It was his turn to steer her now, across the road to another café just around the corner, where he ordered more coffee and where Melanie found herself wondering how much of his time he spent watching people from seedy cafés these days. She still wished he would reconsider. Come back into the force. Surely he couldn't be content with his working life?

'So, what's up, Mel? Why the urgency?'

'It's the Tedbury case.'

'I thought that was all done and dusted? Domestic – straight up, straight down.'

'Who told you that? And why would you even be asking?'

Matthew stared down at his coffee. 'I was on a routine case there myself for a bit.'

'So I hear. One of my witnesses spotted you taking photographs.'

'And how did you know it was me?'

She patted his blond hair and pinged one of the strings at the cuff of his parka. 'You are going to have to do something about that. Seriously. Especially on local cases.'

He dipped his finger into the froth on the coffee and sucked it, making a smacking sound, then took a deep breath.

'I like my parka.'

She smiled. 'So why the photographs?'

'Just research – checking out some locals. Cars. Number plates.'

'So you were getting someone to run number plates through the system? Not sure I like the sound of that, Matt.'

'Oops.' He pulled a face. He had been checking for any previous convictions for fraud or financial wrongdoing, which was standard for his planning cases. 'Look – Mel. My case in Tedbury. It was nothing you need to know about. Routine gig. I promise I would have phoned you if I felt I needed to.'

'So you weren't working for Gill Hartley? Checking out the husband?'

'No. Like I said, I would have told you if it was directly linked.'

'So it was indirectly linked?'

He looked at her. She looked at him.

'I didn't say that.'

'Come on, Matt. I don't want to do this officially.'

'Don't be like that. This is me, Mel.'

'All right. The CPS aren't that fussed. Nor's my boss. Gill Hartley is still in a coma, and chances are she'll be unplugged at some stage, which means there will be no one to charge.'

'So where's your problem?'

'Emma Carter.'

Matthew's face changed and he leant in closer. 'What about her?'

'So you know the name?'

'I didn't say that.' He sipped his coffee, narrowing his eyes.

'I have an instinct about her, Matt. She was the last person to see Gill before the meltdown with her husband, and she was snooping around the hospital for no good reason. There's something not right.'

'And?'

'And I'm asking an old friend, who I rate very highly, if they know anything which might help me.'

'Like I said, I was just on a routine job.'

He looked at her, unblinking now.

'Will you think about it, Matt? If there's anything at all I should know.'

He paused. 'You know this is different for me now, Mel? No police pension. A business to run. A reputation to build. Client confidentiality . . .'

'Someone died, Matt.'

'And the forensics said there was *no one else involved*.'

'So you were worried enough to check for yourself, then?'

He held her stare then, as if struggling with something. 'Look. I need to make some more inquiries my end. Soon as I've done that, I promise I'll call you again, Mel.'

'OK.' She was happier. 'Deal. Meantime – how's the lovely Amelie? She talking yet?'

'As it happens, she said her first word recently.'

'Great. So was it *dadda*, as you hoped?'

'No.'

'Bad luck, Matt. So – *mamma*?'

'*No*.' Matthew's expression was teasing, and so Melanie frowned. 'What, then?'

'Well, she has now deigned to say *dadda* precisely twice. But when I say *no*, I mean that we need to be afraid. Very afraid. Because my daughter's first and absolutely favourite word in the world so far is . . . *NO!*

And now Emma and Tedbury were momentarily forgotten as they both laughed and Matthew took out his phone to share the latest photographs of his daughter.

TODAY – 7.15 P.M.

The doctor and his wife are drinking their coffees. Mark is back from the loo, staring into space, when his phone goes.

I physically start. I want news but I don't want bad news. There is a voice in my head telling him not to answer the phone.

Don't let them say it.

Mark just looks at me and stands to answer the call more privately, walking through to the space between carriages.

The doctor smiles at me. I have put both my hands up to my lips, like I'm praying.

'I am sure it will be fine. The hospital staff are good people. Excellent people.'

I nod, not trusting my voice.

It feels like an eternity but at last Mark is back, putting his phone in his pocket as he sits, his face pale. I am absorbing the fact that he does not speak immediately.

'So what's the news?'

'Nathan is just five minutes away now. He's going to identify the boys and ring us straight away.'

'So that was Nathan?'

'No.' He lets out this odd little huff of air. 'That was intensive care. They've just spoken to Nathan.'

'Intensive care? What does that mean? Why intensive care? Is that normal after an operation? Does everyone go to intensive care after an operation?' I am looking at the doctor but it is Mark who answers.

'One of the boys has had a complication from the surgery. Some respiratory reaction to the anaesthetic.'

'Oh my God.'

'They're monitoring him very closely. It's all a bit hectic right now. They've asked me to ring back.'

'Right. Intensive care. Right . . .' For some reason I am rocking. Forward and back. I am conscious that this is not a good thing and I watch the doctor exchange a look with his wife that I don't like at all.

Next, I do a really stupid thing. I ask to borrow Mark's phone to look something up.

Something which is going to make me feel even worse.

CHAPTER 30

BEFORE

I lay back on the hospital bed and closed my eyes. There had been no bleeding for a week now. Mark felt this was a good sign. He said so again this morning very quietly as we set off for the scan.

There was a man's voice – the doctor? – asking if I was comfortable. *Ready?* I told this new doctor that there had been no bleeding for a whole week. *Sorry. Did we say that already?*

Mark reached for my hand – gently passing each of his fingers between mine – and the doctor's voice was asking me to try to relax but I already knew how I was going to do this; I had decided in the car. And so the voice and the sound of the machine drifted away as I made myself rise ever so slowly from the bed. Floating higher and higher, through the ceiling and the soft haze of cloud, on and on for miles and miles until I could smell the sea. Good. Eyes still closed, I descended to feel the warm sand between my toes, Mark all the time holding my hand tightly in his own.

And now I opened my eyes to see Ben waving from the shoreline, a sandcastle bucket in his hand. The light was hurting my eyes and I had to squint into the sun, but very soon I could feel the tension in my forehead easing. For there was *another* child waving back now. Smaller

– just a silhouette, reaching up to hold on to Ben's free hand. They were laughing together, and I smiled back at them.

Mine.

The voice deep inside my head, whispering beneath the roar of the waves. *Both mine. Please.*

But now Mark's hand was gripping more tightly until the fingers were almost crushing mine. And the space around us thundered with the silence as I strained for the sound of a beat. A rhythm. A heartbeat.

Please.

I squeezed my eyes tighter but still the sound did not come. Mark was asking if the doctor could see anything on the screen. *Any sound wave? Anything at all?* No reply . . . And now the children and the sea were moving further and further away, the sand sucking fast between my toes as I was pulled backwards, backwards. A voice, distant at first, but getting louder and louder.

Are you all right, Mrs Edwards? Would you like a glass of water?

I tried to call out to the children at the edge of the sea, but nothing would come out of my mouth.

Instead there was just a click as they turned off the machine. And the doctor's voice – closer now, saying that they would give us some time alone. *As long as you need.* And then repeating it ever so softly.

How very sorry he was.

But there is no heartbeat . . .

CHAPTER 31

BEFORE

'I'm fine. Really.'

Over and over I said this out loud and also quietly in my head, as the coming days brought a procession of fish pies and fuss. Everyone suddenly so keen to keep me fed.

I mean, it's not as if it were a proper miscarriage. Not really. I kept saying this to Mark and Helen in turn. OK, so I had to have this really horrible procedure to clear the womb, but it was so early, there couldn't have been anything. *Don't you think? Not really. I expect they do that for everyone – even people who've just got their dates in a muddle. I probably just got my dates in a muddle.*

I had this feeling that if everyone could just stop fussing and realise that this was no big deal, I would be completely fine. But I kept catching Helen and Mark whispering as I entered a room, or exchanging knowing glances, and it was making me so touchy that in the end I did something really stupid.

'It's not that I'm not grateful, Helen. You've been wonderful, but I need to sort some things out on my own now.' Even as the words came out of my mouth, I didn't know why I was saying this; sending her away. 'You're not to say a word to Mark but I'm going to press on with looking for some work. I'm going to stall over the deli and see what options I've got. Also – I really want to help Emma with Theo. He's still not talking, poor sausage, and I'm really worried.'

For a while Helen resisted leaving, and so I started decluttering the house, refusing to allow her to help. *I'm fine, honestly. I need to be doing something.* In the end, she quietly packed up the leather suitcase and much-mocked carpet bag, and I don't know who looked more likely to cry. Her or me.

'You absolutely sure you don't want me to stay a bit longer?'

'No. I'm fine.'

'OK. So I'll ring. Every day. And you will answer the phone. Yes?'

'Yes.'

And so I threw myself into helping Emma with Theo, and realised, as I did this, why I had really needed Helen to go.

So has Helen gone, then?

Yes, Emma.

Oh right. I thought she must have had a lot to catch up on. Back in Cornwall. Lovely lady. But quite a bit older than us. I hadn't realised when you said you were close that she would be so much older . . .

The news on Theo wasn't good. Emma had tried just once to coax him back to playgroup but it failed miserably. She was apparently per-suaded to let the staff peel him away from her, crying, the hope being he would 'come around' once she was out of sight, but an hour later there was a phone call to say he remained completely inconsolable. I heard from one of the other mums later that one of the other kids had donned a policeman's uniform from the dressing-up box, and Theo inexplicably went completely bonkers. Emma had to take him home again.

Emma continued to try to play it all down: her strategy – to sit it out. For myself? I just didn't know what to think or advise.

There must be something we're missing, I had made the mistake of saying out loud while Helen was still staying – regretting it immediately. For though I meant something external – that maybe some kid was really bullying Theo – Helen's response had alarmed me.

Look, I don't want to say the wrong thing here, Sophie, but are you sure there isn't something going on at home that we don't know about?

I hadn't liked her tone. Worse still, Helen's next suggestion – that Theo's continuing refusal to speak in front of anyone other than Ben, and him only rarely, sounded very much like a condition called selective mutism. She hadn't liked to interfere initially, she said, but it was a condition which Helen knew a little about through a friend of her late husband's who worked in child psychiatry. If she was right, it was something which would definitely need expert help and which was almost always triggered by extreme anxiety.

I'd never heard of selective mutism and dismissed the amateur diagnosis out of hand. It was the first time Helen had ever annoyed me. She had so clearly failed to take to Emma that I even wondered if, like everyone else, she was a bit jealous.

'I'm sure you mean well, Helen, but Emma is a good mother. Whatever is going on with Theo is not her fault. Nothing at home. I'm certain of that. She goes to incredible lengths to protect him from anxiety. And she's in bits over it.'

'Of course. I'm not suggesting she's deliberately at fault. Look – I'm sorry I said anything. I just felt that if this continues – Theo not talking, I mean – he really ought to see someone. And with all you've been through, I don't think it's something you should be taking on just now. It could well be a great deal more complex than you realise.'

'Look, I'm *fine*, Helen. Truly.'

I suppose that's why I needed her to leave. In case she said the same to Emma and upset her. I was still shocked they didn't get on; dreaded the idea of them falling out openly.

And then two wholly unexpected things happened to pull me right up; to stop all this unhealthy inward thinking.

◆ ◆ ◆

The first was a large storage company van which caused a temporary row over access to Balfour Street. The van parked half up on the pavement outside the Hartleys' pale pink cottage, blocking the way for a tractor and trailer trying to move supplies of hay to a farm on the other side of the valley. The two drivers got quite heated, until a white-haired woman intervened from a dark VW Polo parked further along the road.

I was in the post office buying stamps, and was watching all this through the window when someone in the queue identified the woman as Gill Hartley's mother.

And it wasn't that I had stopped thinking about her. It wasn't that I didn't still see the scene at night when I was trying to get to sleep. The blood on the wall. On my hands. All over my dreams. It was more that I had not let myself think of the relatives; the others carrying this tragedy so much closer and heavier in their hearts.

Gill's mother. Dear God . . .

The update on the Tedbury grapevine suggested financial constraints were forcing the family to let the cottage to cover the mortgage while Gill remained in a coma. Turns out banks and bills don't wait, whatever the tragedy.

But who on earth would want to live in that place after what happened there? I said this over and over to Mark on the phone each evening, and to Helen too – the question answered sooner than I expected when just three days later a young couple with two small children began unloading their furniture and boxes from a large self-hire van.

'I just can't believe it. How will they sleep at night? And with two little children.' My phone calls to Mark each night were getting longer and longer. Gabbled and trivial. The plans for a village parking scheme.

The weather. The interest rate on our savings – down again. Filling all the silences as quickly as I could with gossip and trivia because neither of us could bear to discuss the one thing that perhaps we should. The baby that was gone. That never was?

The second child I was not allowed to have . . .

'Do you think they just don't know? The new people. I suppose if they're from outside the region, there's no way they would know. Though I'm surprised at Gill's mother. It seems a little morally suspect, wouldn't you say? Not to say anything to the new tenants, I mean – if they're from outside the region.'

This puzzle was again answered more quickly than I expected when I found myself standing right beside the new resident the following Monday in the school playground. To my surprise, the two children were neatly dressed in the correct green-and-grey uniform and, though clearly nervous, allowed themselves to be ushered away to class by their new teachers. The younger girl was to be in reception with Ben, and the older boy in year one.

'I hope they'll be OK.' The mother's voice was almost a whisper, so that I was at first unsure if she was speaking to me or to herself.

'Oh – I'm sure they'll be fine. It's a lovely school. I'm Sophie, by the way. My son Ben's in reception. The teacher's really nice.'

'Good. Thank you. I'm Charlotte. Charlie, most people call me. We've just moved in.'

'Yes, I know.'

The woman fell into step with me as we headed to the gate.

'I expect people are a bit surprised.'

'I'm sorry?'

'Us moving into the house, I mean. So soon.'

'So you know what happened?'

'Oh yes. I hope you don't think we're unfeeling. Callous or anything. I mean, I'm not going to pretend we didn't think twice. And of course we're worried how the kids will react but, to be frank with you, we've been trying to get them into a decent school for ages. We can't afford to buy anywhere and our boy was bullied at his last school. We heard about the place being let through a friend. And so when we weighed it all up . . .'

I turned to examine the woman's face – her skin dry and heavily lined for her age. No make-up. Long straight hair, unstyled and uncoloured. She was wearing jeans, an out-of-shape grey sweatshirt and a look of extreme weariness.

'I expect you think it's very mercenary of us.'

I had no idea what to say. I was wondering if anyone had told her that I was the one to find them.

'It's just we didn't know them, so it doesn't feel personal. And they've deep-cleaned – changed the carpets and everything. I mean, all houses must have some bad karma, don't you think? Especially old ones.' It sounded like a speech she had rehearsed.

'And the children?' I couldn't imagine the conversation.

'We haven't told them.'

My worst fears were confirmed the moment Ben got home.

'Do you believe in ghosts, Mummy?'

'No. Why?'

'Well, everyone thinks the dead man will chase those new children. For moving into his house.'

'Don't be silly, Ben. And I do hope no one has been upsetting them. It's not very kind, is it? They're new and they're probably a bit nervous.'

'I didn't say anything. But Emily Price says the dead man is a ghost now. She says there was loads of blood and that you *saw* it. Did you see it, Mummy? Because if it's a lie, I can punch her for you.'

'That's quite enough, Ben. Nobody is ever to punch anyone. Especially girls. *Ever.*' I began to vigorously grate parmesan over his bowl of pasta, my hands trembling. 'Look, Ben. Lots of sad things happen in houses but there are no such things as ghosts. And houses and places and people can be happy again, even after something bad or sad has happened. It doesn't matter what's gone on in the past.'

'Doesn't it?' Ben looked at me very intently and was clearly unconvinced. 'Well, I still think it's scary. And he'd better not invite me to play because I won't go' – widening his eyes – '*especially* not on Halloween.'

The second unexpected distraction came the very next morning, in a mysterious phone call from Mark's secretary Polly. It was a message for me to ring a woman I had never heard of, as a matter of *extreme urgency*. I jotted down the name – Emily Gallagher – but could not place it, nor the number.

'Is Mr Edwards with you at the moment?' Emily was speaking in a hushed tone, adding to the sense of intrigue.

'No. Why?'

'Good.' Emily Gallagher then swore me to secrecy before explaining that she was on the organising team for the forthcoming National Puffa-Flakes Advertising Awards gala in London, and they were extremely disappointed to learn that Mr Edwards was not planning to attend this year.

My immediate response to this was irritation. I guessed that numbers for the awards do were down, and the events team were peeved that Mark would not be spending our son's inheritance on the requisite consolation champagne.

'The thing is, I need you to be discreet here, Mrs Edwards, but in strictest confidence, I also need you to understand that it would be – how can I put this – especially *unfortunate* this year, if your husband were not to attend.'

I sat down at the window seat, gazing out on the square.

'Unfortunate?'

'It would, er, leave a gap.'

I felt my expression change. More curious now. 'You're saying he's won an award?' I turned back to the room.

'Well, I'm not allowed to say too much, *precisely*, of course.'

'How *big* a gap?'

There was a long pause.

'Look – I can go so far as to say that there would be a very large gap and he would be *very, very* sorry afterwards were he not to attend.'

Agency of the Year. Dear Lord. It had to be that Mark had won Agency of the Year. I could hardly believe it . . .

'I'll get him there.'

I phoned Mark's secretary straight back and told her there had been some confusion over a clash with the family diary, and she was to book two tables at the award ceremony immediately. It was to be a surprise, I stressed – so he was not to be in the loop. My call. The staff deserved a treat and so did he. 'Sort out the invites and save a space for me too, but don't tell Mark. Use my company card. He's got so much on just now, and thinks it clashes with something at home.'

The gala was the following Wednesday – just a week away. I had for years refused to join Mark for these events, partly because of Ben but mostly because we both hated the whole drama of smiling through gritted teeth when a shortlisting bore no fruit. Runner-up syndrome had worn very thin since that first awards dinner – the one where we'd met.

I put my legs up on to the window seat and felt this wave of something unfamiliar. It took me a moment to even realise what it was. *Happiness.* So immensely pleased for him. Proud. It was just what Mark deserved – all that driving up and down the motorway – and just what we both needed right now.

But what on earth to do about Ben? It was a teacher training day. I was just wishing that I had not sent Helen packing so hastily when the doorbell went. It was Emma, with Theo alongside, ominously clutching a very large bow and arrow.

'What is it, Sophie? You look miles away.'

'I can't tell you.'

'Don't be ridiculous. Of course you're going to tell me.'

CHAPTER 32

BEFORE

'We need to go to France.'

'Excuse me?'

'I'm serious, Melanie. It's the Tedbury case.'

'Matthew. What the hell are you talking about?'

Matthew Hill was in his study. It was next door to little Amelie's room, and so he was keeping his voice low. In front of him was a file with several pieces of paper. The top sheet had his latest notes scrawled in black ink. *Emma Carter – only renting Priory House . . .*

'Look. I didn't tell you everything, Mel – when we met up before. I couldn't.'

'Tell me what? For Christ's sake, Matthew. I'm through with Tedbury. It's getting late and I'm on my second glass of wine . . .'

'That case I was working on myself in Tedbury?' He felt himself wince. 'It was for Emma Carter.'

There was a pause. Matthew bit into his bottom lip and skimmed through the sheaves of paper again to find the name and number of the nurse in France who had been caring for Emma's mother.

'I'm not following.'

'I swear to God, Melanie, I would have told you everything from the off if I thought it was relevant, but I needed to do some more digging. It's taken me a while . . .'

'Tell me what?'

Matthew ran his hand through his hair and leant back in his chair. He could not bear that he had stuffed up again; still could not quite believe that he had been taken in. He thought of Emma Carter standing in his office. So composed. So elegant. So funny and engaging and quirky too, guessing his birth sign and offering to read his tea leaves. That strange flash in her eyes with the mix of colours . . .

'OK, slurp more wine and try not to be too angry with me.' A deep breath. 'Emma Carter booked me for a standard gig. To do some profiles on the planning committee in Tedbury. Brief was she'd bought some land there in a little consortium and was pitching for planning permission for a small mixed development. Five detached houses and three affordable homes. Wanted to know who had local influence and if anyone had history with similar projects. Any undeclared vested interests. Rival projects. Skeletons in the planning cupboards.'

'Charming.'

'All very routine, Mel. Nothing out of the ordinary in my world. Just a research job.'

'And?'

'I put a file together on anyone who might kick up a stink locally. All the parish councillors. Backgrounds. Political history. Personal stands over local planning issues, blah de blah.' Another pause. Matthew glanced at the baby monitor as it flickered, his daughter making a snuffling noise as she apparently turned in her cot next door. He checked his watch. Sal was out at her yoga class but would be finishing shortly.

'One of them was Antony Hartley, Mel.'

'Oh jeez, Matt. I'm not liking the sound of this.'

'Look, I swear to God, Melanie, I had no idea there was anything amiss with this Emma. This commission. She was completely

241

convincing. Utterly charming. And a bit of skulduggery on planning is nothing unusual. You get a lot of cases where private interests are withheld; people using different names. My job was to dig a bit. All stuff in the public domain if you know where to look. All I did was pull it together to save her time.'

'So what was in the Antony Hartley file?'

'Officially – all very boring. Been on the planning committee for years. No corporate interests or shares. Broke by all accounts, and very anti-piecemeal development in the village. He was in favour of a bigger affordable housing scheme for locals but no one else wanted that, as you can imagine. The locals want as few new houses built as possible.'

'So how is all this relevant, Matt?'

Matthew felt himself suck in his face.

'I did something stupid, Mel. Mentioned something as an aside to Emma when I delivered the report.'

'Go on.'

'While I was researching Antony Hartley, I happened to find out that he had made one of his fellow students pregnant. At the university.' A pause in which Matthew felt himself pull back as if ready for a blow. 'I told Emma.'

'Oh, for heaven's sake, Matthew! The man is dead and you tell me this isn't relevant?'

'I know, I know. But I was praying it was just a horrible coincidence when he suddenly turned up dead. Look – I spoke to forensics immediately and they swore there was no evidence whatsoever of any third-party involvement. A clear-cut domestic. I assumed the wife had just found out, as I did . . . And in any case, I trusted you one hundred per cent to get to the bottom of it.'

'OK. So, first, I'm not happy that my forensics team are talking to you behind my back. But you still should have told me. You must see that you should have told me. And why did you even share this with Emma?'

'Look. She was a client, Mel. Seemed completely straight to me. I gave her the file and we were just chatting over coffee. I said I hadn't found anything amiss. Mentioned that Antony was bound to oppose the development. But he was a genuine guy. And then I just added as an aside – *good councillor, terrible husband.* It was a joke. Stupid of me. I told her about him playing away. As I say – an aside. Inappropriate. My mistake . . .'

'Oh Lord.'

'It gets worse, Melanie.' Matthew was now holding up his notes and flicking through them again.

'I've done some more digging and I've just had a call from a planning contact. It turns out this Emma is a liar extraordinaire. Her property story is all complete nonsense. There *is* a preliminary planning application – I checked that from the off – but I now learn it has nothing at all to do with her. Not only does she not own the land she mentioned, she has no part in the consortium either. She must have just heard about it locally. Oh – and I've discovered this morning that she's as broke as the Hartleys. She doesn't even own Priory House, she's renting it with an option to buy down the line. I've just done some more checks with some financial contacts. She has a truly terrible credit rating.'

'This doesn't make any sense to me. I've called in her bank records too and it's a complete puzzle. Word in Tedbury is there was supposed to be some big inheritance from her mother in France, yet the cupboards are pretty bare. She even took out a loan recently. And if there's no planning deal, why's she even sniffing around Tedbury? Why would she need a cover story to dig dirt on the locals?'

'Exactly what we need to find out, don't you think? And why we need to go to France to check the background on this mother's death too. I've tracked down a nurse there who was treating the mother. Initially I just rang her for background on Emma but the story gets more suspicious. Emma sacked her, apparently – right out of the blue.

The nurse won't talk to me on the phone. Got irrationally upset. I suddenly have a bad feeling about this one, Mel. A very bad feeling.'

Matthew knew what he wanted to happen next. In his ideal world, he wanted Melanie to say she would go to France officially so that he could tag along in the background. But he also knew this was unlikely. Liaising with foreign forces was a nightmare and always painfully slow.

'I can't do anything officially, Matt. No budget. No mandate. In fact, I've been ordered to quieten the Tedbury case down unless and until Gill Hartley wakes up. Meantime I've got a big presentation tomorrow. Zero tolerance on the red-light district.'

'Go sick. We can go together . . .'

'You know I can't do that. And I can't tell them all this either. It'll drop you right in it.'

Matthew could hear a tapping noise. He could picture her exactly, tapping her biro against her wine glass. Old habits . . .

'I just don't get it, Matt. What's all this really about? Was Emma seeing Antony herself? Jealous . . . is that it? Is that why she really engaged you?'

'God knows. But we need to find out. Christ – if I've stuffed up again, Mel.' Matthew let out a long huff of air. Melanie would be diplomatic – and loyal too. She would say nothing. But he knew they were both thinking the same thing; about that terrible time when he left the force. Matthew still felt responsible for that child's death. An inquiry had cleared him completely but that did not help. Matthew stared again at the baby monitor and closed his eyes to the memory. The mother's face at the inquest. The hate in her eyes.

'Seriously, Mel. If you can't come to France, I'll go on my own. Sal will be back from yoga soon. I can make the night ferry if I hurry.'

'I can't let you do that.'

'Look – I don't like that she took me in so easily, Mel. Also – you know they're whispering against you in the department. Rumour is you're seeing a witness. That true?' He winced again as he said this, worried about overstepping the mark but more worried about Mel. Her first case as a DI. He might have thrown his own career away but she mustn't.

'None of anyone's business who I see. OK, so I've had a drink with this guy Tom. Couple of times. He's really nice, Matt, and I like him. So what? He's not involved in the case. There is no real case.'

'I'm not judging, Mel. I'm just sharing what people are saying. A few jealous backstabbers. You know how it goes. So you need to nail this case and I need to clear my conscience. Two birds, one stone. So I go to France. Yes?'

'You're really up for this? You have the time? Won't this be unpaid?'

'Yes, and I'm not pretending it's ideal but I've had a good couple of months so it's fine. Also – this feels partly my mess so I need to clear it up.'

'OK. But by the book. None of your silliness.'

'*Moi?*'

'And you ring me from France – yes? If you need any help, my end I mean. Putting anything through the systems.'

'Course.'

'This Emma, Matthew . . .'

Another pause. The sound of more pen-tapping against the wine glass.

'She came to the hospital to visit Gill. I know we're supposed to stick with facts not instinct, but I got a very odd *vibe* from her.'

'So they were mates – Gill and Emma?'

'No. Apparently not. Only met socially a couple of times. In fact, none of it makes any sense at all, Matt.'

CHAPTER 33

BEFORE

Theo took out his torch from his pocket and shone it at the books. He wished he were big enough to read properly. When they lived in Manchester, Nanny Lucy said you really didn't need to understand all the words when the pictures were so good, but there were some drawings in these books which were weird, and he couldn't understand them at all.

He turned the page and noticed a spider, right in the corner of his cave. Theo wasn't at all frightened of spiders. He didn't understand why Ben didn't like them. He liked the way they scuttled about and then suddenly stood very, very still. If the words weren't all swollen up, deep inside him, he would tell the spider that he could stay in his cave, right here under the bed. Be his pet. He shone the torch on the spider and it ran right up the wall. Like Spider-Man.

Theo had wanted a pet all his life. He had begged for a guinea pig but his mum said they were disgusting creatures, like rats with more fur. Ben had two guinea pigs and three cats – one black and white, one marmalade, and one which was grey and shiny and hissed a lot. Even Slinky – the hissy one – Theo liked a lot. Mummy said it was a spiteful cat and that he had better watch out, but Theo wasn't scared of Slinky. No way.

It wasn't Slinky he was scared of . . .

And so now he snuggled up into a tighter ball in his cave and waited for Ben. Just lately he had become terrified of the doorbell when waiting in his cave, in case it was the police. He saw one of their cars on the square recently and had nearly wet himself. He didn't like the dark and he didn't think they fed you in prison. On the television, people in prison always looked hungry and some of them stole knives from the canteen and put them up their sleeves.

Theo closed his eyes and thought of Krypton. One day he was quite sure that if he waited long enough there would be a knock at the window and it would be Superman. He would have heard all the words which Theo had kept deep and safe inside. He would have picked them all up with his X-ray vision and super hearing and he would scoop him up from his cave.

Then Theo and Superman would know exactly what they needed to do. They needed to get his mummy to Krypton to ask them to give her shiny eyes. They would keep her looking the same from the outside – the face and the hair and everything, otherwise people would know what they had done and the police might come – but they would get her a completely different inside. From Krypton.

An inside like Ben's mummy.

Theo moved very quietly – shuffling across the floor of his cave to find the Penguin biscuit he'd saved from this morning. Ben was downstairs with Mummy, really upset about something, and Theo was trying to make a plan for them. An escape plan.

The trouble was Ben kept crying and Mummy got more cross when you cried a lot. He needed to tell Ben this; that it was best to keep all the worrying and the words and the crying deep in your tummy and wait for Superman.

When Ben's mum got back from London, maybe Theo could go round for tea and cakes. Ben's mum let them dip their chocolate biscuits into their tea. He liked to hold the piece of biscuit in his mouth and suck until all the chocolate had come off and the inside bit had gone soggy on his tongue. One day they had a competition, him and Ben and Ben's mum, to see how long they could leave the biscuit dipped in the tea without a bit falling off and sinking to the bottom. They timed it and were laughing and laughing. And he won.

Ben's mum let him feed the guinea pigs on his own and she let them make a new cave under Ben's bed. They put one duvet cover on the floor to make it soft and Ben's mum hung another one over the side of the bed so that it was all dark inside. Ben had one of those beds on stilts so there was loads of room. You couldn't quite stand up but it wasn't as cramped as the cave under his own bed. This one. Which was actually quite small and not very comfortable at all.

Ben's mum took them to the zoo once, too. It was the first time Theo had ever been to a zoo and he was amazed and just a little bit scared. Ben said he liked the hippo the best but Theo thought it was rubbish. It hardly did anything. Just pooed – a really big, stinky poo.

No. It was the desert that Theo had liked. It was in a dome and was really hot and bright, just like off the television, and there were birds flying about. He watched the birds and thought of his robin flying free somewhere and he could picture the blue sky and the clouds and there was this sort of pressure behind his eyes. He didn't understand because it made him feel really strange – both happy and sad all at once; as if he wanted to smile but also cry every time he thought of his robin far, far away.

There were little lizards in the dome too, hiding behind rocks, and also some really beautiful fluffy guinea pigs.

It was a white-and-brown guinea pig at the garden centre that Theo had wanted for a pet most of all. With Nanny Lucy, when they lived in Manchester, he had asked for the brown-and-white one for his birthday, but Mummy had said over and over that guinea pigs were *absolutely disgusting*.

And when they got home from the zoo that day there was a message from Mummy saying that her headache had gone and that he could come home at five o'clock. And Theo had started to cry and Ben's mum said it was OK. It wouldn't be long until five o'clock. *Gone in a flash.* She had fetched paper and crayons for him and Ben to do pictures from the zoo.

And Theo didn't know how to explain that he didn't want it all to be *gone in a flash*. The truth was he didn't want to go home at all.

CHAPTER 34

TODAY - NOON

I stare at the fruit cake. I don't especially like fruit cake, to be frank. The colour of the cherry is borderline alarming but Mark likes a medley of 'bits' to go with coffee when we travel by train, and fruit cake is always a part of this picnic. For no good reason other than habit and association, I tend to do the same when travelling alone.

'Anything else?' The man behind the buffet counter sounds impatient; only now do I realise I have been daydreaming. Dithering.

'Sorry. Slice of fruit cake, please. And some of the oat biscuits.'

Back in my seat, I check my watch. Should be in Paddington around 3 p.m. Not too bad. I take out my magazine and sip the coffee through the little opening in the lid, relieved the train is so quiet, allowing this rare treat, albeit temporary, of a table for four to myself. Two reservation tickets slotted above the seats opposite confirm company beyond Tiverton, but I will have a good spell of blissful solitude.

I put the ridiculous spare phone on the little table. So stupid of me. When packing earlier, I knocked my smartphone off the dressing table and smashed the screen completely. Only just had time to transfer an old pay-as-you-go SIM to this spare. An ancient model with no Internet. Phone and text only – and not all my contacts have transferred. I can't even find the number for Mark's new work mobile. Of all the days . . .

I check the bars – just about enough – and dial Emma's mobile; thank heavens I jotted her number in my diary. Ben seemed fine when he packed his little case last night, excited even, but this is his first sleepover with a friend. Though Emma said it would be as good for Theo as it was helpful to me, it was still so kind of her to offer.

'Hi. Just being a fussy mother. Everything OK?'

'Sophie? You got a new number?'

'Don't ask. Spare phone. Can you store the details? I'm on the train. So – all OK?'

'Yeah. All good. They've been playing knights in full costume from the dressing-up box and now we're going out for cakes.'

'Theo talking? To Ben, I mean?'

'Nope. Not today. Using a weird sort of sign language but it's fine. Ben is being absolutely sweet about it. Kids are so much more accepting, aren't they? Wish I could be so relaxed.'

'Can I have a word, then?'

'Sorry?'

'With Ben?'

'Well, I think he just went off to the loo, actually. Might be best to let him settle.'

I begin opening the fruit cake, tucking the phone under my chin to struggle with the cellophane. 'Oh, I know I'm being pathetic but you know what I'm like. Call him, would you? I absolutely promise I won't ring again.'

There is a clattering and a click, then a long pause, which I assume means Emma has put the mobile down to fetch Ben. In the distance I can hear some voices for a time and what sounds like crying, then a clatter as Ben is picking up the phone.

'Mummy, I don't want to go swimming.' He is gasping for breath as if in-between sobs. 'I don't want to go out. I want you to come home. You need to come home.'

'Shhh, Ben. Honey. What on earth's all this about, love? You're not going swimming, you're going for *cakes*. You like cakes.'

'Emma says we have to go swimming first. It's a surprise . . .'

'No, no, darling, you must have misunderstood. Emma knows how you are about water, love. Honestly, she does. Look – put her back on and Mummy will sort it all out. You're not to worry now. Emma just wants you both to have a nice time together.'

'When are you coming back?'

'Tomorrow. Just one sleep, remember? Now have a think what kind of cake you would like and give the phone back to Emma. Big kiss. Mummy loves you. To the moon and back – remember.'

There is a pause, then some more clattering and finally Emma.

'I'm so sorry, Sophie. No idea where all that came from. He's got himself into a tizz suddenly. Right out of the blue.'

'You're not going swimming?'

'No, no, of *course* not. I don't do phobias, not even for you, darling. I just put towels in the bag in case we go on to a theme park later. Theo always gets soaked on the rides. Ben must have seen the towels and got the wrong end of the stick.'

'Yeah, that's what I said. Look – will you have another chat with him? Explain about the towels. I know I'm being a pain but he sounded really upset. It's freaked me out a bit.'

'Of course. So will he be all right? With the water rides? We can do something else entirely. I don't want him upset.'

'He should be fine. Ask him. It's only proper swimming that freaks him out. Anything out of his depth.'

'OK. Well, look, I'd better go. I'll settle them both down with chocolate.'

'OK.'

'And you're not to worry. He'll be fine in five minutes. You know what kids are like. Tantrum one minute. All smiles the next.'

'Tell me about it.'

'You have fun now.'

The coffee is bitter and I wince, wishing now that I hadn't phoned. Kids. I break off a piece of cake, remove the cherry and pop it into my mouth. It is my own fault for letting Ben's water phobia go on for so long. We will have to do something about it before swimming lessons start in school. There must be some specialist I can take him to. I've been avoiding the whole thing for too long. Guilt.

I close my eyes and remember that terrible moment of realisation at the holiday villa. *Where's Ben? Oh Jesus, where's Ben?* His tiny face just visible below the surface of the water, looking up. Mark diving into the pool, fully clothed. It was my fault; so very traumatic that I've ducked the whole issue of swimming ever since. Just one minute I took my eye off him. I will never again opt for a villa without a gated pool.

I think of him choking and gasping; of how unbearable it must be to drown. I feel a tightening in my chest and, without thinking, press the palm of my right hand against the top of my lungs, as if to steady my own breathing.

The phone call has pulled me up. Poor Ben. His phobia is getting out of hand. Yes. I will make inquiries about one-to-one lessons as soon as I get back. Find someone really patient and experienced. Fix this.

I open my eyes to look out of the window and try to let go of the worrying. A fine, clear sky and quite warm too, though they are forecasting rain for later. Next, I glance at the case on the luggage rack and wonder what Mark will make of the new dress. It was a shock in the shop to acknowledge how much weight I've lost. I look better for it, but it presents that familiar conundrum – buy the dress in the smaller size which is unlikely to fit for long, or buy my normal size? Given the magnitude of the occasion, I switched several times, eventually throwing caution to the wind and opting for the smaller dress.

The cover story to get Mark to the awards has been tricky. I have arranged for Polly to book a phantom dinner with an important client at a hotel near the ceremony. The plan is for me to surprise him there early with his dinner suit, and then whisk him away by taxi to the awards.

As the train finally pulls into Paddington, I'm feeling quite nervous, wondering if I should simply have tipped Mark off. It would have made things so much easier. But I think of all the driving, all that Mark does for us. I think of what we have been through lately and I really want to see his surprise; to see him happy.

I phone Polly en route and she confirms Mark has already left for a genuine meeting off-site. From there he's going straight to his rented studio flat to shower before the fake dinner meeting at 7 p.m. I decide, while the coast is clear, to pop into the office briefly to check all the other arrangements for our tables at the gala.

Mark's company moved offices just three months back when the old lease ran out, and I haven't seen the new place in the flesh yet. It was a bit of a shock to me, the move, as I was rather hoping the next step for the business would be relocation. But it is what it is. Mark needs to keep his clients happy, and on the website the new premises certainly look impressive – a third of the ground floor of a remodelled building just a stone's throw from Oxford Street.

The reception area is just as depicted online – all steel and white and modern art. I feel a surge of pride. *Good for you, Mark. Nice choice . . .*

Polly, who's covering reception, grins broadly as I struggle in with my suitcase and Mark's suit bag. She orders me a taxi for later while I check over the table plan before setting off for the loo.

Polly directs me along a corridor behind reception. 'Tell me what you think of the new pictures along the wall, will you?' She has stood up. 'I had them framed as a surprise but Mark hates them. Wants them all taken down. I could do with someone on my side.'

'And you think he'd listen to me?' I like Polly and am laughing as I set off along the corridor. A couple of the office doors are open and I feel a familiar surge of excitement at the glimpse of storyboards for new logos and branding.

The series of photographs start just past the offices – half a dozen large pictures in contemporary steel frames which match the stairway. I can see why Polly is miffed. They chart the company's development from the small South London office from which Mark launched the business a decade earlier, to the temporary Docklands studio which saw the second expansion. It is a nice touch, I think, and I can't understand Mark's objection – though maybe he doesn't want clients reminded of the agency's humble history?

There are several posed team photographs from various successful campaigns, alternated with more candid shots, including staff plastered in mud on army assault courses from the corporate compulsion that is 'team building'.

And then, just ahead of the sign for the toilets, I am suddenly stopped in my tracks by the final framed photograph in the sequence.

At first, the non sequitur strikes me absolutely still, like that moment in a dream when you open the wardrobe door to find clothes you cannot recognise. The first evidence that you are not awake after all. Something apparently innocuous but so out of place that it becomes threatening. Shape-changing.

For just a few seconds, it is as if my brain cannot compute the information in front of me and is instead trying, as I feel my brow tighten, to come up with a different image.

And then, with the realisation that the picture is not going to change, however long I stare at it, a cold wave of dread passes through my entire body.

CHAPTER 35

TODAY

Matthew is exhausted as he checks the map on his phone. Next right, then left. There were no cabins left on the ferry and it was impossible to sleep – noisy and crowded.

Sorting out the hire car was the usual nightmare and his head is swimming. He's left the car in the town's central car park and is now on foot, keen to move things forward and get home. His research says Emma's mother used the surname Bell while living in Brittany. Maiden name? Maybe. Her nurse, Aveline, is apparently no longer working with the care agency; she threw in the towel after Emma mysteriously sacked her from the job with her mother. Matthew managed to get all this by sweet-talking the agency secretary. Aveline's husband has a bakery just off the town's main street and she now works there with him. Bit odd. To suddenly give up the nursing.

Aveline had very quickly got terribly upset on the phone when Matthew contacted her from England, gabbling about Theo and then putting her husband on the line – both of them speaking very good English. *Leave her alone, please. This is too upsetting . . . My Aveline. She did nothing wrong. You need to leave her alone.*

But it was all the muttering about Theo which alarmed Matthew. Aveline seemed unnaturally worried about him.

Ten minutes of walking and he can see the bakery just ahead. A smart double-fronted shop with a magnificent window display; he checks the name against his notes and waits until there are no other customers inside.

'Is it Aveline?'

Her wary expression is confirmation enough. Matthew wishes he spoke French.

'Look. We spoke on the phone. Matthew Hill. And I know it makes you anxious to talk about this and the last thing I want to do is upset you, but I am here because I'm worried about what you said. About little Theo, Aveline. I just need to ask some questions about Emma.'

She gasps, hand up to her mouth. 'He is all right? Little Theo? Nothing has happened?'

'No. I mean – yes. He's fine. But why are you so worried about him?'

She rolls her lips tightly together, glancing from side to side. Matthew's instinct is this could go either way. He has just a few seconds to swing this.

'Please, Aveline. I've come all the way from England. Is there something we should know? About Theo? About Emma? Is there something you need to tell us?'

Aveline suddenly heads to the entrance to turn the shop sign to 'Closed' and to bolt the top and bottom of the door.

She retraces her steps and leads him through a beaded curtain to a little seating area behind the shop. There is a small staircase and Aveline calls up the stairs to her husband.

Matthew suspects real trouble now. On the phone previously, the husband was all conflict. But when he appears, the man is a surprise – tall and slim, in contrast to his rosy-cheeked and plump wife, he now looks more resigned than angry as Aveline explains in French what is going on. The husband puts his arm around her shoulders and kisses her on the forehead. They lock eyes for a time and he nods at her as if something has been decided.

'You're not in any kind of trouble, Aveline. We just want to understand things a little better. About how things were when Emma and Theo were visiting her mother. It's to do with a case in England. Also we don't understand why Emma moved to Devon. We're hoping you can help us to *understand* . . .'

CHAPTER 36

BEFORE

Why Devon?

It was the very same question which hung in the air, clashing with the sweet scent of clematis that drifted in and out of the shuttered window as Madame Bell drifted in and out of consciousness those final days in France.

'Why Devon?' The weakness of Emma's mother's voice belied the panic in the tone – clutching at Nurse Aveline's sleeve. 'I heard her on the phone, fixing things. But I don't understand. She hates the countryside. Hates it. So why is she taking Theo to Devon?'

The nurse had tried to calm and hush her – it was always bad after the chemo but she tossed and turned through the memories; the scenes and the secrets stored away with all those papers on Emma's past locked now in the chest in the loft.

Claire Bell – born Sabina to a very different life on the road – had never especially believed in God, but she had once upon a time believed in some kind of natural justice. Balance. That hard work and good intentions would surely in the end be repaid.

She had believed long ago that if she studied well, she could leave behind the taunts and the stares of the *gorgios*, the non-Gypsy children who sneered and laughed in the days when the world beyond the caravans and the camps was closed to her, the days when she could not read.

'Is it my punishment? Is that it?' she whispered to Aveline, who dabbed at her forehead with cool flannels, mistaking her patient's troubles for fever as the old lady's eyes darted around the room. 'For turning my back on my own mother. Is Emma my punishment?'

'Hush now,' Aveline pleaded. 'You must stop this. All this fretting, Madame Bell – it is wearing you out. Doing you no good at all. Emma and petit Theo have gone down to the market for pancakes. You need to rest now.'

'I do love her.'

'Yes, of course you do.'

'I keep hoping, you see, that . . .' In her dreams Claire twisted through the scenes and the scents. Antiseptic . . .

Yes. There they are again. All the midwives in their smart blue uniforms, pink-faced and excited, jostling to see after Emma had been born. *Dear Lord – will you just look at this beautiful baby girl. Have you ever seen such a perfectly shaped head? And so much hair . . .*

It was true. The other mothers on the ward who pushed and shoved and suffered all sorts of terrible interventions had babies with squashed, flat heads – all cross and stretched and strange. But Emma – a caesarean birth – had begun life as she would live it. Bewitching.

'She is too beautiful.'

And now the old lady closed her eyes and was clapping her hands slowly together. Clap. Clap. Tears rolling down her cheeks as if watching some performance from the shadows.

'Shhh, now. Please. Madame Bell. How about I make some tea. Yes?' Aveline gently parted her patient's hands. 'Earl Grey with lemon. Weak and hot. The way you like it in England.'

'Even when she was quite little, I *knew*.'

'Knew what?'

Nurse Aveline's own hands were trembling as she rinsed the flannel in the bowl alongside the bed. 'I really don't think you should be talking to me about this now.'

'I am leaving it all to Theo. The money. I thought it would be *safer*. Changed my will. But she is taking him to Devon and now I am wondering – have I done the wrong thing?' She was again clutching the nurse's arm very, very tightly. 'What do you think, Aveline? Have I done the wrong thing?'

'Shhhhh.'

Claire closed her eyes. The scent of baking suddenly . . .

Flour still on the worktops. A Tuesday. Yes. Emma's eleventh birthday.

The day has started well. There is relief; Emma likes her present – a new pair of jodhpurs and riding boots for the lessons which are her latest fad. It will not last long, Claire knows that. Her daughter's fads never last long, and soon they are bickering.

'You will feed Hot Chocolate before school, Emma. Yes?'

'It's my birthday.'

'Guinea pigs still get hungry on birthdays. And it's his birthday too . . .'

It is true. The impractical gift Emma had pestered and pestered for just last year – a long-haired chocolate brown bundle of trouble who seems to Claire to do nothing very much bar tremble with abject fear.

'I won't do it. You can't make me. I am going to school.'

'You will do it right this minute, young lady, or there will be no tea party with your friends. Go on. Right now, while I check on the cake.'

From the kitchen window, Claire watches her daughter, pouting and still furious, trudging in her furry slippers across the wet grass to the cage by the shed.

She feels a little mean for pressing her daughter on her birthday, but remembers the meeting in school, the look in the teachers' eyes. *Emma needs to learn cooperation, Mrs Bell.*

Emma opens the cage door and glances over her shoulder as if checking for an audience. Then she is taking out a bright pink handkerchief from her pocket, all the while still checking furtively around her.

Claire instinctively steps back to conceal herself behind the curtain and watches as Emma leans deeper into the cage with the handkerchief and then seems to be . . .

. . . *what?*

What exactly is she doing?

A deep knot begins to form in Claire's stomach. She cannot quite see. Is she wrapping up the pet to bring him inside? Cleaning him? What?

Claire runs through to the utility window for a better view but now Emma is suddenly very still, her arms outstretched and her body quite tense. And then, just as quickly, the moment has passed and she is locking up the cage as Claire bangs on the window. 'Is everything all right, Emma?'

Emma turns swiftly to the window, her eyes strange – distant and entirely detached; a look which Claire will come over the years both to know and to dread.

'Everything is fine, Mummy.'

And then skipping back into the house where she screws up the bright pink handkerchief and pops it in the bin. No explanation.

Claire ices the Victoria sponge for the birthday tea and pipes Emma's name with chocolate fondant. Twice during the day she thinks to check on the cage but shakes the thought away.

Then later, after school, she is setting out all the treats on the table in the kitchen as Emma, entirely unprompted this time, skips out to the garden to feed Hot Chocolate his tea.

So that when the scream comes, it is not so much a surprise in itself as a confirmation of a silent scream in Claire's own head. The scream of a mother's world ending; the moment she has been dreading. The moment when she can no longer pretend that she doesn't *know*.

'Mummy, oh Mummy. Come quickly. Something terrible has happened. Hot Chocolate is completely cold. I think he is dead. Oh Mummy. Come look. On my birthday. I can't believe it.'

There were discreet, private therapists. Alarming reports with references to *difficulties over empathy and conscience*. Terrible rows between Claire and her husband, who would believe no wrong in his little princess. Later, after the divorce, the first expulsion from school when Emma falsely accused a teacher of making a sexual advance after he gave her a low grade for a test. But always Claire would cover in the end. Make excuses. Did not want to give up.

Paperwork all locked in the chest with the letters. The records of the secret pay-offs much later, as a string of distraught and angry men turned up on Claire's doorstep, desperate to find the runaway Emma, claiming all sorts. Fraud. Theft of money. Deceit.

Claire had buried Hot Chocolate in the garden that dreadful birthday while Emma changed into a black T-shirt and trousers, seeming to her mother to be almost basking in the drama as her friends arrived for the celebration tea. She had told them that losing Hot Chocolate had made this quite the worst birthday in her whole life, until all the little girls were sobbing and cuddling and soothing while Emma's eyes had shone, soaking up the sympathy and innocent disbelief like some kind of drug.

'My daughter is not like other people, Nurse Aveline. There. I have said it. She is not like us at all. I wanted to bring Theo up myself but she wouldn't have it. We must make sure that he is safe. You must *promise* me that you will help me make sure that he is safe? Yes?'

'Hush now, Madame Bell.'

'He loves her, the poor lamb.' The tears flowing freely down the old woman's cheeks – the wrinkles of her forehead screwed into tight, angry folds and the voice a haunted, panicked whisper. 'But why Devon, Nurse Aveline? Why on earth is she taking him to Devon?'

◆　◆　◆

She will ask the question just one last time when Aveline is gone and the room is dark with the curtains drawn. She is hungry and very thirsty too. Emma is sitting silent by the bed, this terrible and final day . . .

Why are you taking Theo to Devon? Where is Aveline?

But Emma will not answer. She is wearing that blank and disconnected expression on her face that Claire has come to dread and she is holding a large, plump pillow as she stands and walks towards the bed . . .

CHAPTER 37

TODAY – 3.30 P.M.

When I was five, I sparked a major alert involving the police by leaving school secretly in the middle of the day. I had turned up that morning to find that it was the dress rehearsal for the Christmas play and I was the only one who had forgotten my costume. Instead of owning up, I claimed it was in the cloakroom as a sick wave of dread cascaded through me. Then I excused myself to the toilet and set off for home.

Crossing major roads and breaking every rule I had ever been given, the only thought in my head was *home, I must get home* – a picture in front of me of the fairy costume, hanging in a plastic cover on my wardrobe door. Everything else was lost to me. The traffic. The startled pedestrians as I bumped past them along the pavement.

The same sick panic, multiplied a thousand times over, swimming through me now as I push my way through the crowds at Paddington. *Home, I must get home.*

The picture in my head this time: *Ben.*

'Watch where you're going, will you?'

'Oh, piss off.' I shoulder the man out of my way. So angry. So afraid. Then so sorry. 'Look. I'm really sorry. Truly.' Hurrying then, running, towards the board to check the time of the next train. *Damn.* Just missed one.

I try the mobile again. Messaging service. Check my watch. Half an hour until the next direct train. For a moment I think of the airport. Or a helicopter? Can you book a helicopter from somewhere? Then the crazy impossibility of it.

My hand is shaking when the mobile rings again – Mark's name flashing in green. Polly must have called him from reception, given him this number. For the second time I put the call through to messaging. He dials again. I reject it again.

The fourth time, I flash it to my ear, sick of this. 'Stop calling me, Mark. I'm going home.'

My lips and hands are now trembling in unison as I again check my watch. I try once more to contact Ben but Emma's mobile clicks straight through to messaging, and so I head towards a coffee stand, thinking caffeine might help, and sit down with my drink at a grubby table covered in crumbs and rings of sticky brown.

I close my eyes, head down, to picture it once more – that moment staring at the framed photo on the wall at Mark's new office. Emma had short hair, which was the first thing that threw me. A neat, pixie style – dyed a much warmer brown which made her brilliant blue eyes stand out even more. Everyone in the photograph had their arms linked around the next person's shoulder. It was a team shot. Mark's arm around Emma's shoulder.

'This woman. I think I know her.' I had to cough to steady my voice as a tall, lanky man emerged from one of the offices on the corridor, apparently heading to the gents. 'I think I used to work with her.' A lie.

So many lies.

'Emma? Emma Bright? Yes, she was with the company a while ago. Graphic designer. Sorry – I don't think we've met?'

'Oh. I'm Sophie. Just here on a social visit.' I blushed. 'I know Mark. The director.'

'Oh right.' He was on his guard now.

'So – Emma. I'd love to look her up. Do you know where she is now?'

'No. Sorry. She was a freelance. Mark might know. They worked on some sports contracts together.'

'Oh right. Thanks – I'll ask him, then.'

'Bit of a headcase. So was she into tea leaves when you knew her?' He was smiling. 'Used to read all our palms. Could guess birth signs too. Quite impressive until we found out she was getting them all from a guy in Personnel.' And then, laughing, he was shifting from one foot to the other, checking his watch. 'I'd better get on. Do you need anything else?'

'No. No. I was just leaving. Thanks.'

◆　◆　◆

I put the cup of coffee to my lips and open my eyes. I am trying to work out in my head how long it takes for hair to grow. Emma's is way past the shoulder now, so that would be – what? At least a year? More than a year?

The coffee is too hot and so I take off the lid, hand still trembling, and begin to blow on the surface.

More than a year. *Dear God.* I try very hard to calm myself by picturing Ben sitting at a cleaner table eating his cake. Smiling.

Emma doesn't know that I know. And Emma has no reason whatsoever to take anything out on Ben. This has nothing to do with Ben. This is about Mark.

Emma says we have to go swimming, Mummy . . .

Ben had misunderstood. Right? I mean, Emma has absolutely no motivation to upset Ben – and Mark wouldn't allow that.

Mark. Jesus. And now none of it is making any sense. Why would Mark move her to Tedbury? And why would Emma pretend to be my *bloody . . . friend?*

I find my head lolling forward. Physically hurting. A booming ricocheting deep inside. I just cannot make it fit. Any of it.

And then I look up. And there he is. Right by my table. Standing there in the brown corduroy jacket I helped him pick out just a couple of months back in a shop in Exeter. It was before the baby. Before the hospital . . . I remember so vividly looking at his reflection and thinking how great he looked. How lucky I was. How lucky I *thought* I was when I didn't know he was sleeping with some . . . other . . . woman.

I lash out then. Really hard. Swing my hand up so high and with such force that it makes the most extraordinary sound as it hits his cheek – the force magnified because he doesn't even flinch . . . back away. Doesn't even try to avoid the slap. He knows that I know because Polly told him I saw the pictures; that I just fled with no explanation. And so I hit him again and again, around the shoulders and the arm. And still he doesn't move.

People are looking now and I feel dizzy, sick to my stomach, pushing the table away from me so that it makes the most terrible scraping noise as I swing my bag up on to my shoulder and begin to stride across the concourse. Away. Anywhere. Just away.

'Sophie. We have to talk. *Please.*'

No.

I say this in my head, not out loud, hurrying faster and faster towards the display board. I want to be somewhere else – beyond all these prying eyes. I want to crouch into a small ball on the floor. To turn in on myself, into a dark place where this will not feel so bad. I want to phone Mark. To say: *Baby, come and get me right now. Something terrible has happened.* Only this time, for the first time in my life, I can't. Because *he* is the something terrible that has happened. And there is no one else to call. And the realisation of all of this is making everything worse. Second by second it is getting bigger and bigger. And blacker and blacker.

'Sophie, we have to talk. *Please.*'

And now I stop dead, turning so suddenly that he bumps right into me.

'Is he safe? Just tell me if Ben is safe with her?'

'You've left Ben with her?' He looks shocked.

'Yes. I was going to surprise you. And I left Ben with her because you let me *think she was my bloody friend!*'

'Sophie, *please.*'

A lot of people are turning to stare at us now. A woman in a long black mac with a tartan scarf. A man in a smart striped suit paying at a nearby stall for a pack of sandwiches. Two children eating burgers with their father by a newspaper stand.

'Let's get on the train.' Mark is steering my arm now towards the middle platforms. 'It's in early.'

I shake him off, raising my shoulder. 'You seriously think I'm travelling with you?'

'Sophie, it's not what you think.'

'Oh, please. And you haven't answered my question. Is Ben safe?'

'Yes.' And then he stares at his feet. Pauses. 'Yes . . . I think so.'

'You *think* so.'

I hit him again then, so hard that it makes his face turn. I am shocked at the violence. How much I would like to hit him over and over and over, and because I don't want to be a part of that, allow him to reduce me to that, I head towards the barrier as quickly as I can, fumbling in my bag for the ticket. In a seat finally, heart pounding, I put my head between my knees in a bid to ease the dizziness. To get the blood flowing better.

Cake. They will be eating cake. It will be fine. I am trying to push away another picture. Water. Ben in the water. Calling out for me. *Mummy, Mummy . . .* No. He was mistaken. A misunderstanding. No swimming. Emma said so. Why would they? They're probably at a theme park right now. Playing.

I try Emma's mobile again. *The number you are calling is not available. Please leave a message . . .*

Only now do I realise that I am rocking gently. Unable to still myself. I try Heather's number. A new idea. I could get Heather to pop round, see if they have left yet. Make up some excuse. But the number just rings out.

I close my eyes, and for some reason I am remembering again when we bought that jacket. The brown corduroy jacket that Mark is wearing today. He had looked so handsome in it in the shop that I stroked his cheek with the back of my hand. Really tenderly. And the memory of that moment – the intimacy of it and knowing now that it was not how I thought – is so unbearable that I can feel tears streaming down my face. My eyes close until I have that feeling of being watched again. Mark standing right there – again – this time in the aisle, his face grey and awful – inexplicably with two train tickets in his hand.

'I've bought us two first-class seats. For some privacy,' he is whispering.

'Go away.' Again I close my eyes.

'*Please.* For Ben. Please, Sophie. Five minutes.'

Reluctantly I open my eyes, this time to catch a glimpse of a young girl kneeling up on her seat in the section behind us, her mother grabbing her pink coat to turn her around.

'Five minutes.'

He finds us an empty section of a first-class carriage near the front of the train. Sits down opposite, face still grey.

'It's really not what you think.'

'Stop it.'

DI Melanie Sanders is standing outside Gill Hartley's hospital room. Gill has been conscious for two hours – the news Melanie had all but given up on.

Just as the consultant appears at the door to signal she may at last go in, Melanie's mobile rings. Matthew. *Damn. The timing.* She silences it to whisper to the doctor the question burning inside her. 'Does she remember?'

'Unfortunately for her – yes, she does. Don't be long.'

Inside the room, Gill's mother is clutching her daughter's hand. 'It wasn't her fault. She didn't mean to; she was wound up. *Goaded . . .*'

Gill looks across at Melanie, her expression one of sorrow and resignation. Tears drip down her face as she tells how Emma Hartley told her in the tent at the fair that her husband was having a baby with a younger woman. That he had *stolen motherhood* from Gill . . . and didn't care.

I am sorry, but you have a right to know this, Gill. He is laughing at you . . .

What happened afterwards was a terrible blur, but Antony had not denied it or even said sorry; he had simply raged about Emma. *That bitch has been trying to blackmail me . . .*

'Once I realised what I'd done, I just wanted to die myself.' Gill closes her eyes. 'I wish now that I had.'

In her pocket, Melanie's phone is vibrating with text after text. She signals for a pause, apologising, to check the screen. Four texts from Matthew.

ANSWER. URGENT!

◆ ◆ ◆

Mark's face is still grey. Eyes tortured.

'Emma was the worst mistake of my life, Sophie, and there is nothing I can say to make it OK. But it was years back. That crazy, terrible time. When Ben was a baby. When things between us were so bad and I thought you didn't love me any more.'

And now a new sensation creeping up within me. A horrible confirmation of the pictures pressing themselves on to me. Limbs and tongues and Emma's cute pixie hair. Mark's lips on her neck. That thing he likes to do which I thought was a secret.

Our secret.

'I can't listen to this. Please, Mark. I just need to get home. To get Ben. I just need you to leave me alone now. Please.'

'I wanted to tell you, Sophie. Back then. More than anything . . . and when we finally realised it was depression, I felt so ashamed of myself, I knew you would leave me if I told you. That you would *never* forgive me.'

'I hate you.'

'Sophie. I'm so, so sorry but you have to listen to me. I slept with her twice. No more. A mad, stupid blip when I thought you didn't love me. Before we knew you were ill. That's not an excuse. I'm just telling you how it felt. The truth. But I was the one who ended it, I promise you.' He is speaking very, very quickly now – his voice rising. 'She left the company. I never saw her again until she turned up in Tedbury, I swear.'

'I don't believe you.' There are little patches of black on the periphery of my vision.

'It's the truth, Sophie. The God's honest truth. It was the biggest shock of my life when you invited her to dinner that night.'

'And you expect me to believe that?'

Outside Gill's room now, Melanie accepts his next call, raking her hand through her hair.

'Matthew?'

'Listen, Mel. You need to do something about the child. Emma's boy.'

'Speak up, Matthew. I can't hear you.'

'I haven't got long, Mel. I need to try to make the next ferry home.'

'What child? *I can't hear you very well, Matthew.*'

'It's bad, Mel. I found the nurse who was treating the mother for her cancer. She's in a right state. Floods of tears; been in agony about not going to the police before but she didn't think anyone would believe her.'

'Believe her about what?'

'Look – she says the mother confided in her. Was afraid of Emma – a nightmare right from childhood, apparently. Compulsive lying. Shoplifting. Drugs. The works.'

'Christ – but there's nothing on file. You think I wouldn't have checked the files?'

'Yeah, well, she's very clever, this one. She fooled me, remember. Moves about. Changes her name. And the mother didn't help matters. She was always hoping Emma would change, so covered her tracks. But in the end the mother got fed up with people turning up, looking for Emma. Seems there was some run-in with social services when Theo was small but Emma latched on to some wealthy guy in Manchester. He got a nanny in to look after the boy but they eventually fell out. Emma turned nasty, stalked the poor guy and then tried to steal his sister's identity. Then she just disappeared. He's got a profile – political ambitions – so stupidly didn't report it either.'

'Christ.'

'So when the mother gets cancer, Emma suddenly turns up in France all worried about the inheritance.'

'So why the hell didn't this nurse say anything of this before? To the police?'

'Emma sacked her and threatened to report her for theft. To get her struck off. Emma reported some jewellery missing to the police to scare her.'

'Dear God.' Melanie would like to tell Matthew about Gill's confession but knows she should not; not yet. *Christ.*

'The nurse says Theo sees more than he should but the poor little lamb is loyal. Emma can get very nasty. Smashes things up and then blames it on the kid. Sugar – I really am going to have to go, Mel. Get myself a ticket . . .'

His voice is now really starting to break up again, despite Melanie pressing her phone tight to her ear. 'Look, I'm at the hospital. Bad reception here. You really need to speak up, Matthew. Can you get a better line? A landline?'

'No time. I've called in the local police, Mel. The nurse is giving a full statement right now. There was no post-mortem but the mother was expected to live at least another six months. Then suddenly Aveline is sacked and the mother's dead. Emma was *alone with her mother*. And she didn't even hang around for the funeral.'

'You seriously saying she may have killed her own mother?' Melanie glances back through the glass, Gill's mother stroking her daughter's hair.

'And there's more, Mel. This nurse reckons the mother changed her will; has left everything to Theo.'

'Oh – Lord. Right. And does Emma know this?'

'She will by now.'

'She wants money, Sophie.' Mark is running his hand through his hair, face white and his body jolting as the train picks up speed.

A new wave passing through my body now. More cold dread. More black spots.

'Money?'

'Yes. She phoned me at work a few weeks before she turned up in Devon. Right out of the blue. Said Theo was my child, that there was some hitch with her inheritance and she needed to make a fresh start. I didn't believe her about the child. She wanted money , . . a *lot of money*, Sophie. She said that if I didn't pay, she would tell you everything. I told her to piss off or I would phone the police . . . and then suddenly she's in the village.'

'Theo's yours?'

'I don't know . . . I don't know. She says so. But I had no idea she was pregnant.'

'You didn't even use protection? You slept with her without protection . . .' My fists are clenched so tightly that the nails are driving deep into my palms. 'You had another *baby* with her.'

The shape of the train carriage changes somehow as if it is being sucked longer, and I am shrinking smaller and smaller in the middle of it.

Mark . . . has . . . another child? I look to the left and then to the right. *A second child?*

We are completely silent for a time, black dots still forming and flickering on the edge of my vision, so that as I stand, I have to steady myself by holding on to the top of the seats.

'You need to leave me alone now. I'm moving to the other end of the train and I'm going to phone the police.'

'Look – I was just trying to buy some time, Sophie. To get some money out of the business. To work out what to do for the best.'

'For the best? Jesus Christ, Mark. She is *with . . . our . . . son.*'

'I needed *more time*. I told her that. She told me she was nearly out of money. She was getting really pissy but you can't just take big money out of a business overnight. And she wouldn't *hurt* anyone, Sophie. Why would she hurt anyone?' He is speaking very fast now – his arm craned over his head, his forehead deeply etched. 'She's a mother herself. You think I wouldn't have said something, gone to the police, if I thought for one second she was capable of—'

'Ben told me she was taking them swimming.'

And now his face changes completely. The colour draining instantly away – looking down at the ground as if a new picture is suddenly emerging there.

'She made some excuse – fobbed me off – said it was a misunderstanding, but I don't know what to believe now. What she's capable of.

Oh my God, Mark. I think I'm going to be sick.' I close my mouth against the first retch. Hold it in and stagger into the aisle. Mark supports my arm as I flee along the gap, through the automatic doors to the toilet. Only just making it.

Inside I throw up into the tiny stainless-steel sink first. Then again into the toilet bowl. For a moment I stand there gasping for breath. Wait until I am sure there is no more, then try to press the rubber flush with my foot, just as the train begins to move off, bumping me against the back of the door.

'Are you all right, Sophie?'

I don't reply, just stand for a moment, pushing my feet slightly wider apart to steady myself – running the tap and trying the flush again to clear up the mess. And then I hear Mark's ringtone just outside the door – his voice strained and confused.

'Yes. I'm on a train, Nathan. Just leaving Paddington now. Sophie's with me.'

There is a long pause, during which I open the door to find Mark leaning against the wall of the corridor, one arm craned once more over his head, brow pressed to the inside of his elbow. His posture of panic.

'When?'

I can feel my head moving involuntarily, twitching from side to side like a tic. And then the word *no* repeating over and over in my head.

No.

Please, dear God, *no.*

'Durndale Hospital? Right, Nathan. We won't be there for hours. Jesus. At least' – he looks at his watch – 'seven o'clock. Can you ring me as soon as you get there? OK. For God's sake, try to find out what's happening and ring me straight back.'

He hangs up and looks at the floor. A long pause. And then, looking up to me, his eyes terrible and his skin grey.

'The boys . . . There's been some kind of accident, Sophie.'

TODAY - NOW

So – yes. I remember this journey only in parts. As if it happened through some kind of fog. As if I was drifting in and out of consciousness, and now as the fog clears different pictures emerge.

All those phone calls . . . Nathan. The hospital. The police.

At first I refused to sit with Mark, so that later, when I was overwhelmed and in a panic got off the train, I had to go along with his cover story. To explain why we weren't together.

And then, when the doctor was asked to watch out for me, we had to sit opposite each other. *Pretending*. Mark fetching sweet tea and water which I could not drink, sitting instead immobile as different pictures moved in and out of the fog. That picture of Ben with his crooked fringe. The first day we took the stabilisers off his bike and he was shouting, *Watch me, Mummy. Watch me.*

A million stupid pictures over the hours as the rain dripped down the train windows and we sat there opposite each other, me and Mark. Strangers suddenly. Unable to offer each other any comfort at all.

And when the calls came through, piecing together the truth of what had happened, it was good news. Bad news. Good news. Bad news.

At one point I made this terrible mistake and googled drowning on Mark's phone. Some say it is the worst way to die, and so I sat there on the train, imagining it. Holding my breath and counting. Seeing how long before the lungs felt as if they were going to burst, tears dripping down my cheeks.

Until finally we got a phone call which made no sense.

Not swimming. Not water after all . . .

Another lorry on that goddamn hill. A witness said Emma had been leading the boys to her car parked on the village square. They were dawdling – playing up. The boys had towels stuffed under their arms. Ben was crying and Emma had seemed cross, shouting at them to *hurry up*. There was a screech then. Later, much later, we will learn that the lorry's brakes failed.

All three of them ran, according to the witness, but there was not enough time. The tall garden wall alongside Heather's cottage collapsed, huge stones cascading down. *Like thunder*, the witness said.

Emma took the worst of the impact. The boys were further along the wall but were trapped and crushed by the falling stones. I had imagined drowning, that one of the boys had crushed his chest, his spleen, on a rock as he was pushed into a pool, maybe on Dartmoor? But – no. Now I think instead of the awful noise of the stones. The shock. The pain . . .

At first Nathan was told the children were fine. But that was a mix-up. Two children brought in at the same time from a different accident. The corrected news spoke of internal injuries. Surgery. They still could not say for sure which child was more seriously hurt . . .

By the time we finally make it to the hospital, Ben and Theo are both 'stable' but heavily sedated – their beds side by side with machines bleeping and flashing all about them. Tiny, pathetic little bodies – too small for the beds, their faces bruised and patched, with horrid little tubes trailing across the sheets.

I hold Ben's hand for a very long time, stroking the backs of his fingers and whispering in his ear and telling him over and over that everything is going to be just fine now. He had a collapsed lung – fixed in theatre – but is still in pain. And then I look across at little Theo, whose eyes flicker open occasionally, and he looks so fragile too. They have saved his spleen but he has pins in his left leg. Broken ribs. He looks so afraid, poor love, so I whisper to him too – *Mummy will be with you soon, Theo. Everything is going to be OK. I promise.*

And then I see the bag – hanging on the corner of Theo's bed. The nurse tells me that the paramedics brought it in. A dark blue child's rucksack – full swimming kit inside. Two sets of trunks. Two pairs of goggles.

No armbands.

And right then, I look through the window to the cubicles next door where Emma is being wheeled past, and something snaps inside of me so that I am across the room, through the door and lunging towards the trolley bed before I am even aware of this intention.

'You stay away from my family!'

Not my voice. Some other Sophie who almost makes it right up to Emma's bed before someone is grabbing my arms, pulling me back as Emma opens her eyes momentarily – the male nurse then holding on to me so very tightly.

'Come on, this isn't helping.'

'You stay away from my family or I swear to God, I will kill you. You hear me, Emma? You go near Ben one more time . . .'

'That's it. Call security. Will someone for Christ's sake call security.'

EPILOGUE

Some people see music as colours. Synaesthesia, it's called. I read somewhere that it plays right in front of their eyes like a rainbow. A different colour for every note they hear. I have been thinking about that a lot just now, because I have started to see things lately in geometric shapes – triangles especially.

I wonder if there is a name for that too – turning the complex detail and layering of pictures into basic geometric shapes. Like simplifying the views all around into abstract paintings.

Take now. As I look across past the swimming pool (rectangle) all I see are large triangles (the mountains) and two small triangles (Theo and Ben).

Funny how the triangle thing happens with boys. Ben was first – broad shoulders and thin waist, so that when you watch them from behind sitting down, it's all you see: a perfect triangle with a little head (circle) bobbing on top.

Theo took a little longer, not just for being younger but because he had a year of puppy fat. Gone now.

Sitting there this moment, twelve and thirteen – so tall and slim alongside the pool with their legs dangling in the water – it is extraordinary how alike they are. The crowns of their hair swirl in exactly the same way, like the beginning of a question mark. Makes me ask why I didn't see it back then – invisible to me like so many things.

You will be wondering about the water? It surprises me too. A surge in my stomach every time I watch them together like this, not just swimming but diving. Competitive now, as all boys are – wanting always to go the fastest. Highest. Deepest. To see who can hold their breath under water the longest.

Sometimes I have dreams where I float back in time and try to whisper on the breeze to my old self. To tell the Sophie that first day on the village square to *walk away*. To tell the Sophie on the train that it will be all right.

To whisper that in the end Theo will be the one – not some special teacher on some special course, but little Theo who will coax Ben into the shallow water at the beach first. Into the river up to their knees with fishing nets. Then the baby pool at the swimming baths and finally this, which I would never have believed. Sad and silent little Theo. Who in the end would become the motivation for us all . . .

We have been coming here to the Midi every summer for the past eight years. An accidental discovery – through Helen. She has a relative of her late husband's who has a large place in northern France and rents this place every Easter. We decided to steal the recommendation and haven't looked back. It is a second home, with a proper family feel – untidy cupboards, mismatched furniture and a maid who does not believe in cleaning, sweeping the dust under the beds and playing with the children instead.

I love it for the flowers. The villa, white with green shutters, appears held together by a tangle of climbers which twist and turn, stretching up to the sun; and though the wisterias and clematis are all finished by the time we arrive, there is always a profusion of white, bell-shaped flowers which dance in the wind and fill the veranda with the most wonderful scent. I do not know the name but could recognise that scent anywhere.

The boys, indifferent to the horticulture, love it for the pool – bigger and deeper than most and with this spectacular view.

They are especially excited today for Helen arrives tomorrow with her 'beau' George, whom Theo and Ben both adore. They call him *the Boyfriend*, which he pretends to find embarrassing but secretly loves, roaring with laughter. *Hardly a boy any more, chaps . . .*

She met him a good few years back. Such a gentleman. Linen suits. Panama hat. He has a second-hand bookshop in Truro and always arrives with a suitcase full of epics for the boys to read. Also he does card tricks and recitations of comic poems, his face pink and happy after port at dinner – one of those perfect holiday guests who has so many stories to share and so much enthusiasm and energy for everything. Helen positively shines in his company. As do we all.

Ah yes. Helen. What to say? Back in the nightmare all those years ago, I didn't even ring her to confirm what time we would be arriving in Cornwall. Or how long we would be staying. Soon after they discharged the boys from the hospital, I just piled everything into the car and set off – like that journey home for the fairy costume.

'Stay as long as you like,' was all she said, which was just as well because for the first few days all I could do was sleep. It was as if my body had finally given in to an exhaustion so complete that it consumed me utterly.

From the window that first morning I watched helpless as Helen took charge completely – leading the boys to an old garden shed from which she produced a swing that they hung from a large tree overhanging the path down to the sea. And that's where Theo seemed to spend all his time initially. Sad and silent little Theo – swinging to and fro.

To and fro.

Social services were in touch very quickly – sent a nice lady in bright pink clothes from the local office to explain that 'arrangements' could be made just as soon as we were ready. But how could I?

Sad and silent little Theo.

To and fro.

They ran a check for next of kin and at first there was a part of me that was praying there would be some distant aunt or godmother or *someone*. But no. Not a single person in the whole world to take him, and I'm not going to pretend I was some saint about it – that I didn't look at Theo some days and see them together. Emma and Mark. Her eyes looking up at me from Theo's eyes. The shape of her nose in his profile.

But every time it overwhelmed me and I thought it might be for the best – to call the lady in the pink clothes – I would imagine Theo's bewildered face at the car window as she drove him away and I just couldn't do it.

So in the end we had to endure the nightmare of paternity tests. Lawyers. Forms. Meetings. And I had to sit in a room with Mark and find a way to be grown-up, instead of crying and lashing out which is what I wanted to do every time I looked at him in those early days. I remember thinking back then – what if Emma lied? *What if Theo isn't Mark's?*

And then, when the test came back positive – conclusive – I didn't know what the hell to feel . . . or do. Mark couldn't take Theo to London, at least not initially, and so we fudged this compromise – that Theo would stay with us in Cornwall and Mark would rent a little flat in Helston so that the boys could visit him at weekends. *Breathing space.*

Surreal. Like some parallel universe to think of it now. More than a year it went on like that. Mark desperate for me to take him back. Play survivors together . . .

For twelve whole months I said no. Definitely. And then I said maybe . . . and then after two years?

I watched him travel from London to Cornwall. I watched him take them fishing. I listened to the boys' stories. How he taught them to bounce pebbles across the surface of the water. Took them to Kynance Cove; camping on the moors. And some weeks he used the sleeper, sometimes he flew, and some weeks he drove all the way from bloody London to the Lizard. Every other weekend until I just couldn't keep it going.

The pretence of hating him.

But when I finally realised that I didn't hate him, I realised that I was just as afraid to love him. So much sadder and more terrifying – that. For even in my anger I had never quite imagined a version of Sophie without him.

This Sophie who has her own PR agency in Truro which grows year on year. This Sophie who had two staff, then three and then somehow five, with offices and contracts and all the chaos once more.

We live in the heart of Truro now – a three-storey Georgian townhouse with a small, walled garden within walking distance of the city centre. For those first two years the boys spent some of the holidays with their father, during which Helen whisked me away and kept me busy – book-buying trips with George once he was on the scene so that I did not resort to sleeping in their beds. Sniffing their clothes.

For just a short time I tried to see someone else. A restaurateur. Charming. Funny. Divorced. He was setting up a boutique hotel in St Ives and even the boys quite liked him. But then he seemed to get rather keen and it was only then that I *realised*.

Mark wrote me a love letter on each of the anniversaries we were apart. Long letters full of sorrys and memories and his love for the two boys. And me. He was honest about trying to make a fresh start with someone else, but said he could never make that work. And so after that second letter that second year, I thought – *maybe*. Not because I was lonely and not because I was at all sure it could work, but because I understood finally what Emma can do to a person . . .

Still we are weekending. Mark sold the company in London and set up a new, smaller agency in Bristol, where he keeps a waterfront apartment for Monday through Wednesday. The boys describe it as *much cooler than Truro, Mummy*. At least he can work from home too now.

Still a compromise but we make it work. Not enough big-name local clients for a Devon base, alas.

These days, in our new life, I dream less often of Tedbury itself – so that it shocked me to the very core when it popped up on the local TV news last week. Like iced water on warm flesh. The church and the square just the same but the magnolia trees so much taller now. It was the lead item – the village finally getting its bypass after years of setbacks and political rows; bumped up the list of projects one moment then dropped down the list in budget bust-ups. Heather was interviewed and it was so strange but so lovely to see her. We exchange Christmas and birthday cards which she always stuffs with all the news. Last time she wrote, the gossip was all about the family that moved into the Hartleys' cottage. Proper little entrepreneurs. They took over the post office when old Bert retired and are running the deli too. *My deli.* I sold them all the kit and the plans in order to be rid of it all, but apparently they've expanded it to a full village store-cum-diner, with a delivery service of local meat and organic veg boxes. Made a big success of it. Good for them.

Other news we get through Nathan, who has kept up a surprising yet enduring friendship with Theo. Every year he sends a Christmas card – always of a robin – and a generous present. Theo keeps all the cards in a box under his bed.

The other shock is that DI Melanie Sanders has moved into a house on the outskirts of the village, married now to Tom. Who would have believed that?

Nathan visits occasionally too, and it is strange and terribly sad how lost he is. He seems to believe that he was the one who should have seen through Emma. Sussed her. Stopped her. Not hearing when we say that the very same thought haunts us all.

Nathan says that Gill Hartley has been transferred to an open prison and will be due for parole soon. For a time I wondered if I should write to her. But to say what? From the trial we learned Gill had longed for a child for years but Antony said he wasn't ready. And then Emma, from that wretched tent, was so cruel sharing Antony's affair and his lover's pregnancy. *You have a right to know, Gill. If it were me? Humiliated like that? Used like that? The breadwinner while he . . . I can't imagine what I might do . . .*

At the trial they read extracts from Emma's diary, recovered from her computer . . . *Sophie the dopey,* she called me. And Nathan? Turns out she put the brick through her own window to keep him close. Strange and chilling meanderings. Everything like a sum: *A+B = I do this.* She rowed with Antony at the fair but gave up on blackmailing him because he had no money. She apparently stalked me in Cornwall, intending to send the photos to Mark as a threat, but got cold feet, worried he might give them to the police. And so when Mark stalled, she was furious, under pressure from the banks and loan sharks, and lost patience.

Not my fault. Theo has my money . . . MY MONEY!

The last searches on her computer were for spots for wild swimming on Dartmoor. Deep pools. Secluded. Sometimes Ben still wakes with nightmares . . . *She was taking us swimming, Mummy . . . She said it was a surprise for you. That she was going to teach me.*

I have nightmares too, in which I watch her leading the boys down to the water's edge and I am shouting at them to *run! Run away . . .* And then she is coaxing or pushing the boys into the deep water and I am shouting but no words will come out of my mouth . . . And then I am holding my breath and counting. *How long can you last?*

I went through a spell – obsessed with trying to understand how anyone could be that evil. That mad. I mean – why hurt Ben? To punish Mark for failing to pay up? How could anyone seriously hope to get away with that? But trying to understand in the end is both futile and a madness of its own. I traced the guy she lived with in Manchester. *She was so exciting at first,* he said. *Spontaneous. Made me feel so special. And then suddenly she's stealing from me. One night I woke up and she was just sitting up and staring at me with this really terrible look in her eyes.* Later he wrote me letters. Pages and pages. Ranting. Railing. Reeling still. He said he felt not just foolish but afraid. That she had taken him in so easily. Seemed so very normal. *She told me, Sophie, that she had never clicked with anyone like she clicked with me. And I believed her . . .*

In the end I had to phone him. Get firm. *Enough now.*

They ran archive footage of the boys' lorry crash on the news item about the bypass. I had to turn it off then. Unplugged the aerial to make sure the boys wouldn't see.

It was Mark who had to tell Theo. About Emma.

I couldn't do it. They phoned us at home not long before the boys were released and I took them to Cornwall: news of some unexpected complication from Emma's surgery. Lungs gave out. *Gone.* And they were trying to find out about her next of kin – who to call . . .

And if it weren't for Helen – dear God. Her friend Patrick – the retired child psychiatrist – came to Cornwall to save us. I was doing everything wrong with Theo – trying so hard to encourage him to talk. Coaxing and cajoling. Pretending that I didn't understand his nods and pointing. *Please, Theo. Will you please just talk to me?*

But selective mutism is no easy fix; a child so anxious they are afraid even to hear their own voice in public. My prodding was making things worse.

Just love him, Helen's friend advised. *Pretend you don't care either way. Whether he talks or not. Take the pressure off. Give him as much time as he needs.*

Just love him.

And I look at him, over there by the pool right now, loving him as much as I do, and can't believe I ever doubted it. But here's the truth – I kept him with us initially not because I felt I would ever love him, and certainly not because he was Mark's child, but because I felt so very sorry for him. Because I couldn't bear the guilt and the judgement of others if I let them send that car.

I think I imagined that once he was stronger, talking again, Mark would take him to London. Get a nanny?

But a child without a mother has this unbearable ache in their eyes; this way of reaching deep inside you and squeezing so very tight that you cannot breathe.

And in the end I was the one Theo spoke to first. And it was into my bed he climbed in the early hours of the morning, trembling and holding on.

We turned the corner when Patrick taught me the 'sliding-in' technique. I had discovered that on his own in his bedroom, Theo would sometimes whisper to a favourite toy. The little black-and-white monkey with the long curly tail and dark beady eyes; the one I bought at the zoo. Patrick explained that sliding-in involved using indirect communication to coax conversation via an intermediary. Sometimes children with selective mutism will talk to just one sibling or friend. No one else. The trick is to watch and wait and use that bridge.

So one day when Theo was talking quietly to his monkey, I stood in the doorway and asked the toy a question. *Does Monkey know if Theo wants a drink?*

To my astonishment, Theo paused, tilted his head, then whispered into the toy's ear and used it like a puppet. *Theo says yes please. Orange juice.*

And I stood there, trying to look relaxed as it swept right through my body. This deep and shocking realisation of what I had done and what it truly meant.

That Theo was to be my second child . . .

Progress from there was slow but steady. Eventually Theo began to speak openly to me as well as through the toy. And then he would speak through me to Helen, and once more to Ben. It was frustrating but also magical to watch – like a game of Chinese whispers to put Theo back in touch with the world.

We have no idea quite what he must have been through with Emma. What she was really capable of. Papers at the mother's home confirmed years of covering up Emma's mess. Drugs. Fraud. Debt.

There was talk of exhuming the mother's body in France. Aveline, the nurse, was sure Emma was to blame. But in the end the inquiry stalled. I was angry about that. No budget, no one to charge, and worse – no one to care enough. But there were private papers lodged by the mother with lawyers that confirmed Patrick's best guess – that Emma was a sociopath. *High-functioning*.

Report after report from private specialists while Emma was growing up. All with the same verdict: *No conscience*.

Imagine that? No pang of conscience . . . *ever*. No ability, in short, to love or care about anyone but themselves.

There are research papers and books . . . 'The sociopath on your street'. I have read too much. One in twenty-five, some research claims.

I worry that it could be hereditary, but Patrick says *hush*, for Theo is the sweetest and kindest child. And so for him I have invented a different version of Emma.

Tell me about my other mother, he still asks sometimes – too young at the time, thank God, to remember the worst. And so I weave stories of the beach trips that summer and I tell him that he was very, very loved and that she is looking down on him from heaven, watching over him. Every single day.

And sometimes he turns this against me. *My real mother would understand . . .*

Real?

I went on a website for adoptive parents once, and it said this – that some children are grown in their mummy's tummies. And some are grown in their hearts.

And when we are having a tough day, when I doubt whether I am doing a good enough job, when I see him looking at a picture of Emma or find a cutting of a robin tucked under his pillow, that is what I cling to. That I am doing my best. And that he grows in my heart just as I, pray to God, grow in his.

For only now do I understand, through Nathan, about the bird. Poor Theo set that robin free; he watched it fly and he sent his little heart with it. He drew it secretly on his arm, and at night he dreamt of it flying free and safe because that's what he needed himself.

I see Mark's car arriving now. He has driven separately because of work. For years when I watched a car approach the house, in Devon or in Cornwall or here in France, I always imagined it would be *it*. The reckoning. The police.

I always believed they would come eventually; that it was just a matter of time; that someone would find some picture. CCTV? Or a witness?

But now, after all these years? I think it really is probably over . . . finally.

I never planned it. And I still remember it all as if sleepwalking.

At the hospital to visit the boys and passing Emma's room, there was just this moment. This unexpected window. The nurse away from her station. Emma's room unattended. Just her and the machines. The bleeping and the monitors.

And the truth? It was much too easy. To silence the machine. To disconnect the oxygen tube. I really was waiting, all the time, for someone to come in.

To stop me.

But no one came. And so I watched her face change, her head toss from the left to the right. Desperate for air. And I held my own breath and I counted, just as I had on the train. And I knew that in that moment I changed to another person. A person I did not recognise and did not really want to be.

I waited and waited until finally she stilled. Until I was sure. Then I reconnected the tube and I left.

I paced the kitchen at home and waited, again, for them to come for me.

But instead we got the phone call to say that Emma was gone.

I know now, through Nathan and Tom, that there was an internal inquiry. The agency nurse – taking a private call from her teenager – was disciplined. The death recorded as natural causes. Turns out hospitals have scores of incidents involving oxygen every year.

Sometimes I even tell myself that I imagined it all; that she would probably have died anyway.

But the most difficult truth of all? I don't actually care. And I don't feel guilty either. Because the most shocking thing is that if I could go back in time I would do exactly the same thing again.

For I am no longer the person who believes in justice. I am no longer the Sophie who saw things in black and white. Good and bad.

As I watched Emma die, I knew there was no way I dared to let her charm her way out of it all; to come and threaten my family again.

And now I watch Mark's car getting closer, closer, weaving its way past a villa on the opposite hill. A splendid white building with pots of vivid flowers tumbling down its terraces. Pink and red and blue and white.

I have not told Mark, nor will I. Sometimes I think he would understand; that I did it for Ben. For Theo. For love.

But then I think of Emma tossing from side to side as she struggled to breathe. The horror that I could stand there. Do nothing.

Me. Sophie. Ordinary wife and mother . . .

And I see that the lesson and the terrible consequence here is that I alone must somehow learn to live with this.

It is who I am now.

It is what Emma made me.

I really thought on that terrible train journey home that the biggest shock and most important lesson was realising what *other* people are truly capable of.

But – turns out there is a much greater and more chilling shock.

Learning – in the face of evil and in the name of love – what you are capable of yourself.

AUTHOR'S NOTE

Thank you so much for reading *The Friend*. The idea for this book came from my years working as a journalist when, court case after court case, I was so often shocked by how difficult it can be to spot true 'evil' in a person.

When I started out as a reporter I imagined, naively, there would always be some sign – something in a person's behaviour or background to give them away. But then I came across cases involving the kind of people who frightened me way more than the obvious misfits. The wolf in sheep's clothing. People like my fictional Emma.

The 'problem' with having a conscience is you expect other people to have one too, so you analyse and evaluate their behaviour according to your own standards. But true sociopaths have no understanding why we all worry about rules or laws . . . or the lives and feelings of others.

I watched so many witnesses and victims in obvious shock after coming across this kind of criminal and it was that utter *disbelief* – at being taken in – that I wanted to try to capture in this story.

I do hope you have enjoyed reading *The Friend*, and if so, I would greatly appreciate a review on Amazon. They really do help other people to discover my writing.

I also love to hear from readers, so feel free to get in touch. You can find my website at www.teresadriscoll.com and also say hello on Twitter @teresadriscoll or via my Facebook author page: www.facebook/ TeresaDriscollAuthor.

Warm wishes to you all,

Teresa

ACKNOWLEDGMENTS

It is always my family I want to thank first in each of my books, for they are not only my greatest cheerleaders but also the people who have to 'duck and cover' during the inevitable ups and downs of writing and editing each novel.

Pete and James and Edward – I love you so much!

Thanks go next to my second family – all the writers, bloggers and readers who are so generous with their friendship and advice and support. With that goes a particular shout-out to the authors at the Harrogate Crime Festival who were so warm and kind, calming my nerves during my first visit.

Heartfelt thanks also to my publisher, Thomas & Mercer, and my clever and patient editors, Jack Butler and Sophie Missing, who brought wonderful ideas to the table as I worked out how best to tell this story.

And the usual hug of very special thanks to the person who made the whole author dream come true for me – my wonderful agent, Madeleine Milburn.

ABOUT THE AUTHOR

Photo © 2015 Claire Tregaskis

For more than twenty-five years as a journalist – including fifteen years as a BBC TV news presenter – Teresa Driscoll followed stories into the shadows of life. Covering crime for so long, she watched and was deeply moved by all the ripples each case caused, and the haunting impact on the families, friends and witnesses involved. It is those ripples that she explores in her darker fiction.

Teresa lives in beautiful Devon with her husband and two sons. She writes women's fiction as well as thrillers, and her novels have been published in six languages. You can find out more about her books on her website (www.teresadriscoll.com) or by following her on Twitter (@TeresaDriscoll) or Facebook (www.facebook.com/teresadriscollauthor).